ANDREW WEIGHT grew up in Hastings on the East Sussex coast. After graduating from Reading University with a degree in Sociology, he worked in the finance industry in London and Geneva, latterly as a founding partner of an award-winning wealth management business. He left this business and moved to the Swiss countryside in 2009. He has now returned to his roots in East Sussex.

INSTINCT OR INTUITION?

INSTINCT OR INTUITION?

ANDREW WEIGHT

RAKE GALLANT PUBLISHING
Rye

First published in 2013 by
Rake Gallant Publishing
Doucegrove Farm
Doucegrove Lane
Northiam
Rye
East Sussex TN31 6JQ

A catalogue record for this book is available from the British Library.

PAPERBACK ISBN 978-0-9927568-0-2

Typeset by Octavo Smith Ltd

To Della

Sophie looked across the table directly into Henri's eyes. Her heart was pounding, her mouth was dry and she felt the thrill of adrenalin as it coursed through her body. She tried to penetrate his expression, but his eyelids were hooded, almost lizard-like in the way that they covered most of the pupil. This made it hard for her to look deep within him, which was what she needed to do. Then she saw it, just a glimmer, but it was enough. His eyes had betrayed him; now she knew what to do.

They were playing Texas hold 'em with a maximum raise of two pounds in the last round of betting. This had not sounded like a huge sum when they had agreed it, but there were probably thirty pounds in the current pot, one of the biggest of the night, and Sophie needed to win it. She could live quite well for a week on thirty pounds. It was always useful to know an opponent's financial situation, but she had no idea if this was a lot of money to Henri, as she had only met him that evening. What Sophie did know was that poker was a game of patience, and she had waited the last couple of hours for this moment. She had a good hand – ace-king in the hole – which she had paired with the ace and king among the five community cards showing face up on the table. This alone was not enough; to make any money she needed Henri to have a good hand too, only slightly less good than her own. Her interpretation of the glimmer she had spotted

9

in his eye was that his hand was strong but not the strongest. She knew already that she had him beaten, but she tried desperately not to allow her body to betray the way she felt. She looked at Henri again. He had played well that night, pulling off a couple of decent bluffs as well as maximising the amount he made from some good cards. She wondered if he would be smart enough to fold this hand. She loved these moments and milked the fact that men found it more difficult to fold against a woman. She knew what to do.

'Raise,' she said. 'Your two pounds plus another two pounds.'

Henri looked back across the table at her; she could feel him trying to look into her soul. The other two at the table, making up the four, were her flatmate Mark and his friend Johnny. They had both already folded their hands, and it was left to Henri to decide whether or not to bet again. She sensed that he had been watching her not the cards, as the last community card had been placed face up with the other four. Had she given something away? A release of tension as she paired her king perhaps?

'I fold,' said Henri.

He flipped his cards over as he spoke, showing everyone that he had ace-queen. This was quite an arrogant thing to do, but it was calculated. He did not need to show his cards once he had conceded; it was as if he wanted Sophie and the others to know that he had folded a good hand because he knew that she had ace-king.

'Fuck,' said Johnny. 'You folded ace-queen?'

'That's because I know that she has ace-king,' he replied in his slightly accented English, looking straight at Sophie. Her eyes were large and blue, but she did not invite him in. She was too annoyed. She simply raked in the pot and picked up the cards without showing her own hand. She started shuffling the deck, still looking at Henri.

'I suppose we'll never know now,' she said to him.

'I know, and that's enough for me,' he replied.

'Good hand, guys,' said Mark. His natural response to tension was to try to dispel it.

'Thanks, Mark. It's nice to know there's at least one gentleman at the table.' Sophie was smarting from Henri's arrogance. She felt herself colouring slightly; she hated being patronised, particularly at the poker table. She had won the pot, but she had not won the hand, and that was what annoyed her the most. Knowing when to fold was perhaps the most important aspect of poker. Henri had lost some money but had saved himself a lot more; more importantly, he had won the respect of the other players. All of them would be more wary of him now that he had demonstrated an ability to read an opponent's hand so precisely.

'So how the fuck did you work that out, Henri?' Johnny asked.

Henri tapped a Disque Bleue out of its soft packet, lit it and inhaled deeply.

'That is for me to know and for you to find out.' He smiled with a slight sneer. It was an enforced sneer, as a close observer would notice that there was a small scar on his upper lip which held the left-hand side of his mouth lower than the right.

'Yeah, right. Fuck off, you arrogant tosser.' Johnny obviously knew Henri well enough to insult him like that. Sophie smiled to herself; it was exactly how she would have put it herself. She began to deal the cards.

'Right, the next hand is seven-card stud,' she said as she dealt. They were playing dealer's choice; the dealer called the version of poker that they played.

'Antes in please.'

'So did you have ace-king then, Sophie?' Johnny persisted.

'No, I had a pair of twos.' Sophie had met Johnny a couple of times before. He was an old school friend of Mark's. She found him attractive if a little rough around the edges. She looked up at him as she dealt to see if he believed her not. He smiled a half-smile at her; she could tell he was not quite sure what she had been holding.

She smiled an easy smile back. He was a bit of a waster, but she liked Johnny.

It was Mark who had taught her how to play poker. They had met in their first year at University College London, when they were on the same corridor in halls of residence. Coincidentally, they came from the same part of East Sussex, and this accident of geography had helped form an early bond between them. Mark had apparently learned his poker from Johnny when they were at school. Now that Sophie had got to know Johnny a little, she understood how he might have discovered a few vices before Mark.

'I don't think you would have re-raised with a pair of twos, but then what do I know? I'm well down tonight.' Johnny was confident but also quite self-critical, Sophie had noticed. It gave him a slight air of vulnerability to which she was drawn.

'Another whiskey might help,' said Mark. They were sipping their way steadily through a bottle of Jack Daniels.

'Cheers, mate, don't mind if I do,' said Johnny. Mark passed the bottle to him.

'Not for me thanks,' said Sophie.

'Me neither,' said Henri.

Sophie wanted to stay fairly sober, and she noticed that Henri also seemed to be drinking less than the other two. Maybe it was because he was French and not part of the macho drinking culture that seemed to consume English men. Sophie had dealt two cards face down to each of them, and she now dealt one card face up. She announced the cards as she dealt in the style that they all adopted when dealing.

'A small five to Johnny, a pretty-looking queen to Henri, a big fat ace to Mark and an insignificant ten to me. It's the ace to bet. Has everyone anted?'

The ante was fifty pence. Henri was short, and he threw in his fifty-pence piece beside the other three.

Sophie looked at her two hole cards – a three of clubs, a five of spades and the exposed ten of diamonds, three mediocre cards out of suit. She resolved to fold when the betting came around to her. She looked at the other three studying their cards; she knew it was important to watch other players even when you were not involved in a hand. To her left, Johnny's piercing blue eyes zoomed in on his hand; he flicked his fair hair back as he looked. Sophie found herself studying his cheekbones; she had always been drawn to a chiselled set of cheekbones. Johnny's were high and well-carved, giving a gaunt elegance to his expression.

'Whose bet is it?' he asked.

'Why, have you got some cards?' Mark grinned back at Johnny. Sophie smiled to herself. Mark was probably right. A player who wanted to get on with the game normally had a good hand, and as Johnny was not the most patient of players this was highly likely.

'No, I just want to get on with it,' he replied.

'All right. Chill, Johnny. It's my bet because I've got the ace. I bet a pound.' Mark threw a pound coin into the middle of the table.

'I fold,' said Sophie.

She looked at Mark. He was smiling to himself. He had a good hand, she thought, possibly another ace concealed or at least one, possibly two, concealed picture cards, maybe in suit. She turned to look at Johnny, who was next to bet.

'I'll call your bet,' said Johnny. He probably has a low pair, thought Sophie. With anything higher he would have raised Mark's bet. Johnny liked action and tended to bet too often. He picked up a Marlboro Light from the pack in front of him. Sophie watched as he pouted his lips slightly to accept the cigarette. She shifted a little in her chair, surprising herself. Johnny was definitely growing on her.

'I call.' She turned to Henri. He was harder to make out. He may have paired his queen. He may have cards to a straight or flush. He had something. His straight dark-brown hair fell in a fringe just above his eyes. He too was smoking, but his mouth looked too cruel to be sensual.

'Next card,' she said.

She dealt another card face up to each player: a seven of clubs to Johnny, a queen of clubs to Henri and a king of clubs to Mark.

'Highest hand showing to bet,' said Sophie. 'That's you, Henri, with the pair of queens.'

'I bet a pound,' said Henri.

'I call,' said Mark.

Raise, Mark, thought Sophie. I know you have more than a pair of queens. You've probably just paired that king with one in your hand, so you have at least two kings and an ace – or maybe even two aces and two kings.

'With this shit, I fold,' said Johnny, throwing down his cards.

Why did you bet last round, then? thought Sophie. Still, the cheekbones redeemed him.

She dealt the next cards: an eight of clubs to Henri first then an eight of hearts to Mark.

'Check,' said Henri.

'Check,' Mark agreed.

RAISE, MARK. It was so clear to Sophie, but Mark was cautious, and after the last hand he was clearly even more wary of Henri.

She dealt the last cards face up: a queen of hearts to Henri and a jack of hearts to Mark. Henri now had three queens showing.

'I bet one pound.' Henri threw in another pound coin.

'I call,' said Mark.

He really does find it impossible to raise, thought Sophie – but she quickly forgave him, as this time he might actually be behind. She really wanted Mark to win this hand, but now he might lose it. Three queens looked strong. She dealt a last card down to each of them. As she dealt to Henri she noticed again that he was not looking at his card. He was looking at Mark. She dealt to Mark, and, unbeknown to him, both she and Henri watched as he picked up his card. A smile flashed momentarily across his face. Shit, thought Sophie, now Henri knows you've made your hand. She watched as Henri picked up his card, smiling to himself. Sophie knew that Henri's smile confirmed that he knew that Mark was now ahead. Perhaps three aces or better.

'Check,' said Henri.

'I'll bet two pounds,' said Mark with way too much joy in his voice.

'I'll call,' said Henri, 'not because I expect to win, but because I want to see your cards.'

'I've got a full house, aces over kings,' Mark said triumphantly. Three of these cards had been concealed, a wonderful hand to squeeze money from an opponent, particularly one who had three queens.

'That beats me,' said Henri. 'Just the three queens. Good hand, Mark.'

Sophie knew that Henri was aware he could have lost a large sum backing his queens against a better player. He looked at her furtively as Johnny congratulated Mark; the look said that he knew that she also knew. It was conspiratorial. She felt better; Henri was telling her with this look that he knew she was a good player. Mark had had a fantastic hand and had played it just about as badly as he could have done. They both knew that, but it was lost on the others. She held Henri's gaze for a moment, acknowledging the conspiracy.

'Yes, great cards, Mark,' she said still looking at Henri. Then she turned to Mark. He beamed back at her, so pleased with her appreciation of his good fortune. Sophie had got to know that look. She loved Mark like a brother, but she knew that he loved her like a lover.

It was the end of August, and they had finished their final year at UCL. Sophie had graduated with a 2:1 in English and Mark with a 2:1 in Business Studies. Typically, Mark already knew what course his life would take. In September he would begin his training to become a chartered accountant at Coopers & Lybrand in the City. Mark had asked her to stay on with him at the hard-to-let council flat in Wapping that they currently shared with two other friends, Steve and Kate, but she knew it was time to move on. She would give Mark the news soon. He would be disappointed, but it would not be the first time that she had disappointed him. She looked over at Johnny and thought of another way that she might disappoint Mark. She had heard Mark mention Johnny's girlfriend in Hastings, but Johnny had mentioned earlier that it was nothing serious. She wondered if he had registered her own interest.

Johnny had picked up the cards and begun to deal again.

'Right, you bunch of losers, it's time for me to win some money back. Five-card stud. Now we'll see how brave you are.'

'I don't think bravery alone will win you any money, *mon ami*, but if you can add some wisdom to your bravery then maybe you have a chance.'

'Henri, I always said you were smart.' Mark was still full of bonhomie following his full house.

Johnny started to announce the cards. Sophie stopped looking at him and concentrated on the game.

***

It had been light for some time, but as the sun crept higher a burst of sunlight through the window had reminded them that it was probably time to stop the game and get some sleep. They stood around the table, stretching and yawning.

'Right, I'm going straight to bed,' said Mark.

He raked up what little money he had left in front of him.

'What are you guys doing? You're welcome to crash on my floor or on the sofa.'

'I'll take the sofa,' said Henri. He was stowing the money he had won in the front pocket of his jeans. This was taking longer than it had done for Mark.

'I think I'll get some air,' said Johnny. There was less than a pound in change on the table in front of him.

'Do you fancy a walk?' asked Sophie. 'I could do with clearing my head too.'

'Yeah, why not?' said Johnny. 'It'll help me get over my losses.' He was grinning. He had one of those Hastings accents that would not be out of place in south London.

Sophie had been putting the notes that she had won into her bra as the game went on, so she had little money left in front of her. She had noticed Johnny taking an interest in these manoeuvres, and his interest had piqued her own.

The flat was in the middle of Wapping, a stone's throw from Wapping High Street. The area was on the move. As they stepped out into the bright morning light they were greeted by herds of cranes framing the skyline. It was Saturday, so the bird-like machines were quite still, and there was an unpopulated silence in the air.

'This area's like a fucking building site,' said Johnny.

'I'll show you what it's going to end up like,' replied Sophie. 'I don't think our flats will survive much longer.'

She led Johnny through the wasteland that surrounded the flats towards the start of Wapping High Street. She could not recollect being alone with Johnny before. Their lack of familiarity had seemed to make their conversation a little stilted when he had visited Mark.

'You played good cards tonight.'

'I think I was quite lucky.' She tried to rebuff the compliment.

'No, you played well. You were up against decent competition. Henri's a pretty tasty player. You held your own against him. I taught him to play, and I've never beaten him.'

'Well, thank you. I think I made about forty pounds. That's a lot for an impoverished student.'

'I didn't think you were a student anymore.'

'Well no, you're right, I'm not, but I still feel like one. I haven't quite moved on yet.'

'No, and I think Mark would prefer it if you didn't move on.'

'You've noticed, have you?'

'It's not just that I've noticed, he's told me that he only has eyes for you.'

'I told him a long time ago that I'm not attracted to him in that way. It wasn't an easy conversation. I tried to be gentle with him.'

'No, he told me about it at the time. I don't blame you. He's an ugly fucker.' Johnny turned and smiled at her. His eyes glinted in the sun. It cast a small shadow under his cheekbones. He was flirting a little, but she was not quite sure yet how to react.

'Where did you meet Henri?' Sophie wanted to change the subject to give her a little time to decide whether or not to flirt back.

'He came and stayed with us in Hastings as a foreign student. He was there to learn English. I taught him how to smoke, drink and play poker.' He smiled again. It was a winning smile.

'So you corrupted him, did you? He doesn't strike me as someone who'd've been a naïve teenager.'

'No, you're right, I'm exaggerating a little. I really think we hit it off because we had the same interests. He already knew how to smoke and drink, but I did teach him how to play poker.'

As they walked into Wapping High Street the Victorian wharves began to tower over them; the sun disappeared behind the buildings, and they were left in a corridor of nineteenth-century brick. Some of the old warehouses were derelict, but these were in the minority. Many of them seemed to have been renovated, but there were few indications as to their use. The street was deadly quiet, and there were no other pedestrians. The tell-tale sign of occupation of the refurbished buildings was a stainless-steel panel at their entrances with a column of buzzers. Otherwise they seemed lifeless and empty.

'So, is this where the yuppies live?' asked Johnny.

'I think so, but they're quite difficult to spot. I think there's probably a sprinkling of media types too. Maybe they rush off to the country at the weekend.'

'How close are we to the City?'

'You can walk easily; it's maybe ten minutes walk to the Tower of London, then after that the City starts. I rather like this street; it's certainly easier on the eye than it was when we first came. Even more buildings were derelict then, and they looked like they had been for years. At least they're being used now. The buildings on the right front the river at the back. I'll show you in a minute.'

Johnny grunted. Sophie sensed that he was trying to decide whether or not to approve or disapprove of the changes to the area. He seemed to have that educated-working-class spikiness when it came to the well-off.

Further down the street, as they approached the Prospect of Whitby pub, Sophie ushered Johnny to the right. There was a gap between the pub and the last wharf, with steps disappearing between the buildings. She led him down the dank alley of stairs. Suddenly, at the bottom, the sun was back in their eyes as the River Thames opened up in front of them. The bottom of the steps took them on to the banks of the river, a mixture of mud, shingle and rubbish. Opposite lay Bermondsey, skulking in the shadows.

'Fuck. I had no idea the river was so close to us. This is like your own private beach.' Johnny picked up a stone and skimmed it across the water with the practised skill of a regular beach-goer.

Sophie smiled, enjoying the rays of the early-morning sun on her face. A soft river breeze gently diluted the warmth. She was tired but happy. A profitable night followed by the company of a somewhat spiky but rather handsome male. She watched as he skimmed stones. He was slim and wiry, wearing a tight white cotton T-shirt, ripped Levis and a pair of black Converse All Stars. His longish fair hair flicked his cheeks as he threw the stones. She definitely fancied him. He stopped what he was doing and turned around. The tiredness around his eyes made him more accessible.

'I've got the feeling that things are changing a lot lately,' he said.

'What do you mean?'

'Well, look what's going on around here. It's probably been a wasteland since the Second World War, and now suddenly it's all changing. I'm not sure if it's for better or worse, but things are changing. A few people are getting richer; a lot of others seem to be getting poorer.'

'Things are definitely changing for me. I'm going to tell Mark that I'm leaving the flat. I'm going back to Rye before I start my new job at the beginning of next year.'

'Really? That's cool. He'll be disappointed, but I think he knows that you won't be around for much longer. What kind of job is it?'

'I'm going to train to be a clothes buyer for Herberts, the department store in the West End. I've always been really into clothes, and my dad knows one of the directors. I got him to make an introduction, and they decided that they liked me.'

'Oh, right. I should have realised.'

'What do you mean?'

'Well, it's obvious that you're quite posh, so I suppose your parents would be able to help you out.'

'Why is it obvious that I'm posh?' Sophie knew that she was quite well-spoken but had never considered herself to be posh. 'I went to my local comprehensive, and I think you went to grammar school, so how does that make *me* posh?'

'It's not a bad thing. I like it. You enunciate your words, you have nice manners and you've got a confidence that comes from the way you were brought up.'

'Well, that doesn't make me posh.' Sophie now felt flattered but didn't want to concede ground.

'Commiserations on the schooling, though. That place is grim. Why did your mum and dad make you go there?'

'That's another story.'

'Well, I like having a posh friend. Believe me, it's a rarity in Hastings.'

By this time Johnny was standing close to her, looking directly into her eyes. He smiled an easy smile. He touched her upper arm to reassure her. She was wearing a sleeveless top, and the feeling of his hand on her skin took her by surprise. They heard the sound of laughter behind them; there were already some people on the pub terrace.

'What time is it?' Sophie asked.

'No idea, but it sounds like the pub's open. How about a nightcap?'

'Just what I was thinking,' Sophie replied.

***

'I've got a nice buzz going,' said Johnny as they walked back from the pub.

'That might have something to do with staying up all night then having a couple of pints for breakfast,' said Sophie. 'I must say, I feel pretty good too.'

Impulsively, she reached for Johnny's hand as they walked. He took it. She tingled at the intimacy.

'I know what you mean about things changing, Johnny. I feel like I'm at the start of a new chapter.'

'Maybe you are.' He turned and smiled at her.

They arrived at the flat and, stifling their giggles, opened the door quietly. It was dark inside, and they could see Henri asleep on the sofa. Sophie had made up her mind. She took Johnny's hand and led him to her bedroom. He followed compliantly. As the door closed behind them he leaned down to kiss her softly on the mouth. She kissed him back harder and felt him responding to her. Suddenly they were both in a hurry. She pulled his T-shirt up over his head and started to undo his belt and pull down his jeans. He had already taken off her top and released her bra, as if by magic, with one deft movement. She felt his chest on her breasts as they kissed again before he manoeuvred her towards the bed. She felt her body firming to his touch. They could not get much further without taking their shoes off, so they sat on the side of the bed hurriedly unlacing their shoes and taking off their socks.

'I don't have any condoms,' Johnny said in a low whisper.

'Don't worry, I'm on the pill,' Sophie replied.

'What about safe sex?'

'I want you, Johnny.' Sophie could not quite believe what she was saying.

'Yeah, me too.'

They both peeled off their jeans. Suddenly Sophie felt self-consciously naked. The curtains were drawn, but they couldn't keep out the bright light of the sunny day. Johnny clearly had no such feelings; he stood up and took off his boxer shorts. She could see immediately that he was already aroused. He sat back down next to her and began kissing her again. She liked the way he touched her, gently but firmly. Against her better judgement she also liked the way he smelled of sweat and beer with an undercurrent of cheap aftershave. She let him push her slowly down on the bed. His hands began to explore her body, moving slowly down between her legs, where he touched her softly but confidently. She felt relaxed and excited by him, and it felt right to take his penis in her hand. She had a last fleeting pang of guilt about Mark before she abandoned herself to the moment.

HASTINGS AND RYE

10 NOVEMBER 1989

Sophie sat on the sofa in her dressing-gown. Fortunately her mother had gone out shopping and her father was at work in his study. The BBC news was on in the background, but she was finding it hard to concentrate on anything other than the news delivered during her first visit to the bathroom that morning.

This is the middle of the checkpoint, and the gates have been opened. The police are making no attempt to stop people as they go through and come back. I have never seen such elation.

How long was it since she had first slept with Johnny? She went over the dates in her mind again. It had been Saturday 26 August. Today was Friday 10 November. Seventy-six days ago. Eleven weeks, give or take a day. She was not sure why she had not tried the pregnancy test until now. She had even slept with Johnny again a couple of weeks ago, although not with quite the same gusto. The problem was her rather erratic use of the pill. It meant that her cycle was always a little all over the place, so it had taken her a while to realise that she really should have had a period by now. Margaret Thatcher appeared on the television screen.

I watched the scenes on television last night and again this morning. You can see the joy on people's faces. You can't stifle or suppress people's desire for liberty.

What about my liberty? thought Sophie. Johnny had said that things were changing; well, he was in for a bit of a shock. It should have been obvious when the morning sickness started, but even then she had tried to ignore it. There was no ignoring it now. She watched the scenes on the television; thousands of Germans swarming all over the Berlin Wall. Things really were changing. If she was going to bring a child into the world, at least some of the changes seemed to be for the better. She stopped herself. That was the first time she had really begun to think about bringing a child into the world. Until now she had only really thought about whether or not she was pregnant, not the consequences. One thing that she needed to do was share the news. It was time to call Johnny. She picked up the telephone, tapped out the number for his flat in Hastings and let it ring.

'Hello.' A muffled voice delivered the greeting as if from under the bedclothes.

'Johnny?' Sophie asked nervously, although it was unlikely to be anyone else. 'Sorry, were you asleep?'

'Oh, hi Sophie. Sorry about last night. Alex can be a bit of a tosser. Don't take him too seriously.'

'No, I won't. I'm sorry, I didn't call about that. I want to talk to you about something else actually but not on the phone. Can I come over?'

'Yeah, sure, whenever you like. I'm taking it easy today after the gig.'

'I'll come over around lunchtime then.'

'Cool. See you then, babe. Are you OK? You sound a little tense.'

'I'm fine. See you a bit later.'

That had not gone particularly well, she thought as she put the receiver down. She had hardly thought about the exchange of words with that worm Alex. He seemed to think he owned Johnny. Maybe she had overreacted to his weasely remarks and sexual overtures last night, but she had felt better for it. Alex needed to know that he had been usurped in Johnny's pecking order. Her mind turned to more practical matters. What does a girl wear to tell her boyfriend that she is pregnant? She retired to her bedroom to wrestle with that difficulty. She took off her dressing-gown and looked at herself in the full-length mirror on her wardrobe door. She had always thought that her breasts were a little too small, but, was it her imagination, or were they looking bigger? She looked at her stomach; she had avoided having a good look in the mirror over the last few weeks. Now it was obvious. She had grown a small tummy already. She looked at her chin. Was there a little more flesh? Her bobbed hair disguised it if there was. She was pretty sure that Johnny would not notice immediately, but a baggy jumper would probably make sure. She had not even thought about it last night, but the test result had suddenly made her hyperconscious.

***

Sophie's train chugged and rattled its way across the marshes from Rye to Hastings. There was not much change here: the seats were still worn, and you still had to slam the doors as hard as you could to close them. Sophie sat with her back to the front of the train and watched as the spire of St Mary's Church, the highest point in Rye, gradually disappeared into the distance. She had the next twenty minutes on the train to plot her strategy. Now that she knew she was definitely pregnant, she also knew that she wanted to keep the baby. As far as she was concerned an abortion was out of the question. She had been brought up as a Catholic, and while she no longer practised, she found it difficult to go against some of the fundamental beliefs. Abortion was one of them. It would certainly mean goodbye to the job at Herberts and a career in fashion, at least for the moment. But how would Johnny respond? Since the poker game their relationship had been affectionate but sporadic. They had only seen one another a handful of times and slept together only twice, including that fateful Saturday in August. How did she feel about Johnny? Was she in love with him? Did she want him to be a proper father to the baby? Did she want them to live together? There was currently no other love interest on the scene, so Johnny had no competition unless you counted Mark. Now there was a thought. If ever there was a reliable potential father it had to be Mark. But Mark was not the father; it was Johnny, the budding rock star, who was the father. Sophie knew she was not in love with Johnny, but she liked him. He made her laugh, she found him attractive, she liked to spend time with him, but could she spend all her time with him? Where would they live? Not at his bedsit; not with her parents, surely. He definitely would not want that. She had kept him away from them so far. Sophie realised she did not really have the answers to these questions yet. She had not had time to decide what she wanted herself, other than to have the baby. She decided that she would play it another way. She would wait to see how Johnny reacted. She still did not know him well enough to predict what his reaction might be, so she would just keep a completely open mind. She knew that his father had left home before he was born, leaving his mother to bring him up on her own. How had this influenced his views on fatherhood? She had no idea.

The train pulled briefly into Winchelsea Station and continued through the Brede Valley. The beauty of the countryside was less apparent this time of the year under the grey winter skies. The August sun seemed a long way away.

***

He opened the door, his hair tousled as if he had just got out of bed. She knew from the sleep in his eyes that this was indeed the case. He leaned forward and kissed her on the lips. He left a lingering smell of stale alcohol behind him. He was obviously in quite a fragile state. The bedsit smelled of cigarettes and the fug of drunk young male. Fortunately for Sophie it was just about late enough in the day for her morning nausea to have left her; otherwise she might well have been sick on the spot.

'Hi,' he said. 'Sorry, I'm feeling a little the worse for wear. We had a few drinks after the gig.'

'That's OK, I understand. I'm sorry that I stormed out. I couldn't bear the company of that weasel Alex a moment longer. Are you hungry? Maybe we could go out for something to eat.' Anything to get out of here, thought Sophie.

'Yeah, sure. Some fresh air would do me some good. I'm feeling pretty fuzzy.'

A perfect preparation for the conversation we're about to have, thought Sophie.

'How about Dimarcos? I haven't been there in years.' Sophie had a sudden urge for an ice cream float.

'Yeah, great idea. They do a wicked bacon sandwich.'

Johnny picked up his leather biker jacket, patted his pockets to make sure he had his cigarettes, and off they went. His bedsit was at the top of a stuccoed Victorian building behind the station. Sophie imagined that the road had been quite grand at one time, but no longer. Most of the houses had been converted into the small units preferred by slum landlords. No, she thought, this was not an ideal environment for the new baby.

'So what was it you wanted to talk about?' Johnny asked. He had taken hold of her hand as they walked. She gladly accepted it and still felt a bit of a tingle.

'Oh, nothing much,' she said dismissively. 'Let's have something to eat first.'

They turned the corner and arrived at Dimarcos on the seafront. It had been a while since Sophie had dipped into this sixties time warp, all Gaggia coffee machines and nicotine-stained walls. As usual it was staffed by a couple of middle-aged Italians in purple nylon jackets who whiled away their days making lewd remarks in Italian about their female customers. They were accompanied by the palest of surly teenage girls in purple housecoats who did most of the work. Only the men seemed to be allowed to operate the Gaggia machine; the girls appeared to do the rest, hence their attitude. Sophie and Johnny took a seat by the window, which looked out across the road to the promenade and the sea beyond. The wind was gusting, blowing hard at hats and coats as people walked by. Once they had made themselves comfortable at the Formica one of the girls wandered towards them, her plimsolls squeaking on the lino floor as she dragged her feet.

'What can I get you?' The accent was the Estuary English of the south coast.

'I'll have a lime ice cream float please.' Sophie wondered if her unusual order might give Johnny a clue, but it passed without comment.

'Bacon sandwich and a cup of tea please, love.' Johnny suddenly sounded more Hastings than when he spoke to her.

The waitress squeaked back to prepare their order.

'So, what's on your mind?'

Sophie looked into Johnny's clear blue eyes. He was definitely not ready for this, she thought, but there was no way back.

'I've got some news,' she said.

'Well, I've worked that out.'

'I'm pregnant.'

'What?'

'I'm pregnant. I'm going to have a baby.'

The colour had drained from Johnny's face. He looked gaunter than ever.

'How can you be? We only slept together a couple of weeks ago. How do you know already? I thought you were on the pill anyway?'

'The first time we slept together was in August.'

'But that's three months ago.'

'Yes.'

There was a silence. Definitely a pregnant pause, thought Sophie. She imagined the cogs whirring in Johnny's head. About now he would probably be wondering if it was his baby. She watched him take out a cigarette and light it. She thought about the effect that the smoke might have on the baby but said nothing.

'And you're sure you definitely are pregnant?'

'Well, the tests say I am, and I'm being sick in the morning, but I haven't been to the doctor yet. I wanted to see what you would say first.'

'Sorry to ask, but you're sure it's mine, are you? It's not as if our relationship is that serious at the moment. We're just getting to know each other really.'

'I haven't slept with anyone else, if that's what you're asking, and I'm assuming that an immaculate conception can be discounted.' Sophie was mildly annoyed by this line of questioning.

In a rustle of nylon, their food arrived. Johnny was quiet and still as his sandwich and tea were put in front of him. Her luminous-green ice cream float looked just as she remembered. Served in a time-warp glass coffee-cup was a combination of green lime-flavoured syrup and vanilla ice cream. The scoop of ice cream bobbed on top of the fizzy liquid, eluding Sophie as she tried to spear it with the extra-long teaspoon provided for this purpose. She looked up at Johnny. He took a last long drag on his cigarette before stubbing it out in the ashtray on the table. He had something, she thought. She was not sure if it was very fatherly, but he had something.

'This is what happened to my mum,' he said. 'My dad fucked off as soon as he heard she was pregnant. I've never tried to find him, and he's never tried to find me. I don't think that's any way to grow up. But really, I think it's up to you, love. I mean, it's going to affect you the most. What do you want to do?

'I can't imagine not having it, even though I've only just found out. The first thing that occurred to me was that I couldn't possible have an abortion; it's the only thing that I'm sure about.'

'Well then, we'll have to think about what we're going to do. Maybe we should start by getting to know each other a bit better.'

'What do you mean? That you want me to have the baby too?'

'I mean that if you've decided to have it then I'm not going to stand in your way. I'll do what I can to help.'

This sounded slightly unconvincing, but then Johnny reached over the table and took Sophie's hand. He smiled his winning smile, and she felt quite overwhelmed. She wiped away the tears that had welled up.

'Thanks, Johnny.'

'No worries,' he said. 'I think I'll get a cream doughnut. D'you want anything?'

THE M20

1 JULY 1990

Mark Arnold flicked the overdrive switch on the dashboard, eased the gear lever into top and settled into the inside lane of the M20. Now that he had a steady job he had decided to allow himself a treat, a 1967 MGB GT in British racing green with a black-leather interior piped in white. He was enjoying the car but did not want to push it too hard. You had to be easy on these old classics. Still, this was the last part of motorway driving, then he would be back on the A roads that took less of a toll on his pride and joy. He should be there in less than an hour now. He was still slightly peeved that Sophie and Johnny had organised the christening on the same day as the England–Cameroon game. He knew that the invitations had gone out before they had known that England were playing, but if Johnny had been properly organised he would have scrutinised the fixtures in advance and excluded any dates that might have fallen on the same day as an England match. But then Johnny had never been as organised as he was and, in fairness, never as interested in football. The game was at eight o'clock tonight; the christening, he had been told, was at two o'clock. Johnny had assured him that most of the guests would have gone by the time the game started, and that the plan was to watch the game then play some cards. Henri would be coming too, so they could make up the poker four that had been established in Wapping.

Mark felt generally uneasy, but then he often did. He was worried that England might not beat Cameroon; he was worried that he might miss the match; but he was also worried for his friends Johnny and Sophie. Johnny sleeping with Sophie in August had been difficult enough to take, but the pregnancy had really thrown him. Then there had been the register-office wedding – more for Sophie's parents than for the happy couple, Mark had thought – and now there was a church christening. Sophie's mother had no doubt used her connections at the local Catholic church to make sure that her grandchild was properly baptised. He found it difficult to believe that Johnny, the coolest guy he knew – Swerve's guitarist, for God's sake – was now married with a child, living in his wife's parents' annexe. It was difficult to fathom. But Mark was still jealous. Sophie was with Johnny, and Johnny was with Sophie. The two biggest crushes he had ever had, and they were together. He never liked to dwell on the Johnny crush, as this led him down a route that he did not wish to travel. The Sophie crush he was a little happier to dwell on, but it still brought back difficult memories. He conjured up an image of those blue eyes and that wide full-lipped mouth, her face framed by the dark-brown bob, her skin tanned brown, just hinting at a southern-European genetic influence. He had often looked at her secretly when they were living together, as they watched television or as she read a book. She had seemed so confident and self-assured; funny but with a serious side. He had decided not long after they had met that she was his ideal woman; all he had needed to do was convince her that he was her ideal man. He had failed. He was still not quite sure why, but she had at least tried to explain her reasons to him. He had found the conversation difficult.

'Before we move into the new flat together, Mark, I just want to make something clear, so that there are no misunderstandings.'

He appreciated the fact that she had addressed the problem, because it had needed to be addressed, but he had not been ready for what she had said.

'So, you see Mark, I love you dearly as a friend, but not as a lover.

I'm sorry. I just don't feel the spark. I wish I did because you are a wonderful guy, but I'm afraid I don't. I hope you understand, and I hope it won't affect our friendship.'

Not as a lover. Wonderful guy. Love you as a friend but not as a lover. The conversation had been three years ago now, but he still felt the knife in his heart as he looked back on it. At moments like this, when he was alone and began to think of Sophie, the memory often appeared still fresh. Too fresh, thought Mark. He wished he was better at archiving the file, but it seemed to refuse to be stored away. So, instead of what he had hoped for, those two years of flat sharing had been platonic. They had both had other sexual relationships during that time, but these had been short-lived; their friendship had outlasted all of them. Mark still failed to understand the logic. They were quite clearly compatible. While he knew he was not as cool as Johnny, he had been told that he was attractive to women, and he made a point of keeping himself in good shape. Sophie had told him that she loved him, but not like that…

Then Johnny had screwed her in Wapping after the poker. That had been hard to take, but he was not surprised. Sophie was an attractive woman, so in a sense he did not blame Johnny for succumbing to her charms. But Johnny had known how Mark felt about her, and a part of him thought that Johnny had slept with her as a form of one-upmanship. They had always been quite competitive; he had been better than Johnny at sport, but Johnny had been more creative than him. He had actually felt more let down by Sophie than Johnny. No, it was more than that; he had not just felt let down, he had felt that Sophie had knowingly put an end to the intimacy of their friendship. A couple of frosty days later she had told him about moving out, going back down to Rye before she started her new job. By then he was almost pleased that she had decided not to stay on at the flat. He was pretty sure that the Johnny thing would have eaten away at him more if she had stayed. He did still feel a little sorry for them that their drunken tryst had ended in a pregnancy. He had never asked Sophie about the details, but Johnny had told him that he had not worn a condom, and Sophie had apparently not taken her pills consistently enough. He thought that they were mad to keep the baby. He could not imagine being responsible for a child himself. He was just setting out in the real world.

He turned off the motorway at Ashford and followed the signs to Brenzett, Rye and Hastings. He understood why Sophie could not start her new job in London. What he did not understand was why they had agreed to move into the annexe at Clifftops, Sophie's family home. For sure it was convenient and presumably cheap, but it meant living with Sophie's mother. Isabelle Arlington – even Sophie admitted she was overbearing. How could Johnny stand it?

Mark's new job meant that he had to work a sixty-hour week then study at the weekend. But that was not a problem, he was enjoying it, he felt like he was going places. Johnny and Sophie were not going anywhere with a new baby. Johnny had managed to keep Swerve going, and that was the last time he had seen him, over in Brighton at a gig. He had managed to get down to the coast and back in an evening a couple of weeks earlier. Swerve were the support band, so they had had time to chat afterwards backstage while the main band were playing. He remembered parts of the conversation.

'I can't believe you're a dad, mate.'

'Yeah, it's pretty wild. I have trouble getting my head around it myself. It was pretty fucking amazing at the birth, though. You know, when Amy popped out.'

'I can imagine.'

'You feel like this amazing love for this tiny little thing. Incredible.'

'But, what's it like now?'

'Honestly, mate, it's a fucking nightmare. We're both absolutely knackered the whole time. Sophie decided to breastfeed, so she has to do that every few hours, including the middle of the night. I had no fucking idea what it was going to be like. Growing up it was just me and Mum. I never saw what it was like to have a baby around the place. On top of that we have Isabelle sticking her beak in the whole time, telling me to put my cigarettes out, telling Sophie she's not doing stuff right. She does my fucking head in. Luckily I can escape to be with the band. Sophie's the one who's stuck there the whole time.'

'How is she? We haven't spoken in a while.'

'Sophie? I think she's OK. You'll have to ask her at the christening.'

He had felt just a little bit pleased that things seemed to be quite tough for them.

He rounded a corner on the marsh road, and the town of Rye suddenly appeared in the distance, an island of ancient buildings rising out of Romney Marsh. Mark had been down to Rye to see Sophie a couple of times in the past to stay at her parents' house when they were students. The house was at the top of Rye Hill, which was, in truth, more of a cliff than a hill, as he had pointed out to Sophie. From the first floor of the house, as they looked out of her bedroom window at a panoramic view of the sheep-littered marsh with the sea beyond, she had pointed out to him the three rivers converging just below Rye's old town, the Tillingham, the Brede and the Rother. As a result, the coastline in the area had been on the move for centuries as river bed became silt and sea became marsh. The sea was now two miles from the town, whereas a few hundred years before it had lapped up against the cliffs on which the town had been built. Even though he had grown up only twelve miles away in Hastings he was not very familiar with Rye. He found the area unusually atmospheric. It was not something he had experienced before, an area having an atmosphere. It made him feel a little uncomfortable.

***

Sophie opened the door to the annexe with one arm, holding Amy in the other.

'Hi, Mark. Great to see you.' He looked different, she thought, more self-assured. Perhaps it was just the double-breasted navy blazer with gold buttons.

'Hi, it's great to see *you*. And to finally meet Amy too.'

Sophie noticed that Mark was carrying an overnight bag.

'Are you staying the night?' she asked.

Johnny suddenly appeared behind her.

'Yes, I invited him. I thought we might play some cards later, like last summer. Henri's going to be here too. I thought I'd told you.'

'Maybe you did, but I don't remember really. I'm not sure that we're going to be able to play cards.'

'I've taken the day off work tomorrow. I thought it was going to be a late one tonight.' Mark looked a little hurt.

'Don't worry, guys, it'll work out,' said Johnny.

Sophie was too tired to argue. The idea of playing poker between feeds seemed ridiculous, but then the idea of her having a baby had seemed ridiculous the last time they played poker. She also knew nothing about Henri coming along. Or maybe she had just forgotten.

'Mark, how are you? I thought I heard a car on the gravel.'

Sophie's mother had now turned up to greet Mark, dressed as if she were about to attend Lady's Day at Royal Ascot. She was clearly making up for the rather shameful register-office wedding.

'Come in anyway.' Sophie ushered them inside. As she did so, Amy began to cry.

'She's due a feed. I should be able to squeeze it in before we have to leave.'

'Good idea, darling.' Sophie was speechless. Perhaps it was because they had company, but her mother had actually agreed with something she had suggested.

'Anyone fancy a sharpener?' Johnny was looking to oil the wheels.

'He's only just got in the door.' Sophie was irritated by Johnny wanting to play the host.

'I'd love a beer, mate.'

'I really shouldn't, Johnny, but, if you insist, a quick G and T would be lovely.'

'We've got beer, Bulgarian Cabernet Sauvignon and vodka, Isabelle. What do you fancy?' Johnny and Sophie could not afford to keep a drinks cabinet equivalent to that of her parents.

'Oh, give me a vodka with some tonic water then.'

Johnny turned to go and get the drinks.

'I'll have a cup of tea please,' Sophie said to his back.

'Coming up,' he called out.

She sat down in their cramped living space. Mark and her mother sat down on the sofa opposite. She unbuttoned her blouse, unclipped one side of her nursing bra, took out her breast and held Amy next to it. She enjoyed breastfeeding; she loved the emotional connection it gave her to Amy. She looked up to see Mark gawping at her breast. She ignored him and looked back down at Amy.

'It's interesting how fashions change, isn't it? When I was feeding you and your sister, I wouldn't have dreamed of doing it in public. Now it seems to be the most natural thing in the world.' Isabelle had clearly picked up on Mark's interest in Sophie's breast; Sophie interpreted her comments as a reprimand but chose to ignore it. Johnny arrived with the drinks on a tray.

'Ah, getting an eyeful, Mark?' he said as he served the drinks. Sophie watched Mark turn puce with embarrassment. 'Who wants bottle feeding, eh mate?'

'Johnny, really!' Isabelle was unimpressed.

'It's all right, Mum. It's Johnny's idea of humour.' Sophie was in no mood for an argument. Johnny came and sat next to her, putting his arm around her shoulders.

'I'm sorry, babe. You know I can't resist an opportunity to wind my old mate up.'

'My mother used to breastfeed my little brother, so I'm quite used to seeing a baby breastfed, thank you.' Mark tried to defend himself. Sophie noticed that he still looked uncomfortable. She decided to try to help him out; she still felt a little bit guilty about everything that had happened.

'Don't worry, Mark. I feel very comfortable feeding the baby in front of you. You're almost part of the family anyway.'

'Thanks, Sophie. By the way, as there was no formal invitation, I would like an idea of the itinerary for the day.'

Isabelle butted in immediately.

'I told Sophie that there should have been proper invitations. Anyway, the christening is in about an hour at St Anthony of Padua in Rye. We're so pleased that they agreed to let us hold it there. It's a Franciscan Friary. I think the Arlington name helped a little with the monks. Then afterwards everyone is invited back to our house for drinks and a buffet. I think that will ...'

Sophie was starting to zone out as her mother went through the plans for the day, when there was a knock at the door. Her father appeared.

'I found this waif and stray across the drive.' It was Henri. He too had an overnight bag. Isabelle jumped up.

'Henri, finalement on se rencontre! Quel plaisir!' she exclaimed as she rushed over to Henri at the door and kissed him on both cheeks.

Sophie waved in Henri's direction, unable to move while she was still feeding Amy. At least her mother was deflecting the attention; she always revelled in any opportunity to speak French. Isabelle's father, Sophie's grandfather, had been French, although he had lived most of his life in England. Isabelle had grown up in England but had spoken French to her father, and she was more or less bilingual, although Sophie thought her mother's French accent gave away her English roots. Amy had finished feeding on the right, so Sophie decided to retire to the bedroom to finish the feed on the other breast. This way she could avoid showing her breasts to Henri. Once in the peace and quiet of the bedroom her mind turned, despite everything, to poker. She was unexpectedly piqued by Henri's arrival, and it all went back to the way he had folded the ace-queen – that arrogant gesture as he flipped over his cards. Tired or not, she wanted revenge.

She could hear her mother talking to Henri and Mark in the next room. They were speaking in English, presumably for Mark's benefit.

'So you live in Geneva, do you, Henri?'

'Yes, that's right.'

'But you don't have one of those dreadfully ponderous Swiss-French accents. And Le Cerf, your surname, that's a French name isn't it?'

'You are quite right. My parents are from Paris, but I grew up in Geneva. My father is a lawyer working for the United Nations. He works for the United Nations High Commissioner for Refugees.'

'Oh, how interesting.'

'I suppose it must be, but he doesn't talk that much about it.'

'Did you go to school in Geneva then?'

'Yes, I went to the International School, which allowed me to learn English but also to take my exams in French. They teach in both languages. My parents wanted me to have the advantage of growing up bilingual.'

'And what are you doing now?'

'I'm studying philosophy at Geneva University.'

'Oh, how wonderful. You must talk to my husband Charles; he's terribly interested in aesthetics. He's an art historian, although it's more of a hobby, really. He's never had to work as such.'

Sophie cringed in the bedroom, but at least she now knew a bit more about Henri. Her mother always found a way of letting people know that they were independently wealthy within minutes of meeting them. Sophie had not really noticed that her father did not have a proper job when she was growing up; she had thought that his job was reading books in his study and going to museums. As she entered her teens she had overheard enough conversations between her parents to understand that her father had inherited enough money for them to live on, but not quite enough for her mother to live in the way that she thought she should. This was why Sophie and her sister Amanda had attended the local comprehensive. There was not enough money around for school fees, but there was enough for them to live in genteel poverty. It also explained the shabby-chic appearance of Clifftops. The house had been an Arlington family seaside retreat that Charles had inherited when still a young man. This stroke of luck at an early age seemed to have rather put the kibosh on his desire ever to seek gainful employment.

'And, Mark, how's the world of money?' Sophie's mother was as interested in money as Mark was but had a knack of distancing herself from the toil that produced it.

'Oh, it's all going rather well thank you, Mrs Arlington.'

'Call me Isabelle please.'

'Yes, sorry, Isabelle. I've passed my first lot of accountancy exams, so only two more lots and I'll be a chartered accountant.'

'How nice. Well, I think we must start to think about leaving. Where are Sophie and Johnny?'

Sophie could feel Mark smarting from where she was in the bedroom. Isabelle was not interested in chartered accountants and was not really interested in Mark. She had made this quite clear by asking him a question without really bothering to listen to the answer.

Sophie decided not to reveal her whereabouts immediately. She imagined that Johnny was outside smoking a roll-up, drinking a beer and avoiding Isabelle. They had only been living together at the annexe for a matter of months, and she already wondered how long this cosy arrangement might last. She looked down at Amy suckling; she needed to try to make it last a little longer for her sake.

**

For a football match, it had actually been quite exciting, enjoyable even. Amy's newly baptised head lay on the pillow of her crib in the bedroom next door, her parents were recovering from the rigours of the day in the main house, and Sophie was able to allow herself a glass of Bulgarian red while the boys watched the game. These kinds of moments had been few and far between recently.

'So what happens if it's still 2-2 at the end of extra time?' Sophie asked.

This was the first World Cup match that she had watched this summer. She had gathered that England seemed to be doing a little better than usual, and the names Gascoigne and Lineker were coming up a lot. She had a soft spot for Lineker's tanned legs but found Gascoigne's antics a bit childish.

'It goes to penalties,' said Mark. They were sat next to one another on the sofa. Henri and Johnny were stood by the window, smoking out of it rather than into the room as a concession to the baby's health.

Suddenly Mark was on his feet.

'That's a penalty!' He was bawling at the television.

'He's given it,' said Johnny. 'He's fucking given it.'

'*Vous avez de la chance, mes amis,*' said Henri. He had been siding with Cameroon on the basis that they were francophone.

It was Lineker who had been fouled, and it was also Lineker who dusted himself down, picked up the ball and placed it on the penalty spot. Mark and Johnny were both stood right by the television, almost shaking with nervous anticipation as Lineker turned away from the ball, walked back to his mark then turned again towards the ball, composed himself and ran forward before crashing the ball into the middle of the goal.

Mark and Johnny emitted caveman screams and threw themselves into one another's arms. It was almost homoerotic, she thought; the air was thick with testosterone. Henri had sat on the back of the sofa to watch the penalty more closely. He leaned down and moved his mouth right up close to her so that his low voice tickled her inner ear.

'*Ces Anglais,*' was all he said. 'These English.'

He moved his head back a little, still close, and lingered smiling at her perhaps a second longer than was decent. Then he stood up and began to clap Mark and Johnny on the back.

'It's not over yet,' Mark kept saying deadly seriously.

Sophie was not concentrating on the football. She was still thinking about the moment she had just had with Henri; she was slightly annoyed that something had stirred within her for the first time since she had had Amy. She hoped that feeling might come back when she was close to Johnny. She knew that Johnny was keen to restart their sex life, but so far she had put him off.

***

Sophie looked across the table at Johnny. She had folded her hand before seeing the three shared community cards known as the flop, so she was trying to study the remaining players as the hand developed. They had only been playing for about half an hour or so, but she was already finding it hard to concentrate. Somehow a game of poker seemed a little futile in the face of a bringing a new life into the world. Even the incentive to stick it to Henri seemed insufficient. She felt the pull of her bed and a couple more hours of snatched sleep before the next feed. The other issue was money; this was something she had never worried about before, but she and Johnny were skint. They were surviving on benefits and Johnny's sporadic cash-in-hand payments from gigs. This kind of hand-to-mouth existence had felt fine when she was a student, but now that she was responsible for Amy it felt uncomfortable. Her father would always help if she asked, but it was enough that they were living in the annexe. She had learned that the more help she received from her parents, the more her mother expected to be able to take control.

'Raise a pound,' said Henri.

'Your pound and raise another pound,' said Mark. 'Your bet, Johnny.'

Mark was raising? Sophie looked at her husband. She knew that expression. She had seen it at the poker table before. Thankfully she was yet to see it in their relationship. It was an expression of a kind of defeated stubbornness. Sophie quickly realised that in the current context it meant that he knew he did not have the best hand but was chasing a flush or a straight. They were playing Texas hold 'em, and the three cards in the flop lay face up on the table. If Sophie was right, Johnny had two more chances to hit his flush or straight. His problem was that the other two would most likely continue raising, making it more and more expensive for Johnny to pursue his dream.

'Call,' said Johnny, putting in two pounds to match the other bets but not to raise them.

This was the weakest response. It confirmed what Sophie had thought. The three cards showing were an ace of hearts, a king of spades and a five of hearts. Sophie suspected that Mark had at least one ace in his hand, giving him a pair of aces; he certainly would not be raising with anything less. Henri was harder to read, but he might also have an ace or a king or possibly a pair of fives in his hand. Johnny either had two hearts and was trying to find a fifth heart to make his heart flush or was trying to make a straight using the ace and king. Sophie knew that the odds of making the flush or straight with two cards left to be dealt were reasonable but less than fifty-fifty. A good chance but not odds-on. She looked at Johnny again; he was staring at his cards, his shoulders slightly hunched. A long way from his normal relaxed, open body language.

'I've been doing some research, Johnny, and the odds of hitting a flush or a straight with two cards to come are about two to one. So, I'm going to bet that you don't make it. Raise.' Mark had a smug look on his face that Sophie did not like. Passing some accounting exams seemed to have given him a new confidence that bordered on arrogance. He was definitely trying to needle Johnny.

'Raise,' said Henri.

'Fuck you guys – particularly you, Mark. Call.'

The die was now cast, thought Sophie. Johnny would chase his card to the end. If he did not find it he would fold and lose everything he had invested. If he found it his body language would betray his luck, and he would not win as much as he should have done. Johnny would never back down to Mark, and Mark's new-found confidence meant that he was finally ready to exploit this trait. However, Mark's confidence might yet be his undoing. In his haste to unseat Johnny he had taken his eye off Henri. Mark may have done his technical analysis of the probabilities, but she was pretty sure that he had not suddenly become a student of people. She had no doubt that Henri would come out on top when they counted their money at the end of the night. She did not have the energy to try to stop- him, and she was pretty sure that the other two did not have the ability. It all seemed rather predictable from where she was sitting. She had already decided that she would not play for much longer; her heart was simply not in it, and she could not bear to watch Johnny pissing away their disposable-nappy money.

The fourth card, the king of clubs, did not help Johnny, and he was squeezed again on the betting. The fifth card came down. It was the eight of hearts. Sophie was looking straight at Mark, whose expression immediately changed from smug to sulky. She looked at Henri, whose expression had not changed. His fringe of dark hair cast a shadow over those hooded eyes. She then looked at her husband; he seemed disconsolate. She could not understand why. He had the perfect opportunity to represent a flush now, even if he did not have one. Mark would certainly fold against a move along those lines, despite his apparently improved play. She realised that Johnny had probably not made the straight he had been chasing and had not even considered representing the flush as he had not even noticed it was there to represent.

'It's your bet, Mark,' said Henri.

'I know, Henri. I'm thinking.'

'Well, try to think a little more quickly.' A smirk crossed Henri's face as he said this. He looked at Sophie still with a half-smile and winked at her. She smiled a tired half-smile back.

'Check,' said Mark. No bet. Either an admission of weakness or a trap. Mark had never trapped anyone, so it was an admission of weakness.

'I raise,' said Henri.

'Well, I missed my straight, so I fold.' Sophie's heart sank as Johnny capitulated.

'I thought you had made the flush,' said Mark. 'Right, Henri, I'm still in the running. I'll call your bet. What have you got?'

Henri flipped over his cards. A king and an irrelevant two. With the two kings on the table he had three kings.

'You jammy bastard,' said Mark. 'I've got two pairs, aces and fives. That's a nice pot you've won there.'

'Yes, thank you, gentlemen,' said Henri, raking in the money.

'Anyway, nothing can ruin my night after that football result, eh Johnny?' said Mark.

'Too right, mate. Englaaand!' he cried out.

A baby crying cut through the fug of the poker table. It was the first time that Sophie had been pleased to hear Amy crying.

'Oh shit.' Johnny was still not used to having a baby in the house.

'Well done, Johnny. I'm sorry, guys, I'll have to feed Amy, and then I think I'm going to go to bed.'

'That's a shame, babe. We're only just warming up. You don't mind me playing on, do you?'

Sophie would have preferred that they stop playing, not least because she knew it was going to cost her money if Johnny carried on. But that was something she could not say.

'No, carry on. I'm sorry I'm so tired. No more football chants, though, please.'

Sophie retreated to the bedroom where Amy was still crying. She quickly changed into her pyjamas then picked Amy up out of her cot and sat with her back against the headboard of the bed feeding her. She felt the usual fierce emotional bond as she fed her baby, but simultaneously she felt melancholy. She realised that tears were trickling down her cheeks. She was tired, a deep inner tiredness from which it would take months to recover, but it was not just the tiredness that was causing the melancholy. She felt as if she were grieving for her youth. She was only twenty-two years old, but her youth had already disappeared. The day that she discovered she was pregnant she had become an adult. Her youth was a ghost that was sitting at the card table in the other room still playing cards, laughing at her friends' stupid jokes and getting drunk. This was exactly what Johnny was doing. It had taken a while to admit it to herself, but she resented the fact that she had become an adult, but Johnny had not. She had also realised that she resented him for causing the pregnancy in the first place. She did not resent Amy, only Johnny, and for the moment this resentment was preventing her committing to him. It was starting to eat away at her in an unhealthy way. She looked down at Amy. Although the sight of her baby made her feel calmer she knew that the bad feeling towards Johnny would remain simmering away under the surface.

Later she woke up to the sound of Johnny stumbling out of his clothes. She could smell the booze and tobacco at a distance. She lay inert with her back to his side of the bed, hoping that he would not notice she was awake. He sat on the edge of the bed wrestling with his jeans for a while. Then he stood back up and stumbled off to the bathroom next door. She listened to him brushing his teeth. It would have little impact on the smell, she thought. She wondered if he might start pawing her when he came to bed. She hoped he would just pass out. She felt lonelier than when she had slept alone.

Johnny sat playing a twelve-bar chord progression. The tinny sound of the unamplified guitar jangled in the small undecorated room. He liked to strum his battered old Telecaster immediately before going on stage. It calmed the nerves that he still felt at every gig. Tonight he felt them more acutely, as this was the biggest venue they had ever played. Thanks to Alex they had managed to get a spot as second support to the Jesus and Mary Chain. They were well down the bill, it was a one-off and they only had a half-hour spot, but even so, for them it was a seriously big deal.

'How long do you reckon we've got to go now?' asked Rob. He was pacing around the small room like a zoo animal waiting to be fed. He clutched his favourite drum sticks in one hand and a bottle of Holsten Pils in the other.

'We must be on soon,' said Alex, pulling deeply on a spliff before taking a draught on a bottle of Jim Beam. Not exactly the best preparation of the vocal chords, thought Johnny but left it unsaid.

'Well, they said ten minutes about half an hour ago.' Rob was impatient. Johnny wondered if he was speeding. More than likely, he figured.

'Chill, Rob,' said Johnny, regretting it instantly.

'Fuck off, Johnny. We can't all be as fucking sanguine as you.' Rob grinned at him. He had the slightly crazed look of the amphetamine habitué.

'Or as wired as you,' said Johnny, grinning back. He sparked up a Marlboro Light. Rob chose to ignore the loaded remark.

'Guys, we need to focus. This is our biggest gig ever. Do you two have to fuck around the whole time?' Alex, their self-appointed leader, seemed more nervous than usual.

'Come on, Dave, focus,' said Rob.

Johnny looked over to where Dave Simpson, their bassist, was slumped in a battered leather armchair. He looked asleep or stoned or both, but it was difficult to tell as his eyes were hidden behind a pair of wraparounds. He remained motionless. The others laughed, Alex despite himself.

The door opened, and the head of a security guard appeared.

'You're on, lads. Follow me,' he said.

Johnny's stomach flipped just to remind him how nervous he was. He downed the can of Foster's he had been nursing and got to his feet; he would continue with the Marlboro until it was finished. Rob shook Dave's shoulder. His long denim-clad legs slowly unravelled themselves and brought him to his feet.

'Must have dropped off. Sorry, lads.'

They trooped out of the dressing-room and followed the security guard up the corridor. Rob at the front, and Alex at the back.

'"Lost in Space" is up first, guys. Let's give it everything.'

They approached the side of the stage. Johnny caught Sophie's eye standing just offstage with Mark and Henri. He had wanted them all to be there for his big moment. Sophie looked nervous, but she smiled a broad smile as he almost jogged past. He had not seen that smile for a while.

The stage seemed huge. Their gear was dwarfed by the main band's banks of speakers, which would be used later. The lights were down. Johnny he dashed over to his amp, plugged in his guitar, pressed his foot on the fuzz box and was straight into the opening chords of 'Lost in Space'. The physical sensation was instant; the distorted notes enriched him in a raw, animalistic way, pumping adrenalin through his system. His nerves were forgotten, replaced by a rush of pure energy. The sound of the bass and drums kicked in as he started the chord progression for a second time, adding to his feeling of euphoria. Finally, at the end of the second chord progression, Alex's vocals began right on the button:

> 'I'm alone,
> Suspended from gravity,
> Away from reality.
> Is my mind playing tricks?
> Am I losing my sanity?
> No, I'm lost in space,
> I'm lost in space.'

Johnny mouthed the lyrics while Alex sang in his haunting style. He looked out from the stage for the first time and saw that right at the front there was a group of their hard-core fans singing along. Behind them there were gaps, but from what he could make out it was still easily the biggest crowd they had played to. He turned and looked at Dave's dishevelled figure strumming away at his bass. Dave winked at him. Johnny saw straight away that he was in the groove. He glanced at Rob behind his drum kit, his arms pumping, grinning like a Cheshire cat. The surge of energy he had felt at the start of the song stayed with him, the music shook through him; everything felt right, they were going to fucking rock Brixton Academy.

Sophie looked on from the wings. She had not seen Swerve since she discovered that she was pregnant, about a thousand years ago. The band seemed to be about a thousand times better too. She was astonished at the new level of maturity and confidence the band were displaying, and, for the first time, she felt a real pride in Johnny. She watched as his wiry body moved in time with the music.

He was in his own world, at one with his instrument; it was the only time she had seen him do anything with this level of intensity. It made her realise that she had probably been unnecessarily hard on him for the last couple of years or so. She suddenly felt quite overwhelmed. Swerve were better than good; they really were an excellent band. All this had been going on under her nose and she had been too busy and, worse still, too dismissive, to take proper notice of what had been happening. The music was making her tingle with excitement. She turned to Mark next to her, who was bouncing up and down in time to the music, singing along to the lyrics.

'They're really good, aren't they,' she shouted into his ear.

'I kept telling you to go and see them again,' he shouted back to her.

Sophie had to admit that Mark had been a much more loyal supporter than she had. He seemed to know the words to most of the songs, so he must have been to a lot of their gigs. The music was still quite hard-core, but there seemed to be less feedback and histrionics and more melody. Alex could really sing, and his vocals had a resonant quality that added a depth to the sound that was driven along by Johnny's soaring guitar and backed up by the relentless bass and drums. She sensed how the endless practice and the long-standing bonds between the band members were reflected in the tightness of the music. She felt a pang of guilt when she remembered how difficult she had made it for Johnny at times to go to his practice sessions. She had always thought that the band would disintegrate, and Johnny would then have to do something serious for a living. Now she was witnessing with her own eyes how far the band had come, she began to take her husband seriously for the first time.

She looked at Henri next to Mark; even the languorous Frenchman seemed to be transfixed by what he was seeing. His foot was tapping to the beat, and his head nodded as the guitar ebbed and flowed. It was the first time that she had seen him since the christening, about eighteen months ago. It was a while since she had thought of the feeling he had provoked in her. Had it been innocent on his part? She had never quite worked it out. Anyway, her husband was a rock star, why would she be interested in Henri?

She looked over at Johnny in his tight black Levi's, hunched over his guitar, eyes closed as he strummed out the last chords of what seemed to be the last song. The half-hour set had flown by in an intense, euphoric wall of noise. It had gone by too quickly. Sophie looked on as the band took their bows at the front of the stage, their arms around one another. The original fifty or so fans at the front had been joined by other new fans from the main throng, and they were giving the band a rousing send off. As they left the stage Johnny's eyes sought hers, and they embraced with a rare spontaneity and warmth. Johnny took her by the hand, and they followed a small crowd back down the corridor to the dressing-room. Rob and Alex were shouting and whooping as they went. Alex was with his girlfriend Charlotte just ahead. Rob seemed to be alone. Back at the dressing-room a table in the corner was piled high with booze.

'Right, you lot, it's time to party,' Alex yelled. His declaration was met with loud cheers. Sophie was still not sure about Alex; she looked at him fighting with a champagne cork before he popped it with a flourish. At times she felt like he wanted to own Johnny – perhaps she was simply jealous that they spent so much time together. She realised that she was next to Charlotte – or Charlie, as Alex called her.

'Well, that was fantastic, wasn't it?' Sophie said to her.

'Yeah. Amazing. Alex was brilliant. I love him so much.'

'Ladies, champagne.' The man of the moment arrived to hand them each a glass. Sophie had to admit that they made a great rock couple. Alex was dark, almost Mediterranean looking, with tousled shoulder-length brown hair but blue eyes. Charlotte had a kind of hippy English-rose look, soft, pale, flawless skin, a scattering of freckles over a pert nose, floaty fine blond hair and a rose-petal mouth. Sophie could imagine them in a soft-focus seventies advert with a Labrador puppy and lots of toilet roll.

'That was fucking amazing, Alex.' Johnny had joined them.

'I loved every minute of it,' Alex replied.

'Charlotte and I were just saying how much we enjoyed it.'

'It's Charlie, Sophie. Nobody calls her Charlotte anymore.' Alex was quick to make his point.

'Oh, really? I hadn't realised.' Sophie noticed that Charlotte herself had remained silent and was looking down at her feet.

'That's probably because you don't normally come and watch the band.'

'I'm sorry, Alex, but I do have a toddler to look after. Fortunately my mother's babysitting tonight, but I don't like to ask too often.'

'Come on, guys, let's enjoy the moment. No bickering.' Johnny was clearly uncomfortable.

'Yeeeah,' Alex yelled then hugged Johnny and took a swig on the champagne bottle he was holding. He then grabbed Charlotte with his other arm and looked back at Sophie triumphantly. Clearly there was animosity there that she had previously been unaware of. She wondered if he still bore a grudge over her rejection of his advances back at the Old Golden Cross in Hastings. She had not really had the opportunity to have a proper conversation with him since then. She tried to keep Amy away from the band.

Johnny broke free from Alex and came over to Sophie, kissing her hard on the mouth. She kissed him back, and tried to push Alex's display to the back of her mind. This was helped by the arrival of Mark and Henri with big grins and cans of free beer in their hands.

'So, this is what it's like to be a rock star?' said Henri. 'It doesn't look so bad. Not quite as glamorous as the life of a private banker, but not bad.'

'Well done, Johnny, you were absolutely brilliant,' said Mark and gave him a big kiss on the cheek. Johnny looked pleased but turned puce. Thankfully Alex and Charlotte had evaporated into the background.

'No, really,' Mark continued. 'That was the best I've ever seen you play. Forget the venue, forget who you're supporting, it was so tight but still really powerful.'

Sophie stayed quiet; this was only the second time she had seen the band live. First there had been Amy, and now she had the shop. But these were excuses, really; the band was something she had begrudged Johnny until now. She had not been to any gigs because she thought the whole thing was frivolous; now she realised that she had been unfair.

'Thanks, Mark. It was fucking amazing playing a venue like this. I know there weren't that many people actually watching us, but the vibe of the place was amazing.' Sophie had rarely seen Johnny so buzzed. She watched as he lit a cigarette, pursing his lips as he pulled hard on it, his eyes darting.

'I think more and more people came towards the front as the set went on. There were loads of them clapping by the end.'

Sophie listened to Mark. He had always hero-worshipped Johnny a little, but she could see that he was already starting to treat Johnny differently, with an extra reverence. She looked around the cramped room as the hyperbole continued. There were probably twenty or so people in the small room. She knew Rob and Dave, the other band members; they were in a corner together, chatting to a couple of pretty girls she had not met. Alex was holding court to a larger crowd; Sophie smelled a strong whiff of sycophancy coming from this group. Again the pretty girls were to the fore, and she noticed that Charlotte was clinging to Alex, making sure that they all knew who he belonged to. The girls in the room were all sporting a similar look to Charlotte's with lots of long straight hair, pouty lips, floaty dresses teamed with boots. Sophie made a mental note for the shop; grunge was definitely starting to influence fashion.

She needed to update her own look too; she felt a little out of place in her jeans and leather jacket.

'So, what's the plan?' said Mark. 'How are we going to celebrate Swerve taking Brixton Academy?'

'I'm really sorry, but I'm going to have to go soon. I've got to get back down to Rye tonight. I need to relieve my mother, but I'm also opening the shop tomorrow.'

'But tomorrow's Sunday,' said Mark.

'I'm opening for a few hours on Sundays in the run up to Christmas. I'm not sure if it's legal, but I haven't been arrested yet.'

'Well, that's a shame. It's been so long since we've had a proper night out together.'

Sophie could tell that Mark was genuinely disappointed.

'I'm sorry also,' said Henri. 'I have a date tonight.'

'That's the first I've heard of it, Henri. Who's the lucky lady?' asked Johnny.

'A gentleman never discusses such matters.' Henri put on his poker face and then broke into a smile. 'I'll tell you all if it's a success. I'm seeing someone from my old school in Geneva who now lives in London. I'll be late if I don't leave soon.'

'So, no chance of a game of poker.' Mark really was disappointed.

'We'll leave you two to party like rock stars.' Sophie felt middle-aged as soon as she said this.

'Well, we've been invited to the Jesus and Mary Chain after-party, as a matter of fact,' said Johnny, looking smug.

'That's the first I've heard of that,' said Mark. 'Fucking brilliant.'

'That's the first I've heard of it too,' said Sophie, looking quizzically at Johnny.

'I'm sorry, babe. We only found out tonight. You knew I was staying up here tonight, didn't you?'

'Yes, but I didn't know you were going to be hobnobbing with proper celebrities. I thought it was a night out with your boring old bandmates.'

'Yeah, well, that was the original plan...' Johnny's voice tailed off as he took a drag on his cigarette.

'Don't worry, I'll look after him.' Mark put a proprietary arm around Johnny's shoulders.

'Thanks, Mark. You're a real friend.' She was disappointed and a little envious. Mark's gesture and her sarcastic reaction were testament to the direction their relationship had taken. Mark competed with her for Johnny's attention; Johnny himself probably didn't even realise. Tonight Mark was winning; he was the one off to the celebrity party while she would be on the train back down to the south coast.

'Are you going back to central London, Sophie? *On peut y aller ensemble si tu veux?*'

'That's a good idea, thanks, Henri. The age of chivalry is not dead.'

'Do you mind not propositioning my wife?' Johnny was grinning but did actually seem to be slightly put out. The fact that Sophie spoke fluent French had always slightly rankled with him.

'I just asked if she wanted to go up to central London together.'

'Yes, I know. I do speak a bit of French, if you remember.'

'It's a shame we won't be able to play poker this time,' said Sophie, deliberately changing the subject.

'I agree,' said Mark. 'I've read a couple more books. I'm really getting on top of the probabilities now.'

Henri raised an eyebrow at Sophie.

'Well, I'll look forward to testing your knowledge. You know we haven't played since the christening, and I seem to remember that I bailed out early that night.'

Sophie looked at Johnny. He wasn't really interested in the poker conversation; his eyes were on Alex and his coterie. It was time for her to leave him to it. She wished now that she could stay.

***

The Victoria Line tube from Brixton up to central London was busy with an expectant Saturday night crowd heading up to the West End. There were no seats, and she had to stand nose to nose with Henri. She was close enough to smell the sophisticated scent that he was wearing, which almost masked the alcohol and Disque Bleues. He was tall – over six foot, she reckoned – and slim but not skinny. Toned would be a good way of putting it. She realised suddenly that they had probably never been alone together before. She felt her heart race a little at this revelation.

'So, you have started your shop now, I think?' he said.

'Yes, I've been going for a few months now.'

'I think you are very brave.'

'Thanks, but there's nothing brave about it. I'm just trying to make a bit of money.'

'Starting your own business is definitely brave. Most of them fail.'

'So did you mean that I was brave or foolhardy?'

He smiled a warm smile. Even his eyes joined in. 'I think both. Foolhardy, this means imprudent?'

'More like *aventurier*.'

'Yes, exactly. Foolhardy because you are young, inexperienced and likely to go bust, but also brave because you are doing something that I would not dare to do.'

'I don't feel like I'm doing anything very daring.'

'Maybe that is something to do with your English phlegm, no? That's the right word?'

'I understand what you're getting at, yes. You know, I didn't really have a role model for work. Neither of my parents worked. My grandparents were quite work-shy too. I think my dad's brother, my uncle Geoffrey, works in the City, but I don't know much about what he does. He's quite partial to a gin and tonic at about eleven-thirty in the morning, but I don't suppose that counts as work. I don't think I really count the shop as work.'

'That's exactly what I mean. My parents are defined by work. My father is a United Nations lawyer. All he knows is work – as a student, then when he was trying to qualify as a lawyer, then when he worked in Paris as a civil rights lawyer, now working for the UN. Work is treated seriously in our family. They would think that you are doing something frivolous.'

'I don't doubt that I am. Is that why you went into banking? To avoid frivolity?'

'Private banking is a career in Geneva that is highly regarded.'

He sounded very precious all of a sudden.

'It sounds a little dull. Is it?'

'I wouldn't describe it as dull. It's serious, but it's not dull.'

Sophie became aware of people in their crowded carriage listening to what they were saying. She had forgotten how little people spoke on the tube, not least because the rattling of the carriages meant that you had to shout above the noise.

'But you play poker. Isn't that frivolous?'

'It depends how you play.'

'What do you mean?'

'If you play like Johnny it's frivolous. If you play like you and me, it's serious.'

She smiled inwardly at the compliment. Outwardly she jumped to her husband's defence.

'Johnny's just more impulsive.'

'That's one way of putting it.'

'So, what did your serious parents think of him then?'

'Well, Johnny's very charming, and he knows how to use his charm. They like him very much, but they would not want me to be like him.'

'Yes, he is very charming. He certainly charmed me.'

The train jolted as it came into Victoria Station. Sophie lost her footing and was thrown towards Henri, who caught her adeptly. She unavoidably joined in the embrace and felt her breasts push against his chest. The train came to rest in the station, and Henri let her gently back down and out of his arms.

'I have to get off here,' she managed, breathlessly.

Henri smiled his lop-sided smile at her, and then before she knew it she was on the platform watching him disappear into the tunnel. He made a telephone with his hand and put it to his ear, just before he vanished. What did that mean? Call me? I'll call you? Or had she imagined it? She certainly had not imagined falling into his arms and the effect it had had on her. She still felt slightly light-headed. Why was this happening now? She was just starting to feel a new respect for her husband.

***

Mark sat on the balcony of his new Wapping flat, sipping on a mug of coffee, looking out over the river. To his left the sun was starting to peep above the horizon, and to his right Tower Bridge was beginning to reflect back this pinkish dawn light. It felt like there had been a frost; the air was dry and smelled clean and crisp. He was wearing a woollen hat against the cold, and he warmed his hands on the mug. He had left Johnny sleeping inside. He had definitely needed some air. He had woken up with quite a start. If his memories of the previous night were broadly accurate, it had been more than eventful, it had been cataclysmic. They had moved from the backstage party to the Limelight in Shaftsbury Avenue, a group of maybe twenty of them. Someone had blagged them into the VIP area, which, from what he could remember, had been full of VIP spotters rather than actual VIPs but still a step up from the Audit Department Friday-night drinks, the event that normally rounded off his week. A lot more booze was consumed, and there were drugs around, but he had been too scared to take any of those; he was pretty sure that Johnny had, though. At the club, the main thing he remembered was a couple of girls who had taken a shine to him and Johnny – well, probably Johnny. He remembered their long hair, floaty clothes and fragrant smell. Holly and Lindsey. He was pretty sure that Johnny had been kissing Holly and that he had wanted to kiss Lindsey, but she had not been quite as keen. The girls seemed to know Alex and Charlie somehow or other. The next thing he could recollect was leaving the club, Johnny wanting to extricate himself from the situation. Maybe he had experienced a pang of guilt. Then what? A cab back here, and then it had happened. It must have been very late, both of them had just wanted to fall into bed, and they had both fallen into Mark's bed half clothed. Then it had happened. It had not been in the slightest bit romantic. They had not kissed or hugged, but he clearly remembered that he had given Johnny a handjob. He could not even remember them speaking while it happened. When he had finished Johnny had just rolled over and gone to sleep. Mark had at least washed his hands and put on his pyjamas before he too fell asleep.

Now he had to face Johnny in the cold light of day. Mark did not consider himself to be gay or even bisexual, but occasionally he felt a sexual attraction to another man. For him, this had always been an undercurrent in his relationship with Johnny. Until now there had been no physical expression of this feeling, even when they were adolescents fumbling their way through sexual development. He had experienced a couple of incidents at university, which he had stored away in the deeper recesses of his memory, but otherwise these occasional urges had remained unfulfilled. He wondered what had led to this happening now. It was not as if they had not shared a bed together before; this had happened plenty of times after nights out when they were growing up. Maybe it had been the euphoria of the gig; certainly the booze had also played a part. What was he going to say to Johnny this morning? He was about to find out, he thought, as he heard the sliding door to the balcony opening behind him.

'Morning, dude, where's the coffee?'

'I just made some. I'll get you a cup.'

Mark went back into the flat to find Johnny some coffee, and Johnny followed him. Mark avoided looking at him as he poured the coffee. Johnny lit a cigarette and drew deeply on it. Mark thought he seemed strangely relaxed.

'That was pretty fucked-up last night,' Johnny said.

'What do you mean?' Mark tried not to sound too anxious.

'Well, everything really. The gig, the party, the club, the girls, the booze, the drugs and then finally you tossing me off.' Johnny was laughing. 'How the fuck did that happen?'

'I can't remember much, to be honest.' Mark felt himself turning crimson.

'No, it's probably better that you don't. Still, I don't remember objecting. I'm just glad that it wasn't one of those girls. Then I would have felt really bad about it.' Johnny giggled. 'I think I'm still a bit pissed.'

Mark could not believe that Johnny was brushing off their sexual intimacy quite so easily.

'No, I mean, if we'd brought those girls back here, I'm pretty sure I'd have fucked one of them, and then I would have felt bad this morning. A drunken fumble with you seems like nothing in comparison.'

Johnny passed through the open plan from the kitchen area to the living space and let himself fall on to the big leather sofa.

'Still, amazing gig. I still can't believe Swerve have played Brixton Academy.'

'No, neither can I. It was pretty phenomenal.' Mark was glad in some ways that the subject had changed but felt almost disappointed that Johnny had brushed off the previous night with such ease.

'I'd better think about going for my train soon.'

For once Mark was relieved that Johnny was leaving. It would give him more time to get used to what had happened.

'Sophie's hands are pretty full these days, with Amy, the shop and everything. I don't like to leave her on her own for too long.'

'Sure. I understand. How are things with Sophie anyway?'

'It's a funny one really. I still feel like we're only just getting to know each other. Everything happened so quickly. I don't really feel like we're a married couple; it's more fragmented than that. The priority has always been Amy. I do sometimes wonder if we'd have had a proper relationship if it hadn't been for her.'

'I didn't have much time to talk to her yesterday. She seemed OK, though, apart from when Alex was around. What's going on there?'

'Alex thought I was crazy to get married. He's always believed that Sophie got pregnant deliberately.'

'Really? That's pretty unlikely.'

'Yeah, I know. But you know what Alex is like; the band comes first. He also tried to grope her at a gig a couple of years ago. She told him where to go, so maybe he hasn't forgotten that. Alex is a proud man; he doesn't like losing face like that. I suppose he might also think that Sophie could get in the way of my involvement. He's a selfish fucker when it comes down to it. A great front man, though. He's trying to line us up with a tour at the moment. I think it might happen after last night. That would be difficult to explain to Sophie.'

***

Sophie had not slept well. After leaving Henri she had got the last train back to Hastings, then a taxi from Hastings back to Rye. She had relieved her mother from babysitting Amy and then collapsed into bed, but her sleep had been fitful. Henri had been the cause; that confident swagger of his was annoyingly alluring, and it seemed to have crept into her consciousness, keeping her awake. Still, at least it would be a while before she saw him again. She could concentrate on things closer to home. She was reminded of this as Amy banged her breakfast bowl on the tray of her high chair. Sophie looked at her and smiled. Thankfully her daughter had an easy-going disposition, and she smiled back. She must have inherited that from the Jones side of the family; the women on the Arlington side were not quite as affable. She was going to have to face her mother's acerbic tongue in a few minutes when she dropped Amy off at the main house. She had not been impressed when Sophie had arrived home without Johnny the previous night.

'Good morning, darling – or darlings, should I say?' Her mother seemed quite chirpy. 'We've been invited to the Snettertons' for drinks this morning, so I thought I'd take Amy along. You don't mind, do you?'

'No, of course not.' Sophie realised immediately that her mother's good humour owed itself to the opportunity she had to show her granddaughter off.

'Good. We'll see you later then.'

Sophie strode down towards the centre of Rye. She loved this walk; she had been walking the same streets since she was a young girl, but she never tired of it. It was just a few minutes down the hill in the winter sunshine to Landgate, the last remaining ancient gate in the medieval town wall. It was still known as the entrance to the citadel, which conjured up images of warring knights in far-flung kingdoms. This was the gateway to Rye's old centre, a hotchpotch of English architecture through the ages: black-and-white beamed post-medieval buildings, their bowed roofs sagging under the weight of the passing of time; Jacobean brick houses with dark mullioned windows, keeping their secrets within; elegant Georgian town houses, promoting their Palladian roots; hulking Victorian mansions, pronouncing their owners' wealth. There was something for everyone. As Sophie walked along the High Street where her shop was located she felt a sense of well-being, a strong connection to her surroundings, a sense of a birthright among these old buildings. She reached the shop and looked in the window, as she did every morning, checking that everything was in order, that people might be enticed by her wares. It was not a glamorous West End store, but opening a clothes shop in Rye had gone some way to making up for the career as a buyer that she had never even started. She had a local clientele, but she also tried to appeal to the well-heeled weekenders, perhaps staying at the Mermaid Inn or the Hope and Anchor, who might be tempted to make an impulse purchase. The window currently had a couple of mannequins showing off two sixties skirt-suits – one by Jaeger, tailored in a light Prince of Wales check, and one by Chanel, black and white with a round neck – that were seeking to attract these kinds of buyers. The tailored suits were juxtaposed with a third mannequin sporting an original Sex Pistols T-shirt and a pair of ripped Levi's. Sophie enjoyed the irony of punk and couture sharing the same window, post-modernism at its best. She hoped her potential clients viewed it in the same way.

She opened up the shop and began to busy herself. The odd customer dropped in for a browse, but otherwise the morning passed uneventfully until a familiar face appeared at the door.

'Morning, babe.' Johnny's lithe form entered the room. She skipped over and embraced him, kissing him on the lips. He seemed a little half-hearted in his response.

'What's up, Johnny? You seem a bit grumpy.'

'Well, I came back as early as I could so that I could relieve your mother and spend some time with Amy. No such luck. There's no one at the house.'

'Oh, yes. She's taken Amy with her and Daddy to the Snettertons' for drinks.'

'So that she can show off her granddaughter in front of her posh friends, I suppose.'

'Probably. I'm sorry, I didn't know that you'd be back this early.'

'Well, I'll just go round there and get Amy. Where do they live?'

'You don't need to do that, Johnny. They'll be back before lunch. It's just drinks.'

'I don't give a fuck. Amy's my daughter. I should be able to see her when I want.'

'I know my mother can be a pain, Johnny, but she babysat last night and then again this morning. I couldn't have opened the shop otherwise.'

'She loves it. It's a power game. If I ever suggest that my mother comes over to help if it's too much for Isabelle, she immediately says that it's no bother.'

The shop doorbell rang to announce a customer. Johnny lowered his voice to a loud whisper.

'Look, Sophie. I'm tired after the gig. I just wanted to have a relaxing day with Amy.'

'The Snettertons live at 17 Church Square. Go round there if it's so important. I'm going to be busy here until this afternoon.'

'I might just do that. See you later.'

The customer must have sensed an atmosphere, as she followed Johnny out of the door. Sophie could have screamed. Why was Johnny suddenly being so precious about spending time with Amy? Why did he allow her mother to get between them? Why did they have to live in that fucking annexe? She knew the answer to that. They were skint. That was one of the reasons that she was in the shop on a Sunday and Amy was with her mother, because they didn't have any money. They were scraping by on Johnny's dole checks and the small profit that the shop made. Maybe the success of the gig had made Johnny feel empowered to confront her mother's manipulative ways. Whatever it was it was pissing her off. She hoped he didn't make a scene at the Snettertons'. She could really do without her mother having the ammunition to take more moral high ground.

Two hundred yards further down the High Street, at the George Hotel, Johnny took a sip on the pint of Harvey's bitter he had just ordered. The opening of the doors to the bar on the strike of midday had tempted him in; once inside he had quickly decided that a quiet pint or two would do more good than a confrontation with Isabelle Arlington at a stuffy drinks party. He pulled hard on his Marlboro and felt himself begin to calm down. He had always had a bit of a temper, and a hangover really did not help. He had been furious when he had arrived home to find that everyone was out. He still had a cold toxic sweat brought on by alcohol, amphetamines and the sleazy memory of that unpleasant handjob. He had tried to brush off the incident with Mark, but internally it had induced a deep self-loathing. A couple of beers and an afternoon with his daughter would sort that out – at least, he hoped it would. He regretted venting his anger at Sophie. They had to move house. Maybe if the band started to take off they would have more money to rent a flat or perhaps even to buy something. The current arrangement was not working. He hated the idea that Isabelle had them, and particularly him, under surveillance the whole time. Sophie was right, it would be impossible for them to do what they did without her help, but that did not stop him resenting it. He wished his mum could be more involved, but she worked full time; Isabelle, of course, was a lady of leisure. He should go and see his mum to talk things over; she would have some wise and calming words for him. Maybe not today but next week. He drained his glass and ordered another beer. He felt a little better already.

Sophie decided to call it a day around three o'clock. She locked the shop and walked home back up the hill. She wondered what Johnny had decided to do earlier. She suspected that he had thought better of dragging Amy away from the Snettertons', although he had seemed pretty angry. She could not help but smile at the thought of the enraged young rocker confronting the great and good of Rye over their Sunday-morning gin and tonics. She herself had stewed for a while, but then she had sold a couple of nice items, the original Sex Pistols T-shirt and a pair of jeans, enough to have made it worth while opening. She hoped that Johnny had calmed down now that he had seen Amy. She arrived back at the annexe where a clapped-out Mini was parked outside. She knew who that car belonged to.

She opened the door to be greeted by the sight of Alex Middlehead sitting on her sofa, deep in conversation with Johnny. Charlotte was sitting on the carpet playing with Amy. There was a bottle of Jack Daniels open on the table.

'Hi, babe. Alex has brought round some great news.' Sophie could tell that Johnny was quite pissed. Her heart sank a little.

'Yeah.' Alex was less pissed but seemed hyper. Either adrenalin or speed, Sophie thought to herself. 'It looks like we're going to get a deal. I talked to Charles Cooper-Smythe last night after the gig. He loved our show, and he wants to try to put together a deal for us. He's the founder of Paisley Records. Pretty amazing, eh?'

'Fucking incredible,' said Johnny.

'That *is* amazing news,' said Sophie. Despite herself, she gave Alex a hug and then kissed Johnny. Maybe things were going to take a turn for the better.

HIGHBURY, NORTH LONDON

9 MAY 1992

'So, how come you Brits voted in this man Major again? This is incredible, no?' Henri expressed his incredulity with an exaggerated raise of the shoulders and outstretched hands.

'Well, you know what, Henri, I'm what they call a floating voter. I never make my mind up who I'm going to vote for until just before the election.' Mark was opening a bottle of champagne, and he stopped speaking momentarily as he popped the cork. Sophie noticed that he had started to thicken around the waist. Life was obviously treating him quite well.

'I had actually decided that I was going to vote for Labour until just before the election, and then I saw that goon Kinnock on TV pretending to be a rock star at a political rally. Just embarrassing! I'm afraid I switched to the Tories after that. Not that it would have a made a difference around here. Islington North is a Labour stronghold. It has been for decades.'

'You fucking traitor. Have you forgotten what happened in the eighties?' Johnny had always been vehemently anti-Thatcher. Sophie found it a little tiring, particularly when he was a bit pissed, which seemed to be the case a lot of the time these days.

'No, of course I haven't forgotten, but I also haven't forgotten some of the sleazebags on the Labour left either. The economy is in a mess; the last thing we need is the return of nationalisation.'

'You Tory twat! I wish you could hear yourself, Mark. You do remember going to those gigs to support the striking miners, don't you?'

'Yes, I do, but that was a different time.'

'Yeah, a time before you became a boring fucking accountant.'

'OK, guys, I only asked a question.' Henri tried to take the heat out of the argument. Sophie had seen this sort of exchange between Mark and Johnny before and realised it was not a big deal. She was also keeping her head down as she too had voted Tory in the hope that it might help small businesses. It had been a pretty selfish vote, but she had a family to feed. She also knew for a fact that Johnny had not even voted. He had been in London recording and had not got round to organising a postal vote, so he was hardly arguing from a position of strength. Dare she mention it?

'Did you vote, Johnny? Weren't you in London on election day?' She couldn't resist.

'Well, no, I didn't actually vote. I was too busy. But if I had I would have voted Labour, obviously.'

'So you felt so strongly about it that you couldn't be bothered to get a train from London down to Rye?' Mark was now crowing as he poured the champagne. This was not what Sophie had wanted either.

'Come on, you two, enough bickering.' Sophie tried to take the wind out of Mark's sails. Johnny grinned at her sheepishly.

'Yeah, sorry, babe, I got a bit carried away there. I should have known that Mark would go over to the other side now that he's a home-owner.'

'So you still think property is theft, do you, mate? I thought you told me that you might buy a flat in London yourself.'

'That's news to me,' said Sophie.

'Well, the other boys are all living in London now, and as I have to be here for recording and stuff it would make things easier if we had a place up here. I was going to mention it to you when we had some time on our own.'

Sophie was still taken aback at the speed at which Johnny's career seemed to be moving since the Brixton gig. She needed to hang on, or it would speed away from her – and Amy too.

'Can we at least remember why we are here, guys, before we have another argument,' said Henri. 'We are here to see Mark's new apartment, to congratulate him for buying it – but most of all we are here to play poker.'

Sophie had been looking forward to the evening for weeks. Now that Johnny was embroiled in recording Swerve's first album up in London her daily grind had become exactly that, a grind. She was looking forward to pitting her wits against her three adversaries. She felt less concerned that she was married to one of the other players now; Johnny had been paid what seemed to her a stupidly large advance by the record company, so, in the short term, cash was no longer a problem. Any money he lost tonight would probably have been squandered in any case. He had very generously put the advance in their joint account in any case, so she could spend the evening squandering it with him. It would make a change to play without worrying about how much she lost.

'The flat is lovely, Mark.' Sophie was admiring the view from the tall Georgian windows out across Highbury Fields.

'I agree it's a nice flat, but isn't Islington a bit trendy for you, mate?' Johnny continued to try to bait Mark.

'I think you'll find an eclectic mix of population in the area, old chap. We accountants have to live somewhere. Who says we can't live next door to the chattering classes.'

'I think you've made a great choice, Mark. I really like it.' Sophie was actually quite envious. 'It beats Wapping anyway.'

'Well, I'd become quite attached to Wapping, but, believe it or not, a nice one-bedroom flat on the river there was too expensive. I did look around. It was quite a lot cheaper in Islington, particularly the Highbury end. I was lucky to find this place, though, right on Highbury Fields; someone had to sell quickly, and I was ready to go.

Now that I've passed my exams I'm considered a good credit risk.' Sophie thought Mark seemed more mature all of a sudden, more grounded.

'Well, I think you've done the right thing. It's fabulous. We might have to move in next door. What do you think, Johnny?' she said.

'Yeah, brilliant! Let's do it.'

'My problem is that I'm a bit too attached to Rye, particularly now the shop's going well.'

'Well, I don't think either of us is attached to that fucking annexe, are we?' Johnny was definitely pissed already.

'I wouldn't have put it quite so bluntly, but no, we're not very attached to the fucking annexe. Still, it was a godsend when we were skint.'

'That's true. I'm sorry, babe.' Johnny got up and gave Sophie a kiss on the cheek. She was relaxed enough to return his embrace.

'Maybe you guys need two houses. One here and one in Rye,' suggested Henri.

'Excellent idea, Henri. Maybe if I win enough of your money tonight we might just do that.' Johnny grinned at Henri.

'On the subject of cards', said Mark, 'I'd like to make a proposal.' He retrieved a leather case from under the table that they were sat around and snapped open the locks to reveal a very professional-looking collection of gambling chips.

'Rather than playing with our usual motley collection of loose change and screwed-up banknotes I think we have reached the stage in our lives where we should have a proper bank, buy in our chips and play like adults.'

'Fantastic,' said Johnny. 'If we're going to play like adults then we should play for proper stakes as well. How about Texas hold 'em pot limit?'

'Fine with me,' said Henri.

'What does that mean exactly?' asked Mark.

'The highest raise you can make is the amount in the pot at that point.'

'But that could be a lot of money.' Mark was clearly uncomfortable.

'Yes, that's the point,' said Johnny.

'I'll do it if you will,' said Sophie. 'But I don't want you to be uncomfortable, Mark.'

'No, that's OK, let's go for it. I've been reading up on my stats again, so that should help.'

Sophie was comfortable with the increase in stakes. If she considered herself to be the best player at the table then she should be in favour of playing for higher stakes. Now all she needed to do was prove that she was the best player.

They took up their places at the round table that Mark had positioned by the window. A hush fell over them as they readied themselves for the game. Sophie felt composed. Amy was down in Hastings with Johnny's mother, they were staying overnight here at Mark's place, and she had decided not to open the shop tomorrow. With Johnny's advance in the bank there was no need to worry about their finances, but there would be no harm done either if it were topped up a little. Mark started to give out chips in exchange for cash.

'OK, Henri, now you're on a private-banker's salary, how many thousands of these do you want?'

'I'm afraid I'm still a lowly assistant at the bank, Mark. I'll start with one hundred pounds in chips.' He passed him five twenty-pound notes.

'Cheapskate. Give me two hundred quid, Mark. I'm feeling lucky,' said Johnny. Sophie winced a little as Johnny threw over four fifty-pound notes.

'Just a hundred for me, Mark,' she said. 'By our old standards that's still a lot of money.' Sophie smiled at Mark, who grinned back at her.

'Just a hundred for me too,' he said.

Mark ceremoniously unwrapped a brand-new pack of cards, and they were ready to go. Sophie sensed a tension in the air that seemed new. Perhaps it was the higher stakes they were playing for; perhaps the boys had more to prove to one another. She instinctively felt that it was something that might work in her favour.

Mark dealt the first hand of two cards face down to each player, and Sophie glanced at Henri as he received his cards. He picked his cards up almost furtively and then hunched over his hand, his dark fringe almost covering one eye, the other barely visible because of its hooded lid. She looked momentarily for his reaction to the contents of his hand but saw nothing. She picked up her own cards: a seven and a three unsuited. She would not be going far with those. That was not a problem; she was happy to play a long game, happy to scrutinise the others while they played, waiting for her moment. Henri was to the right of the dealer, Mark, and was first to bet. They were playing with a blind of two pounds and a small blind of one pound. These bets had to be placed before any cards were dealt by the two players to the left of the dealer. The first player to bet was the one to the left of the player who had posted the blind. This was Henri, who had to match the blind of two pounds to stay in the hand.

'I call,' he said, putting in two pounds.

Mark was next.

'I fold,' he said.

Next was Sophie.

'I fold too,' she said. This meant that she automatically lost the small blind of one pound that she had already put in, but this was better than losing more later in the hand.

Johnny was the last to bet. He had already put in the blind and so did not need to bet to stay in, he could just check to do that. Alternatively he could raise by putting in an additional bet. This would then have to be matched by Henri if he wanted to continue.

'Maximum raise, the pot. Five pounds.' Johnny threw in his

chips with a flourish. Sophie felt a mixture of admiration and anxiety as she watched her husband.

'I call the five pounds, and I raise it ten,' Henri said flatly.

'Call,' said Johnny.

The two players would now see the first three cards in the flop. Sophie looked at each of them as Mark dealt these cards, hoping to spot a tell, any indication in their body language that they liked what had been dealt. She concentrated on Henri, trying to penetrate that gaze, looking for that barely perceptible glimmer in his eyes that she had seen for the first time in Wapping. Nothing. She would just have to be patient; she was confident that if she had seen it once she would see it again. Johnny, on the other hand, was a picture of confidence. She was pleased to see him playing confidently; she just hoped that the confidence did not turn into petulance.

'Left of the dealer to bet. That's you, Johnny.'

'I bet the pot.'

'I fold. It's your money, Johnny.'

Johnny eagerly raked in the chips. Sophie hoped that he realised that he had put a lot of them in himself – but still, he had taken some money from Henri, and that was no mean feat. She wondered if Johnny had been bluffing and realised she was not sure. She also wondered why Henri had bet so much before the flop only to fold when confronted by a big bet from Johnny. She was not sure of the answer to that either. It was going to be an interesting night.

Sophie sat for the next hour or so waiting for some decent cards to come along. If she had won a couple early on she might have considered trying to bluff one of her more mediocre hands, as the other players were always more wary of someone who had just won. However, if you started to bluff without the benefit of already having won a few hands, generally the other players were on you like vultures. You had to prove your worth at the poker table before you were allowed to consider bluffing. Even if you knew the other players and had played together many times before, the player with the most chips on the table in front of them was always given that little bit more respect, even if he or she was not necessarily the best player. This was the case now, as Johnny sat with the biggest pile of chips in front of him. Sophie thought he was playing with more confidence than normal, which, when matched with his unpredictability, was proving to be a successful combination. Henri had challenged him a couple of times, and each time so far he had come up with the goods. Henri had even had to change up some more cash, another hundred pounds, and Sophie thought that he was starting to look just a little bit peeved that his old friend Johnny was taking money off him. Henri would have known that any display of emotion at the poker table was a sign of weakness.

Henri was dealing the next hand. She picked up her two concealed cards, a pair of kings, her best first opening cards of the night. She was also in the big blind and so would be last to bet, giving her a further advantage. The hair on the back of her neck stood up a little, signalling her excited anticipation; she needed to make sure that this eagerness she now felt did not manifest itself to the other players. She looked at Johnny, who was first to bet.

'Call.'

He caught her looking at him and smiled back at her with genuine affection. No poker face for him. She smiled in return and shifted in her seat slightly. That languid smile could still have an impact. She concentrated on the matter in hand.

'Call,' said Henri.

She studied him. He was looking down at his cards, hunched, inert – nothing much to read there. It was Mark's turn to bet.

'Fold.'

'Check.' Sophie decided not to raise at this point. She was planning a softly-softly approach to this hand. She wanted to maximise the value of her kings.

Henri dealt the flop: a seven of hearts, two of clubs and a king of hearts. Seriously good news, three kings. She tried to keep a straight face and looked down at her cards. She was the first active player left of the dealer and therefore the first to bet.

'Check,' she said again.

'Raise the pot.' Johnny was in no mood to hang around.

'I call your raise, and I raise the pot too.' Henri also seemed to be in a hurry.

Sophie was pretty confident that she had the best hand at this point, unless one of the others had two pairs, but that was a long shot. The most likely situation was that one of them was chasing a flush and the other had an ace and another high card. Bluffing at this point was foolish with three people in the hand. Henri, certainly, would not raise the betting with rubbish at this point. The odds were that at least one of them had a very good hand that they wanted to see through to the end. The pot had contained seven pounds at the end of the first round of betting. Johnny had then raised seven pounds. Henri had called that seven pounds then raised twenty-one pounds, the amount of the pot before his raise. She now had to put in twenty-eight pounds to stay in: Johnny's bet of seven plus Henri's bet of twenty-one.

'That's twenty-eight pounds for you to call, Sophie,' said Mark.

'Call.'

'I'll call as well,' said Johnny. His expression was a little meeker. He seemed to be slightly taken aback by Henri's aggressive betting.

Mark dealt the next of the shared cards face up in the middle. Sophie did not look at the card. She looked at Henri and then Johnny. There was no reaction from Henri, but Johnny, she could tell, did not like what he had seen. It was a two of hearts. She felt an immediate adrenalin rush. It was the best possible card for her. Not only had she made a full house, kings over twos, but she suspected that one of the other two had just made the heart flush they had been chasing. Her concealed full house beat the flush, but the holder of the flush would struggle to work out what she had. Both Johnny and Henri would be pretty certain that they were holding the best hand. The best thing she could do was to continue to try to conceal hers.

'Check,' she said.

'I fold,' said Johnny. 'Where are the beers?'

This was a surprise. Johnny had obviously decided to take a beer break. So it was Henri who had the flush, she thought.

'I raise ten,' said Henri. That was a little tentative, thought Sophie, for someone who had just made their flush. Maybe he was pretty certain of his hand and did not want to scare her away.

'I call,' she said.

She would save her ammunition for the last card. Again, she decided not to watch the card but to watch Henri. She had made her hand already. She wanted to see if he was still waiting to make his. As Mark dealt the card her eyes met Henri's; he was looking at her rather than the last card. For a split second she looked into his gaze as deeply as she could until he looked away. There was no sign of weakness. She read him for an ace-high heart flush. He probably thought that she had made the flush, but she could not beat him because he had the highest flush.

The last card face up on the table was an irrelevant ten of clubs. Sophie took a moment to think about the hands that could beat her. Four twos was the only hand she could think of. He could not have four of anything else, he could not have a royal flush or a straight flush and he could not have three of anything higher than kings. She was pretty sure that she had him beaten. She looked at him again, straight in the eyes. He was looking down at his hand. What she did not want was for him to fold his flush and say that he knew she had him. Not this time.

'Check,' she said. The old check-raise routine. She hoped he would now raise, then she would come back at him with an over-raise.

'I raise fifty.' Henri seemed to be playing his part. He might have raised even more. There was no going back now.

'I'll call your fifty and raise a hundred. I don't have enough chips, but I'm sure Mark can sort that out.'

Mark exhaled loudly.

'More chips coming up,' he said.

'Go for it, guys, this is proper poker,' said Johnny, downing his beer and sucking on a cigarette.

Henri looked at Sophie now, and that was when she saw the glimmer of weakness in his eyes again. It was the first time since she had seen it in Wapping. You had to know what you were looking for, but it was there. He was looking for weakness in her, but he would not find any. He did not have four twos, he had the flush, and she had him. She was also pretty sure that he would feel obliged to pay the one hundred pounds to see her hand, even if, deep down, he knew that he was going to lose. Mark passed them each another hundred pounds in chips.

'I call,' said Henri.

'Full house, kings over twos,' said Sophie. She was bursting with pride but tried to hide it.

'Well played,' said Henri. 'I had the top flush. You hid your hand very well. It was only right at the end that I thought maybe you had me beat.'

'It was a good job I folded,' said Johnny. 'I had fuck all. I was well lucky to be out of that. Great cards, babe. I never read you for the full house.'

'Well played, Sophie. I think we can safely say that's the biggest hand we have ever had. Maybe that will calm everyone down a bit.' Mark, as ever, was the voice of reason.

'I'm sorry, Henri, it's not often you get a concealed full house when someone else has a flush. I was very lucky.'

'You played it well.' Henri looked pretty hangdog. Sophie almost felt sorry for him – until she remembered how he had made her feel all those years ago in Wapping. 'But maybe the pot limit was not such a great idea.' Henri allowed himself a wry smile.

Sophie raked in her chips. There was well over three-hundred-pounds' worth, equivalent to a very good day's takings at the shop. But it was not really about the money; it was winning that thrilled her. Winning a big hand against Henri, the man considered by Mark and Johnny to be the best player in their group. It would take him a while to come back from this. She looked over at him again. He caught her gaze and smiled. For the first time his smile showed her genuine respect. That was all that she had wanted.

They carried on playing for a couple more hours, but that one big hand had changed the game. The bets were lower – even Johnny had been shocked into playing less aggressively, and Henri was clearly finding it tough to overcome the big loss he had taken. They played the last hand around one o'clock, and the game petered out. Sophie had finished well ahead; Johnny, she noticed, had also done pretty well. Mark had lost steadily, and Henri had taken the big hits early on and never really recovered.

'How about a glass of champagne to round off the night?' Mark offered.

'What a lovely idea, Mark,' said Sophie.

'Yeah, *lovely*, mate.' Johnny mimicked Sophie's accent as he said the word lovely.

Sophie stuck her tongue out at him. He grinned back at her. He was drunk but a nice kind of drunk. She was pretty drunk too but mentally still on the ball. That big win had seemed to keep her sharp for the rest of the game, however many glasses of wine she drank.

'I have to go,' said Henri.

'Don't you want to crash here?' Mark asked.

'No, I'm staying with Emily. She wanted me to come back whatever the time was.'

'Who's Emily?' asked Johnny, quick as a flash.

'She's my friend from Geneva who lives in London.'

'Friend?'

'Yes. My friend.'

Sophie felt disturbingly put out by the revelation that Henri was staying with a female friend.

'It's an ambiguous word in French,' she said. '*Amie* can mean friend or girlfriend.'

'So which is it, Henri?' Johnny persisted.

'Maybe I'll find out when I get back to her place,' he said, smiling his lopsided smile.

Sophie was now even more peeved.

'What do you mean?' she asked.

'I'm not sure whether I will be on the canapé or in the nice warm bed,' he said.

He had made the nice warm bed seem pretty appealing, Sophie thought.

'Well, good luck with that, mate,' Johnny said.

Soon after Henri had left to find a taxi Sophie called it a night. She hoped that Johnny would follow quickly. The discussion of Henri's sleeping arrangements had uncovered an itch that she was quite keen to have scratched. The only issue was that they were sleeping in Mark's bed; normally this would have been a passion killer, but she was too pissed to care.

She went to the bedroom, changed into a long T-shirt that passed as nightwear and went down the hall to the bathroom. She was encouraged to hear Johnny saying goodnight to Mark. As she finished cleaning her teeth the door opened and Johnny came in with his toothbrush, grinning. He kissed her on the mouth, first softly then harder.

'If you can eradicate the smell of beer and Marlboro Lights you might just get lucky,' she said in a loud whisper, touching his bottom as she eased herself past him back to the bedroom.

She got into bed and lay waiting for Johnny. Images of Henri came into her mind, his hard stomach against hers, his firm buttocks in her hands, those inaccessible eyes covered by the fringe of dark hair, his cruel mouth. Johnny came into the dark room; she could hear him undressing hurriedly. He lay down next to her. She immediately stretched out her hand to touch his chest, his nipples, gradually moving down his stomach to his penis. It was hard already. She pulled off the duvet, hitched up her T-shirt and mounted him, facing away from him. As she eased herself up and down on his erection, firstly slowly then more quickly, she could still imagine Henri's mouth kissing her hard. It was not long before she had rhythmically and silently moved them both to orgasm.

***

Henri sat in the back of the black cab, reflecting on the evening. He could not see any real weakness in his play; he had been unlucky, particularly against Sophie. He still knew that he was the best player at that table, and he would not play the hand differently if he played it again. The odds on her having the concealed full house were tiny; he had been the odds-on favourite with the top flush; he had been absolutely right to back his cards to the hilt. It was only at the very end that he had seen something in her body language that had rung alarm bells. Should he still have paid the one hundred pounds to see her cards? He thought he should have; they would play one another again, and he had needed to have the confirmation that the slight descent of her shoulders meant that she knew she had a winning hand. It was a subtle movement, but it was if she felt the pressure releasing at the moment of victory. He would try to remember it for next time. He really did find her quite attractive. She was smart – smarter than Johnny, probably, and he was no fool – and she was also funny. He liked the way she teased them all a little, but there was enough vulnerability in her face to make him feel drawn to her, to make him want to protect her. He felt she needed someone stronger than Johnny. Johnny was a good guy, but he was unreliable. He thought of her big blue eyes and those full pink lips contrasted with her brown hair and tanned skin. She was a beautiful mixture of Anglo-Saxon and Mediterranean French. Not a classic beauty, but she had something special. He thought it inevitable that they would sleep together; it was just a question of how and when.

The taxi dropped him in Marylebone High Street where Emily had her studio apartment. He had a strange relationship with Emily; they had been friends in Geneva, but since she had moved to London they had also become lovers. His feelings for her were not very deep, but he enjoyed coming to London both to see her as a friend and to sleep with her. She had given him a set of keys, and he let himself into the small flat as quietly as he could. He heard nothing, so presumably Emily was asleep. He crept into the bathroom and washed and undressed there, trying not to wake her. He picked his way naked in the dark to the bed that was at one end of the large studio room. Once he had found it he slid quietly under the duvet. As he lowered his head on to the pillow he felt the ends of Emily's long blonde hair lightly touching his face. He could sense the warmth of her body, but he did not touch her; he lay there listening to the rhythm of her breathing. It sounded as if she was still sleeping. His mind was full of Sophie; she had produced in him a yearning that he felt in his stomach. He noticed Emily moving, then she turned to face him; he felt her breath on his face, tickling his skin. To his surprise she moved her hand to his face and touched it softly then leaned into his ear.

'Fuck me,' she said, her voice gruffly full of sleep.

'Avec plaisir,' he replied softly.

He found her face with his hands and kissed her softly, inquisitively. She smelled of orange peel, warm and exotic. He began to touch her breasts and felt her kissing intensify as he did, her hands behind his neck, pulling his mouth closer to her. They kissed for a while, their urgency increasing.

'Turn over,' he said to her – an instruction, not a request.

She rolled on to her stomach, and he moved to kneel behind her. He lifted her hips slightly with both hands and began to touch her sex, encouraged by her quiet moans as he did so. He felt her reaching for him, pulling him gently towards her until he was inside. This was how he wanted Sophie, needing him, desperate for him, dominated by him. His hips moved backwards and forwards, spurred on as he pictured Sophie naked and submissive. Before long he was spent.

He collapsed back down on the bed with Emily beside him. She sought out his hand and held it.

'You were different tonight,' she said. 'I've never known you to be so physical.'

'Did you like it?' he asked.

'Yes, I liked it. It just wasn't very loving. I wouldn't want you to be like that all the time.'

He kissed her softly on the mouth.

'I'll try to be more loving, *ma chérie*, but sometimes I just really want you.'

She kissed him back; it seemed as if the white lie had worked.

'It was a bit weird,' she continued. 'It was as if a stranger had come into the flat and got in my bed. It excited me, but I didn't feel any connection to you.'

'Do you normally feel a connection?'

'Yes, I think so. Don't you?'

'I always feel very close to you.' Henri liked Emily, but he always found these moments awkward. He was not in love with her, and knew he never would be. While she never pushed it too hard, he felt as if she wanted something from him that he could not give her.

'Me too,' she said.

She lay with her head on his chest. He looked down at her petite, almost boyish body. He wasn't sure what it was that made him so ambivalent about her. She was pretty as well as sexy; she was sophisticated, educated and good company. What she was not was challenging. She was just a little too compliant. He had always found himself drawn to strong women. It was not because he wanted their support; it was because he wanted to conquer them, almost to the point of domination. With Emily this was too easy; Sophie, however, was a different proposition. Her strength was an aphrodisiac. He could feel Emily's breathing starting to rise and fall more regularly as she fell back to sleep, still resting on his chest. She was a sweet girl, too sweet for him, and that was the problem.

***

Sophie cut up the buttered toast into bite-sized chunks and then poured the baked beans over them.

'There you go, kitten,' she said to her daughter as she put her supper in front of her.

'What's that?' asked Amy.

'You know what it is. Beans on toast. I thought you liked baked beans.'

'Is Daddy coming home for tea?'

'No, not tonight, honey, but he'll be back soon.' Sophie hoped she sounded convincing.

'When's soon?'

The telephone started to trill, releasing her from another conversation about when Daddy was coming home.

'Hello, babes.' Johnny sounded quite sober. It was still quite early, though. 'How are things back at the ranch?'

'Amy's tucking into baked beans without much gusto. It's funny, she just asked if you were coming home for your tea then you rang.'

A brief pause punctuated Johnny's guilt.

'We're just having a break from recording. I was just trying to lay down the solo for "Lost in Space".'

'Oh, that's my favourite song.'

'OK, I'll try to remember that when I have another go.'

'That's nice.' Sophie realised she really meant what she had just said. 'When do you think you'll be back down here next?'

'I'm not sure. I'll try to get down at the weekend, but things are a bit nuts with the recording. We're up against a deadline now. They really want us to get finished. I think the studio time is costing the record company an arm and a leg.'

'OK. Amy really misses you, but I'm sure you know that already.'

'Yeah, I'll talk to her in a minute.' Johnny paused again. 'Have you thought any more about moving up here? I think Alex and Charlotte are getting a bit cheesed off with having a permanent lodger, and I don't think it would be a good idea to move in with Rob and Dave. It's a fucking madhouse round there.'

'Couldn't you stay with Mark for a while?'

There was a pause.

'No, I don't think that would work. Maybe I could rent a place on my own, and then you guys could come up and stay here sometimes?'

'You know it's difficult for me to do that with the business.'

'Why don't you open a shop in London? Then we could all move up here.'

'You know how I feel about living in London. Particularly for Amy.'

'I know, but I wish you'd give it a try. There's nearly ten million people up here, you know. They can't all be wrong.'

'I'll think about it.' There was no way she was moving up there, particularly not as a rock-star's widow, waiting for Johnny to come home every night.

'Daddy!' By now Amy had realised who was on the telephone.

'You better put me on to Amy. Just one thing, I saw Henri last night. He's in London again for a couple of days. He said he wanted to call you. It's about your business.'

'Daddy!' Sophie gave up and passed the telephone to Amy.

She wondered why on earth Henri would want to speak to her. Just thinking about it gave her butterflies. What was it about him that made her feel uncomfortable? Perhaps it was something about the intent in the way that he looked at her. It attracted and worried her simultaneously.

She watched as Amy spoke to her father, her pretty face suddenly alive at the sound of his voice. Amy needed to see him more often. They needed to agree between them where they were going to live, but she was finding it hard to make a decision. She knew why. The obvious thing for them to do was to live in London while Johnny's career was taking off. She just could not bring herself to commit to it. Now that the shop in Rye was working, albeit on a small scale, she had put all thoughts of a glamorous career in the capital behind her. She was quite happy the way things were. In a way, moving to London to be with Johnny was a bigger decision than getting married to him. Deep down this dilemma made her realise that she was not sure that her relationship with Johnny would last. If it did not, she was better off staying in Rye, keeping her business and keeping her family close to her. She was also not sure about Swerve – or, more specifically, Alex Middlehead. She did not want to feel that her life was in any way dependent on his egocentric whims. Whether Johnny wanted to admit it or not, Alex ran the band, and if he decided that Johnny was to be replaced by the latest hot guitarist then Sophie's instinct told her he would just do it.

'Daddy's gone. He's got to play his guitar.'

'Right, you can finish your baked beans then.'

They went back to the table. A couple of minutes later the telephone rang again.

'Hello.'

'*Ma chérie.*'

'Henri. Johnny told me you were going to phone. To what do I owe this pleasure?'

'I think I have some friends in Paris who might be able to help your business. They buy and sell vintage clothes. I thought this might be interesting for you.'

'Well, it sounds interesting. Do you know what kind of clothes they deal in?'

'I don't know so many details, but I know the two girls. They're very trendy but more on the high-quality side than street fashion. One is an old friend from Geneva, and the other is Parisienne. Do you know Paris very well?'

'Yes, I do actually. We have some family there.'

'Well, I'm going to be there soon on business, seeing some clients, so maybe I could arrange to introduce you to my friends at the same time. Is it easy for you to get to Paris?'

'Well, yes, I suppose I would just take a plane, or maybe even the ferry and a train.'

'Cool. It would be nice if you could come.'

'Well, I'm not sure how soon I'd be able to get over. I'd need plenty of notice.'

'The best thing would be to stay the night if you can. We could meet the girls during the day, followed by dinner, and then you go back the next day. What do you think?'

Sophie paused.

'Well, maybe. I'll see what Johnny thinks.'

'I mentioned it to him already. He thought it was a great idea.'

'Right. Why don't you let me know the next time you're going, and then I'll see what I can do?' Sophie was really not sure about this. She wondered what Henri's real motive was. He did not strike her as someone who did favours for nothing.

'Absolutely. It should be quite soon. I'll call you again to let you know the dates.'

'Thanks, Henri, it's very kind of you.'

'Maybe I'll organise some poker too. That way I get to look into your eyes.'

Sophie was a little taken aback. Had he really said that? She was both outraged and flattered at the same time. She felt like she was heading down a dangerous path. She ignored Henri's comment.

'Well, it would be nice to take some more money off you, I have to admit.'

'*Touché*,' he said, chuckling. 'I'll call you again when I know more.'

Sophie heard the telephone click. Apparently there was no need for him to say goodbye. She did not quite know what to make of it all. He was clearly flirting with her, in a very Gallic kind of way, but was he really attracted to her? And if he was, did it not bother him that she was married to one of his best friends? And who were these mysterious Parisian high-end vintage fashionistas? It sounded glamorous and exciting. More so than the life of a rock widow, she thought, as she made a final attempt to persuade Amy to finish her baked beans.

Johnny sat at the bar of the Compton Arms, puffing on a Marlboro Light and sipping at a pint of London Pride. He was due to have lunch with Mark. He also thought that they were probably due to have an uncomfortable conversation, so he had chosen somewhere quiet to meet. He was early deliberately, so that he could ease his anxiety with a couple of beers. He felt awkward about the previous night; he had arrived late, pissed, at Mark's flat without prior notice. Mark, decent guy that he is, had welcomed him in despite the late hour and invited him to crash. Over a nightcap one thing had led to another, and they had ended up in Mark's bed again. He had a vivid recollection of Mark's head bobbing up and down on the end of his cock. He had enjoyed it at the time, but now he felt fucking awful about it. It was the third time it had happened. The first two were handjobs, now a blowjob. He had woken up late that morning to discover a note from Mark asking Johnny to call him at the office to arrange to meet for lunch, if he had the time, so that they could catch up properly before he went away on tour. The Compton Arms was a shortish bus or cab ride from Mark's office in the City, so he had been quite happy to meet there.

It struck Johnny that life was full of irony. Here he was, twenty-five years old, on the cusp of fame, leading the life he had always dreamed of – except that somehow he had ended up married to a woman that he liked, maybe even loved, but hardly saw, as well as fathering a daughter he loved desperately but also hardly saw. On top of that he was in the middle of a bizarre homosexual dalliance with his best friend. This was not the life he had always hoped for. This was seriously fucked up. To cap it off, right now, he had a ferocious hangover, which was being temporarily eased by the intake of more alcohol. It was a finger-in-the-dyke solution, he knew, but it was relieving his cold sweat.

So how did he tackle the man-love issue? He ordered another pint and sparked up another cigarette. The only way to tackle that was head on. It had to stop. He did not want to ruin his relationship with Mark, but the late-night fumbling had to come to an end.

'Morning, old chap, you're looking a bit pale and interesting.' His love interest had arrived on cue.

'Hello, mate. Yes, I'm struggling a bit. Thanks for putting me up last night.'

'No worries. I'll have half a lager if you're getting them in. And a roast-beef sandwich with mustard. Shall we sit down?'

Johnny ordered for Mark and added a bacon sandwich for himself. He sat down next to Mark in the corner of the small pub. They almost had the bar to themselves, so Johnny decided not to hold back.

'About last night, Mark ...'

'Yes, I'm afraid I rather took advantage of you again.' Johnny was surprised to hear Mark acknowledge what had happened. He must have sensed what was coming.

'Well, I wouldn't quite put it like that. I think I knew what was happening, but yeah, I was quite pissed. Anyway ...'

'I agree with you. We shouldn't do it again.'

'I haven't said anything yet.'

'I know you haven't, but it's pretty obvious that it's on your mind. We shouldn't do it again if it makes you uncomfortable.' Mark had rather taken Johnny by surprise.

'Well, I don't want to seem ungrateful. No, that's not the right word. I don't want to seem disloyal. I'm not sure what to say to you; it's something that I seem to enjoy at the time, but it makes me feel uncomfortable afterwards. I mean, after all, I'm not queer, I shouldn't be letting you suck me off.'

They both looked up at the bar suddenly, realising that Johnny had made this last remark a little loudly. There was no one within earshot, but they carried on in loud whispers.

'I know it might seem strange to you, Johnny, but I've always felt attracted to both boys and girls. It's a huge relief to be able to talk to you about it, to be honest. I always fancied you a bit when we were at school. I still do, but if you want to stop the physical side and just stay friends, that's fine.' Mark seemed very matter of fact about the whole thing.

'It's not that I don't like you, Mark. You're my best mate, so of course I do, but I'm married. I shouldn't be cheating on Sophie, especially with another bloke.'

'As I said, it's up to you. Don't feel like you're beholden to me in any way.' Now Johnny felt even more uncomfortable. By saying that he wasn't beholden Mark had clarified something in Johnny's mind. He *was* beholden to him, because Mark could tell anyone what had happened. He now had a hold over Johnny that had not existed before.

'No, it's not that,' he lied, 'it's just that I don't feel very comfortable with it. It's hard to explain, but I would prefer it if we stopped the physicals and just carried on as before.'

'That's fine,' said Mark, although it was clear from his tone that it was not. He decided to change the subject.

'So, do you think you'll make it to any of the gigs? There's going to be a few in the South-East.'

'That's cool. So what's happening exactly?'

'Well, "Lost in Space" is coming out as a single on Monday, and we start touring the same day.'

'Do you know where you're playing yet?'

'It's mainly universities and polys from what I remember, up and down the country. Sometimes we're headlining, sometimes we're supporting. Monday is Newcastle University, then we go up to Scotland, come back down to northern England, the Midlands then the south. The finale is a big gig in London before Christmas. That's at Brixton Academy again. We're supporting the Ramones. All the dates should be in the *NME*. I think that gig might be the 20th of December.'

'The Ramones. Wow, amazing.'

'Yeah, pretty fucking cool, eh? I'll get you a ticket for that one, if you like.'

'Like? I'll definitely be at that. Can you get me two tickets?'

'Why, who are you bringing?'

'I've just started seeing someone, a girl in the office. I'd like to bring her along if things work out.'

'Well, you kept that quiet.' Johnny felt oddly piqued by this revelation. Was he jealous? The visions of Mark's head bobbing up and down returned. He tried to put them to one side. 'How long has that been going on?'

'I've been kind of admiring her from afar for a while. Then we went away together on an auditing course, in Brighton, actually. I suddenly realised that she was keen on me too. But we have to pretty careful. It's frowned on in the office, fraternising with colleagues. We're having to be a bit cloak and dagger about at it all for the moment.'

'I can imagine. You're not in the most easy-going of professions.'

'I've told her about you and Swerve; she hadn't heard of you, though.'

'Hardly surprising. What's her name?'

'Victoria.'

'A nice, solid, middle-class name.'

'Yes, she's quite posh actually. More Home Counties than Hastings.'

'That's not such a bad thing. How come we both ended up with posh birds?'

'No idea. How is Sophie, by the way? I haven't phoned for ages. I feel a bit guilty.'

'Well, don't ask me, I hardly ever see her either. I am going down to Rye today, though.'

'Yes, you mentioned that last night.'

'Did I? I don't remember that, to be honest. Anyway, we're having a weekend together before the tour. I haven't been down there for a couple of weeks, what with finishing the album and everything. We're meeting at my mum's; she looks after Amy sometimes while Sophie's at the shop. One of my mum's old-fashioned teas is on the agenda.'

'Sounds lovely.'

'I'm a bit nervous to be honest. I'm kind of growing out of the family thing.'

'My advice would be don't arrive pissed and don't arrive late.'

'Well, I'm already a bit pissed, and I'll probably be a bit late. Talking of which, fancy another?'

***

As the slow train from Charing Cross pootled down the track between Crowhurst and West St Leonards Johnny gazed out of the window as countryside gradually changed to housing estate. He had an afternoon-beer buzz, which he had been topping up surreptitiously with a small Jim Beam-filled hip-flask. He felt quite mellow but knew he was probably just a little too drunk to be able to feign sobriety. With any luck a couple of his mother's industrial-strength mugs of tea would help straighten him out by the time Sophie arrived. He decided on one last sip from the flask before he got to his stop. The playing fields of his childhood appeared at the window, signalling that it was time for him to get off. As he got up, the same fields also reminded him of Mark. He pictured them as boys kicking a ball around: Mark the better player; Johnny more adventurous. He had certainly always had the better haircut – he still had the better haircut. He smiled to himself at the blissful ignorance of youth.

He left West St Leonards station and walked the short walk down to his mother's flat, which was above a newsagent on the main road between Hastings and Bexhill. As he got to the bottom of the hill the wind whipped up; he felt its salty freshness on his face and in his hair. He had grown up here, a stone's throw from the beach; he could even see the sea from his bedroom. When he managed to bury the resentment towards his absent father his memory was that his childhood had been happy. There had not been much money but plenty of love. His mother had been devoted to him, and he in return had loved and protected her; he had been so protective that it was only since he had left home that she had managed to get a steady boyfriend. He had put a stop to a handful of other short-lived romances as a child. He had known what he was doing; he simply had not wanted their cosy twosome to be interrupted. He felt a little guilty about it, but his mother was still a relatively young woman, and it had not taken her long to find someone once he had gone. He nipped into the newsagent below the flat to buy her a box of Milk Tray before he went up.

'Johnny!' Harry Briggs gave him his usual effusive welcome as he entered the shop. Harry smoked like a chimney, an occupational hazard, and as ever his craggy face was barely visible through the grey fug.

'Harry, how the devil are you?'

Harry coughed an acrid cough before he replied. His cigarette remained attached to his bottom lip.

'All the better for seeing you, old son.'

'A large box of Milk Tray please.'

'I know who that's for. Your lovely mother.'

'Have you seen her? She's looking after Amy today.'

'They came in this morning. Your mum was treating the kid to some jelly babies. She told me you were coming down later. She's worried about you, son. She thinks you don't see enough of that posh wife of yours. She thinks those bright lights up there have sucked you in.'

'I can understand why she'd say that, Harry. I've been really busy with Swerve. We're going on tour next, all round the country.'

'Well good for you, mate, but don't forget your own. Keep them close. That's my advice.'

'I'll have twenty Marlboro Lights as well please.' Johnny knew Harry was right. He always was. He had looked out for Johnny as he was growing up; his avuncular advice was normally pretty sound.

'And maybe take a little more water with it.' Harry put the cigarettes on the counter next to the chocolates and winked at him.

Johnny felt both angry and embarrassed as he left the shop. He walked next door, through the front door and up to his mother's first-floor flat, the flat that had been home to him for most of his life. Harry liked a drink himself, so for him to comment on Johnny's sobriety was a little rich. But still, it must have been pretty obvious that he was a little the worse for wear if Harry had noticed straight away.

His mother opened the door and threw her arms around him. Amy was not far behind. He picked his daughter up and threw her in the air, revelling in her squeals of delight.

'I'll put the kettle on,' his mother said. She was from a generation where a cup of tea was the catchall response to any situation.

Johnny left his leather holdall in the small hallway and followed his mother into the kitchen. Amy held his hand and chattered to him, the odd phrase making sense.

'It's lovely to see you,' Mary said, turning to look at him as she busied herself at the sink.

Her face was lined now but still handsome, with strong bones and an almost Scandinavian look. Her blonde hair was greying a little at the edges, but her good looks still filled him with pride. He remembered as a child how proud he had been to have the youngest, prettiest mother waiting for him at the school gates.

'How's London?' she asked.

'Great,' he said, which it was for the most part. 'How's Sophie?' He knew his mother would have seen her that morning when she picked Amy up.

'She seemed a bit preoccupied this morning. She looked tired too, to be honest, love. I'm not going to tell you everything's great when I don't think it is.'

'What time is she coming over?'

'I think she'll be here soon. She was going to shut the shop early and join us for some tea.'

Johnny had always talked to his mother about everything: adolescent worries, first girlfriends, his fear of the dark. For a moment he considered talking to her about Mark. He had some time before Sophie arrived.

His mother sat next to him at the kitchen table.

'What's on your mind, love?'

'Nothing in particular,' he lied. 'I'm excited about the tour, but I'm worried about Sophie and Amy. I feel distant, and it's only going to get worse.'

'Nothing else?' She really could read him like a book.

'No, not really. I'm drinking too much, but it's an occupational hazard.'

'Yes. Your father was a drinker. He was easily led, like you. Be careful, won't you, love.'

It was rare that Mary mentioned his father. He had given up years ago asking her to expand on these occasional comments. They both let them float away just as his father had done.

'I'm OK, Mum, I've just got a lot going on. You will keep an eye on the girls for me while I'm touring, won't you?'

'Yes, I'll try. I'll still be looking after Amy on Fridays. I've agreed that with Sophie. It gives Isabelle a break too.'

'It gives Amy a break from Isabelle as well.'

'I know you don't like Isabelle, Johnny, but she does a lot for your daughter.'

The doorbell rang. Johnny was slightly relieved. He got up to greet Sophie, tottering only very slightly. He threw the door open, probably a little too theatrically, and put his arms around her, kissing her hard on the lips. He felt her wince slightly. Not the best start to the weekend. She seemed happier to see Amy, who squealed delightedly. Sophie picked her up and held her. He felt as if she was keeping her close to keep Johnny away. His mother had been right, she looked tired. He was going to have to tread carefully this weekend.

'How are you, babe?'

'I'm knackered.'

'Well, come and sit down.' He patted the seat next to him. She put Amy down and sat beside him. He put his arm around her; he felt her stiffen slightly.

'Make yourselves comfortable. I'll put some music on while I'm getting the tea ready. We might hear Johnny!'

'We've had a couple of radio plays already. "Lost in Space" comes out on Monday.'

He shifted away from Sophie and lit a cigarette.

'That's great, Johnny.' Sophie seemed genuinely pleased and smiled at him for the first time.

'In fact, Amy, I've got you a present.' He unzipped his weekend holdall and pulled out an advance copy of the new CD for Amy.

'Oh, wow, that is seriously cool.' Sophie was clearly impressed.

'Cool, cool,' chanted Amy.

'I'm so proud of you, Johnny,' his mother said as she put her arms around him. 'We've got to put it on.'

'Yes. We have to.' Sophie seemed genuinely keen too. He basked a little in the adulation as his mother put the CD on.

Soon the familiar guitar riff filled the room as the song opened. Sophie and Johnny sat grinning at each other; for the moment, the music had broken the ice. His mother insisted on putting the song on a couple of times more; on the third rendition he got up, lit a cigarette and looked out of the window at the back of the flat. He surveyed the wasteland where the old lido of his childhood had once stood; he could see himself diving from the high board, showing off to his friend Mark. Mark had never overcome his fear of diving from that height, but Johnny had forced himself to. Time never stood still. He was on the cusp of something big with Swerve; he would try not to be carried away on the waves of it. He felt a small hand in his as Amy dragged him back to the sing-a-long. For Amy's sake he would try not to be carried away.

***

Sophie was a nervous flier. The worst moment for her was the landing. She already had the jitters; she was anxious about coming to Paris on her own, about leaving Amy with her mother for a couple of days, but most of all about meeting up with Henri. It had taken months to organise. She had been reluctant at first, making excuses when Henri had called to let her know that he would be in Paris. But he had been persistent. He had phoned for a third time on Sunday evening. His timing, as ever, was uncannily precise. She had just said her goodbyes to Johnny at the annexe as he left to go on tour. The weekend had left her feeling a little bit empty. She felt as if she and Johnny were going through the motions for Amy's sake. The spectre of physical contact hung over them in the evenings like a dark cloud. He had stayed up drinking on both Friday and Saturday nights, leaving her alone in bed tossing and turning, wondering what state he would be in by the time he did join her. By contrast, he had been pleasant company during the daytime as well as affectionate and tender with both her and Amy. Still, there was no mistaking the emptiness she had felt, and she would hardly see him until Christmas because of the tour. It was almost like a trial separation. The plane started its descent. She felt sick to her stomach.

She gripped the armrest as she felt the beads of sweat rising on her upper lip and her forehead. Only a few minutes and then she would have her feet back on the ground, she kept telling herself.

She felt so much better once on solid ground. Henri was meeting her at Charles de Gaulle Airport. Apparently it was not too far from his friends' shop at Clignancourt market. She hurried through the tiled corridors. She had thought long and hard about what to wear to on the trip; she would only be there for a couple of days, and she wanted to travel light and create the right impression. In the end she had decided on a short black-and-white-patterned A-line dress, a short double-breasted sailor-style coat with gold buttons and a pair of motorcycle boots to which she had recently become very attached. She felt ready for any eventuality; the dress was chic enough for a restaurant, but the look was street enough to pass muster in the fashion world. She had also not wanted to try to look too chic, as this would only be tempting failure in the chicest city in the world. She had been growing her hair longer, and her bob had now grown out so that she could have it in a freer shoulder-length style. She liked the feeling of it bouncing as she walked. She had her toiletries and a change of underwear in a seventies shoulder bag, and that was it. She was at large in Paris.

She spotted Henri before he saw her. He was in a private-banker's suit, looking slightly rakish, smoking a cigarette. She realised that it felt good to see him, her tour guide for the next couple of days. Despite herself, she bounded up to him with a big smile.

'*Salut, brave,*' she said, kissing him on both cheeks.

'*Salut,* Sophie. Welcome to my city.'

'I thought you were from Geneva. I've got as much claim on this place as you have.'

'Yes, of course, I was forgetting your French heritage. Welcome to our city then. I think we'll take a taxi down to Cligancourt to meet Véronique and Juste. I would offer to carry your bag, but you don't seem to have one.' He half smiled at her – a half-smile as his eyes were concealed by his fringe and those reptilian eyelids. He was as difficult to read in life as he was at the poker table.

They were soon in a taxi speeding towards the city.

'So, how's our favourite rock star?' Henri asked.

'He's OK – at least, as far as I know he's OK. He went on tour on Monday, so he's currently at a university somewhere in the north of England, playing to drunken students at a freshers' ball.' She looked at her watch; it was only two o'clock. 'No, I tell a lie, he's currently recovering in a tour bus from last night's after-gig party somewhere in the north of England. He'll be playing at the next freshers' ball a little bit later.'

'You don't make it sound a very attractive prospect.'

'I'm sure he's having a wonderful time; it just doesn't appeal to me.'

'And how is the lovely Amy?'

'She's being looked after by my unlovely mother.'

'But Isabelle is charming.'

'She can be, but I can assure you that absence makes the heart grow fonder.'

'So, you're free from all that for a couple of days.'

'How about you? Aren't you here on business?'

'I saw some clients this morning, and now I'm free until tomorrow morning. I'm all yours.'

Sophie felt herself redden slightly. He had a habit of flirting a little too obviously. Fortunately they were approaching Clignancourt, and the conversation was interrupted while Henri gave directions.

'So, we haven't really discussed my friends. Véronique and Juste. Véronique is the woman, and Juste is the man.'

'But you said they were both girls.'

'Yes, they are, but they are a couple, and I'm just explaining how their relationship works.'

'Right. So how did you meet them?'

'In the lesbian bar in Geneva.'

'And what were you doing there? Are men allowed?'

'Of course men are allowed; they're not men haters. It's a fun place, and I was there with a lesbian friend of mine. It has a very French, kind of old Parisian feel to it. They seemed quite at home there.'

Sophie wondered if Rye could accommodate a Parisian-style lesbian bar. Probably not, was her rapid conclusion.

'Anyway, we met, stayed in touch, and now I often see them if I'm in Paris.'

There was more to Henri than she had thought.

The taxi pulled up outside quite a large shop in a narrow street in part of the market complex. VJ was painted in large art-nouveau-style letters on the shop front. She followed Henri inside, and they were immediately set upon by its owners. The conversation was all in French, but Sophie just about managed to keep up.

'Henri, mais c'est fabuleux. Comment vas-tu?'

Juste was more vocal than Véronique. Sophie held back a little and took them in. Their appearances could not have been more different. Juste had short-cropped blonde hair and wore a tight black T-shirt, tight black jeans held up with a large studded black belt and big black boots with large steel toecaps. Véronique was more in the style of Vanessa Paradis or a young Jane Birkin. She wore suede hipsters and a cropped T-shirt, showing off her admirably flat tummy. They greeted her warmly, and she felt Juste in particular eyeing her up from head to toe. It was more obvious than a woman would normally be; not as obvious as a man but still overtly sexual.

'And this must be Sophie. You didn't tell us how beautiful she was, Henri. Enchantée, Sophie.' Juste kissed her on both cheeks. Véronique floated over silently and did the same thing.

'It's wonderful to meet you too.'

Juste then continued fussing over Henri, who was clearly enjoying himself. Véronique floated off to find some champagne, leaving Sophie alone to feast her eyes on the clothes. It was an Aladdin's Cave of French fashion. The clothes seemed to be broadly arranged chronologically from about the thirties to the eighties; a tour through Chanel, Dior and Givenchy right up to Yves Saint Laurent and Thierry Mugler. There were not only clothes but shoes through the decades as well: from forties platforms to seventies platforms; fifties stilettos to eighties stilettos. She was in heaven. As the others chatted over their champagne she lost herself in twentieth-century French fashion for the rest of the afternoon.

***

'What a beautiful room,' Sophie exclaimed as she sat down opposite Henri at Maison Prunier that evening. The day had been a whirlwind. She had been whisked from VJ to Hôtel Le Meurice and then on here for dinner. The room was a shrine to art deco: soft black marble, cream porcelain tiles laid out in perfect symmetry.

'I think art deco is my favourite period of architecture. I love the clean lines. I think it appeals to the Cartesian in me,' said Henri as they sat down.

'I love it too, but what do you mean by Cartesian? I've read about Cartesian logic, but what does Cartesian mean to a real Frenchman?'

'Well, I think we French have a much more mathematical education than you Brits. We have a reputation for being passionate and creative, whereas the reality is that the emphasis at school is not on the arts, it's on maths. Perhaps that logical foundation allows us to be more creative when we do break out of it.'

Two glasses of champagne arrived.

'Shall I order for you?' Henri asked.

Sophie would not normally have dreamed of allowing a man to order for her, but she found herself agreeing rather meekly, a little overawed by the surroundings.

'We'll have a dozen of your Breton oysters to start, then two whole grilled Dover sole with allumettes and a bottle of Sancerre.'

'Perfect,' she said, despite herself. 'So, do you think your Cartesian education makes you good at poker?'

'That's the first time you've admitted that I am good.'

'Well, you're better than Johnny and Mark.'

'I think that is what you English call faint praise, no?'

She smiled at him, looking deep into his eyes. They seemed more open than normal, more receptive.

'Would I be right in thinking that Mark is more Cartesian than Johnny?' She giggled at the idea of Johnny possibly being described as Cartesian.

'Maybe if you could add them together it might make a good poker player,' he replied.

'So what does make a good player?'

'I think you already know the answer to that.'

She felt herself colouring a little at the compliment.

The oysters arrived quickly with the Sancerre, and they began to devour them. Sophie had eaten oysters occasionally in France before with her family, but they seemed different in a chic restaurant in the company of a charming Frenchman. There was something very physical about eating an oyster, pulling it from its muscle, tilting the shell to your mouth, letting it slide in, the salty juices dribbling just a little down your chin. It felt intimate.

'So, how's your girlfriend in London?' She wanted to know more about Henri.

'I think you mean Emily. She's fine. I'm not sure that she's my girlfriend, though. It's not an exclusive relationship, not for me anyway.'

'So, do you have other girlfriends?'

'No, nothing serious. What about you? Is Johnny an exclusive relationship?'

'Of course he is. We're married.'

'I'm sorry, I didn't mean to offend you. I think we French have a different view of marriage. We accept that sometimes a relationship with one person is not quite enough.'

'Well, I suppose I'm English on that one.' Sophie had found Henri's comment gauche, but she was still enjoying herself. She decided not to spoil the evening by taking offence and smiled back at him.

'We have our ups and downs, though, Johnny and I. It hasn't been easy. In fact, it's still not easy.'

'I can imagine. Easy and Johnny are mutually exclusive. Exciting and Johnny go together much better.'

'Yes, the problem is Amy. Johnny loves her, but his lifestyle's not that suited to childcare. He's hitting the booze quite hard these days too.'

'I noticed the last time I saw him. Do you think it's becoming a problem?'

'I think it's an occupational hazard. Being on tour with Swerve isn't going to help. Anyway, I'm here to enjoy myself not to worry about that.' She really was not sure where things were going with Johnny, but she saw no reason to tell Henri that. She had already decided that she would confront that problem once he was back from his tour. Henri had also seemed to have picked up that the Johnny subject was closed for discussion.

'So, what do you think, *ma chère*, shall we take up our friends' kind offer to join them at their club after dinner?'

'I can't see any reason to turn them down. I've done some great business with them today. I know the pound collapsed this week, but the prices are still OK. I've bought things that I can sell for three times the money back in England.'

'Yes, your government tried pretty hard to bankrupt the country, but I think it's a short-term thing. I think Mr Major and company are over the worst. Your English pounds should still be able to buy you more French fashion.'

'Good, because I'm already planning to come back to Paris. I'm kind of liking it.'

She lifted her glass and chinked it with Henri's. Yes, she really was liking it.

***

Juste and Véronique had suggested that they meet after dinner at the nightclub Cheroot, which was apparently just off the Champs Élysées. They had chosen to walk from the restaurant in Avenue Victor Hugo, as it was a warmish dry evening, and Henri had recommended that they take in some Parisian street life. As they ambled along Sophie felt more relaxed than she had done in a long time; there was something about Henri's manner tonight that put her at ease. The streets too seemed friendly; the buzz of conversation hung in the evening air with clouds of laughter floating every now and then into the night. The streets, Henri's manner, the wine, the seafood, the lack of responsibilities, it had all given her a nice mellow buzz. Before she could stop herself she had taken Henri's hand in hers as they walked along. She tingled with the thrill of it. He accepted it without comment. Had he felt the same tingle? She turned to look at him; he turned too and smiled at her. Even his eyes were smiling, but had he felt the tingle? For the moment she could not tell. She felt a pang of guilt but fought it off.

She let go of his hand as they arrived at the club and made their way in. There was a queue outside, but they walked straight past it and right up to the doorman. Henri said a few words in his ear and they were ushered inside. Sophie recognised 'Be My Baby' by Vanessa Paradis playing loudly in what was quite a small room for a nightclub. The décor was definitely Baroque with a capital B: lots of gilt and red velvet; a little kitsch but fashionably so. She soon spotted Juste waving at them from a prominently positioned semicircular booth, Véronique by her side smiling in a slightly vacant fashion. There seemed to be an assortment of extravagantly dressed friends draped around them, most of them women but a couple of men too. They joined them at the table amid lots of cheek kissing. She was introduced to the rest of their gang and sat down wedged between Juste and Henri. A bottle of vodka in an ice bucket arrived at the table with lots of ceremony and several flunkeys carrying mixers and glasses. Apparently Henri had ordered it, and he began to pour drinks and hand them round. Juste was talking in Sophie's ear, but she was finding it difficult to hear what she was saying. What she did notice was how close she was getting to her ear and neck, almost touching her with her lips as she spoke. She turned to Juste's ear and tried to explain that she couldn't hear. In the end they just shrugged and smiled at each other. Juste took this as a sign of encouragement, and put her hand furtively on Sophie's thigh under the table. Next she felt Henri's arm around her shoulders as he sat back against the padded velvet of the booth, sipping on his vodka and Coke. She was receiving more attention than she had done in quite some time. Not quite sure what to make of it all she decided that a visit to the ladies would give her some respite.

In the relative quiet of the loos she sat in a cubicle with her knickers around her ankles, reflecting on the situation. She had made a pass at one of her husband's best friends, and one of *his* friends, a woman to boot, had made a pass at her. It was all pretty harmless so far, but she was starting to feel a little out of her depth. She needed to relax and go with the flow; she should have a couple more drinks and it would all seem quite normal. She stood up, rearranged herself and left the cubicle. Straight in front of her was the vested back of her seductress, standing at the mirror.

'I knew it was you when I saw those boots under the door,' said Juste, without even turning around.

'Why were you looking for me?' asked Sophie.

'I wanted to tell you how beautiful you are. You didn't seem to be able to hear me in the club.'

Sophie shuffled a little; she had no idea what to say. Juste turned round to face her and then put her hand to Sophie's cheek, touching it softly. She moved closer to her.

'Have you ever been with a woman?' she whispered into her ear.

As if on cue the door to the ladies slammed open.

'*Saloparde!*' yelled Véronique as she stormed towards them. Sophie stepped away from Juste, realising quickly that she was not the object of Véronique's ire. There's nothing more dangerous than a woman scorned, she thought, as she slipped quietly back out into the club, leaving Juste to fend off Véronique rather feeble blows.

It was time to call it a night. She moved quickly back to the table, caught Henri's eye and pointed to the exit. To his credit he followed her out.

'I seem to have come between your friends,' she said once they were on the street.

'What do you mean?' asked Henri.

'Well, Juste made a pass at me in the toilets, and we were caught by Véronique.'

Henri began to laugh. 'You are one of a long list of conquests,' he said. 'Juste is constantly straying, and Véronique is constantly catching her. It's like a game to them. They're probably already kissing and making up.'

'Oh well, maybe it's not as bad as I thought, but do you mind if we go anyway?'

'Of course. Le Meurice is just down the road.'

He put his arm around her shoulders as they walked down the Champs Élysées to the hotel. She put hers around his waist.

'Did I tell you how much I like the hotel?'

'I'm glad. I thought you'd like the English connection.'

He really was very slick, she thought, but with a dangerous edge. She had always been drawn to dangerous men.

***

Their rooms were next to each other, and as they approached the doors their banter stopped as they both seemed to acknowledge that decisions were imminent. Henri stopped next to her by the door to her room. He was close, closer than a friend would be.

'So, this is where we decide when we are going to say goodnight,' he said quietly.

His face was inches from hers. She leaned forward and kissed him on the lips tentatively; he responded immediately, kissing her back hard, his tongue finding hers. He tasted acrid, of cigarettes and alcohol, but she did not mind. In fact, she quite liked it. He pulled away from her.

'Are you OK with this?' he asked.

'I'm not sure,' she said, putting her hand behind his neck and kissing him again.

This time she pulled away to open her door.

'Come in,' she said.

They slipped through the door into the hotel room, both looking down the corridor as they did so, as if they were being watched. Once they were inside he pushed her softly but firmly against the wall and began kissing her again, but this time also touching her breast firmly, his groin pressed against hers, his body pushing her back and buttocks hard against the wall. She could feel him bursting out of his trousers. She was at the point of no return. Without any warning she pulled away.

'I'm sorry, Henri, I can't do this. You're a very attractive man, and I want you, but I can't do this. Not to Johnny and not to Amy. I'm sorry.'

They were both breathing hard. Henri was still inches from her. She felt suddenly vulnerable, unsure how he might respond. The room was sparsely lit by a couple of table lamps, and his face was shadowy, his fringe flopped over his eyes. She put her hand on his cheek.

'I'm sorry,' she said again.

'OK. I'll go,' he said, and with one quick movement he disappeared.

Now she felt guilty for leading him on. She stayed still for a minute or two then realised that she was still standing up against the wall with her dress above her knees where it had ridden up as he pressed against her. She went and sat on the bed. She felt a strong urge to speak to Johnny, but she had no idea where he was – no doubt trashing another hotel room somewhere in the north of England. She had not brought the list of hotel numbers for the tour with her, so there was no chance of calling him. There was something between Johnny and her, she could feel it now, and it was that something that had made her pull away from Henri. What a day. She needed to try to sleep. Would she be able to face Henri at breakfast? Why not? She had done the right thing. She just wished it had not been her that had kissed him first.

BREDE VALLEY, EAST SUSSEX

31 DECEMBER 1992

Sophie went through to the kitchen to check on the meat. She was still not used to cooking with an Aga, so she kept checking the lamb shoulder, which she was slow cooking in the bottom of the two ovens. She was trying to produce a piece of meat that fell off the bone like they cooked in Greece or Morocco. She stuck a knife into the meat again, and it slid through the flesh easily; the slow oven seemed to be working. The evening seemed to be working too. She thought it might have been a little uncomfortable with Henri, as it was the first time she had seen him since their rather frosty breakfast before she left Paris back in September. Thankfully, he had been warm and friendly, or about as warm as he ever was. He did not seem to be bearing a grudge. She was meeting Emily for the first time too; so far she seemed good company. She was very pretty and had enough poise and style not to be dominated by Henri. Sophie even felt a little jealous at quite how pretty she was. She was not jealous of Victoria; not because she was ugly, but she could not imagine being jealous of a girl who was in a sexual relationship with Mark. Victoria was attractive in a handsome rather than a pretty way. She was perfectly polite and pleasant but seemed a little overawed by the situation, and particularly by Johnny.

It had been Johnny's idea to rent the new house. He had called one night from the tour and suggested that Sophie find them a place in the country. His reasoning was that they had the money now, and he really could not face going back to the annexe. Sophie had jumped on the idea and had quickly found Cadborough Cottage, nestled into the north side of the Brede Valley, a couple of miles from Rye, with stunning views out over the marsh to Winchelsea and beyond to the English Channel. The move had transformed their lives, and since Johnny had come back from the tour their relationship seemed to be right back on track. They had spent a quiet Christmas in the countryside with Amy and had made the odd family visit. It had been a time for them both to recharge and get to know one another again. It had been Sophie's idea to invite their friends down for New Year; it gave her a chance to show off the new house but also to show them how well she and Johnny were getting on. She was enjoying this opportunity and felt herself smiling as she went back into the dining-room, thrilled at the prospect of being at her own first proper grown-up dinner party.

'It was amazing,' Mark was saying. 'Imagine being at a party stood right next to Joey Ramone. Amazing.'

'Sounds amazing,' said Henri with a certain amount of disdain.

'You can scoff, Henri, but the Ramones are seriously cool guys, I'm telling you.'

'I can well believe it.' Henri gave Sophie a conspiratorial look. So they were friends again, she thought, smiling back and affecting to be well above Mark's naïve enthusiasm.

'In fairness, Henri, I have to agree with Mark,' said Johnny. 'They were pretty fucking cool guys. It was the highlight of the tour for me, meeting those guys and playing the Academy again.'

'It was absolutely rammed with people that night,' Mark continued, 'and Swerve were brilliant. They really rocked.' However hard he tried, thought Sophie, Mark still sounded a bit stiff.

'It was probably our best gig. We were really tight that night, and the atmosphere was amazing.'

'Amazing,' Henri repeated.

Emily dug him in the ribs. 'It's more interesting than talking about the economy, which is all you seem to want to do. I love "Lost in Space". It's amaaazing.'

Everyone laughed. Sophie was warming to Emily despite her excessively beautiful looks. She seemed to be able to put Henri in his place from time to time, which was no mean feat.

'I must admit, there is something about that song that is catchy.' He started singing, his French accent somehow amplified now that he was singing.

"'I'm alone, suspended from gravity ...'" he sang. The others joined in around the table. Sophie looked at Mark, belting out the words in a slightly off-key baritone; he was a bit of a nerd, but she had a soft spot for him. Even Victoria was joining in. Sophie was glad that Mark seemed to have found someone who could reciprocate his affection.

'Well, that's a pretty good sign, Johnny. Everyone knows the words,' Sophie observed.

'Yeah, it's been massive on the tour that song.'

'So how was the tour anyway?' asked Henri. 'Or should we ask you when Sophie is out of the room?'

You wanker, thought Sophie.

'Ask away, I'm just going to sort out the main course.' She went into the kitchen; she had no desire to listen to Henri trying to embarrass Johnny into telling everyone tales of groupies and drug-taking. She knew there would have been girls around on the tour; she hoped that Johnny had been faithful, but if he had not, she really did not want to know. Henri was deliberately stirring things up; he clearly had not forgiven her for the Paris incident. She tried to put it to the back of her mind while she sorted out the lamb.

'Can I give you a hand?' It was Emily. She had surprised her again; she did not look like the type to don an apron in a crisis.

'Oh, that's very kind.'

'I'm sorry about Henri. He likes to wind people up.' She was perceptive too.

'Don't worry about Henri. I know him well enough by now. I would say that he doesn't mean anything by it, but I think we both know that he probably does.'

'Yes, I'm afraid so.' They both laughed.

'So why do we put up with him?' Sophie asked.

'Oh, he has other ways of making up for it.' Emily smiled at her. Sophie could tell that Henri had not told her what had happened between them.

'Good,' she said, 'I'm glad to hear it.'

***

'Mummy, can we go out soon?'

'Yes, darling, after breakfast we're all going to go out for a walk.'

'Shall I wake everyone up then?'

'Well, you can go and wake Daddy up. He can come and give me a hand.'

Amy ran off, and Sophie went back to frying bacon. She had a very fuggy head, but it had been worth it. Everyone had been in great form all evening; no one had got too pissed, even Johnny, and Henri had finally mellowed out after a couple of bottles of wine. Now the plan was a hearty breakfast followed by a walk down the Brede Valley to Winchelsea and the sea beyond. She looked out of the window in front of her, which framed the glorious view they had from the cottage. Straight down the valley she could track the river Brede meandering towards Rye with Winchelsea high up above the right bank, the old port now a stranded island surrounded by marsh. Then there was the sea beyond, an ever-changing gateway to adventure. She really loved this new house.

The rest of the group gradually straggled down to breakfast. First, Victoria and Mark – she looking bright and breezy, and he a little less so – then Emily appeared, looking exquisitely hung over, followed by Johnny and finally Henri, looking slightly contrite.

'J'ai vraiment mal à la tête.'

'That's because you Frogs can't take your booze,' said Johnny.

They sat around the kitchen table, bantering over breakfast.

'So, who's coming for a walk?' Sophie asked. 'Amy's been waiting all morning.'

'Walk, walk!' Amy jumped up from her seat and began pulling Johnny to try to get him up.

'I'm not sure I've got the energy, babe,' he said. 'There's some football on TV I wouldn't mind watching. I think I'll stay here.'

'Well, I'd love to come,' said Emily, catching Amy in her arms as she ran over to her.

'*Moi aussi*. I need something to clear my head,' said Henri.

'Yes, a walk sounds like a good idea. Some air would be very pleasant. How about you, Mark?' Victoria asked.

'I think I'll stay here and watch the football with Johnny.'

'Well, don't drink too much beer. You're going to have to drive later.' Victoria clearly had Mark in hand. Not that he would have had too much beer anyway if he was driving.

***

After they had been walking down the valley for twenty minutes or so Sophie realised that she had underestimated how cold it was. The sun was shining, but it was low in the sky; it was one of those still, frosty winter days, the temperature barely above zero. It was nice to be out, but she wished she had put on a hat.

'Mummy, my ears are cold.' She had forgotten to put Amy's hat on as well.

'I think I'll have to go back to the house for Amy's hat,' she said to the others. 'If you carry on slowly I should be able to catch you up again.'

'No problem,' said Henri, taking hold of Amy's hand. She took it quite happily.

She set off back to the house at a fast walk.

A few minutes later she was walking down the path to the back door of the house. The hats were hanging up in the boot room. She picked hers up and put it on then stuffed Amy's in her pocket. She walked through to the hallway and checked her hat in the mirror. She could hear the football commentary blaring from the sitting-room, as the door was half open. There was no need for her to go in and talk to Johnny and Mark; she needed to get back quickly. Then, as she tucked her hair into the woollen hat, she saw something moving in the mirror; it was reflecting an image of the sofa in the sitting-room. She felt sick to her stomach as she realised that what she could see was Mark's head quite clearly moving rhythmically up and down on Johnny's cock. Johnny was lying on the sofa, his head back and his eyes closed, moaning softly, quite clearly enjoying himself. She was transfixed for a moment and then came to her senses. They had not seen her, and she must not let them see her. She turned and moved as quickly and as quietly as she could out of the house. They must not know that she had seen them. She fast-walked back down the garden path, out of the gate, and, once she was shielded by the hedges, she began to run, tears streaming down her face. As soon as she was a few hundred yards from the house and on the footpath she stopped, knelt down and vomited into the bushes. She stayed kneeling on the footpath, breathing hard, the tears still coming. She tried to start to fight them back; for Amy's sake she had to pull herself together. She had to try to put this to the back of her mind until she had more time to think. She stood up, breathing heavily. She realised she was in a state of shock, but she had about fifteen minutes or so to calm herself down before she caught up with the others. She walked down the path, taking deliberate and deep breaths. She managed gradually to stop crying as she continued along. Sooner than she would have liked she could see the backs of her friends walking slowly down the valley. She had to forget what she had just seen. She had to.

***

Mark lifted his head for a moment from what he was doing.

'What was that? I thought I heard something.'

Johnny did not move.

'I didn't hear a thing. Don't stop now.'

Mark was convinced he had heard something from the kitchen, but if he had it seemed to have gone now. He put his mouth back on Johnny's cock and carried on. A short while later he brought him to a climax. He loved to give Johnny pleasure like this. The fact that this time they were in Johnny's house only added to the thrill; he felt as if he was usurping Sophie, paying her back for that night in Wapping. The problem was how guilty Johnny felt after their occasional sessions. It was strange, but Mark did not feel any guilt himself; he had more or less admitted to himself recently that he had been in love with Johnny for years. As far as he was concerned it was perfectly natural to have sex with someone you were in love with. In fact, if he analysed it honestly, he knew he would rather have sex with Johnny than with Victoria. But he did like Victoria, and he did like having sex with her; he just did not have that all-encompassing, obsessive feeling that he did with Johnny.

'Fancy a beer, mate?' Johnny asked, doing up his flies.

'You heard what Victoria said. I've got to drive later.'

'One beer won't do you any harm.' He walked out to the kitchen and came back with a couple of bottles of Grolsch and two pint glasses.

They poured their beers and settled back on the sofa to watch the football.

'So, how's it going with Victoria anyway? She seems like a decent sort.'

'We seem to be getting on pretty well. She's my kind of person really: intelligent, organised, neat and tidy. I like her.'

'Has she moved in yet?'

'No. We have discussed it, but we don't think it would be appropriate.'

'What d'you mean not appropriate, you old fart?'

'Well, it might raise a few eyebrows at work. Relationships between colleagues are frowned upon.'

'What do they expect from a load of people just out of college?'

'Yes, I know, it is a little old-fashioned, but it does lead to problems sometimes. I'm afraid my working environment is not quite the same as yours.'

Johnny chuckled. Mark liked to make him laugh. He knew that he was not the funniest bloke in the world, but Johnny seemed to appreciate his dry sense of humour. They had always been able to laugh together, and laughing was not something that came easily to Mark.

'While we're on relationships, how are you and Sophie getting on?' he asked.

'Funnily enough, pretty well at the moment. This house was definitely a good idea. I think absence really does make the heart grow fonder too. After the madness of the tour it's been a real oasis of calm. The tour really was amazing, but I needed to straighten myself out afterwards. The boozing was pretty crazy, never mind the charlie.'

'So did you stray at all?'

'Not what I would call straying. I had a couple of drunken goes at groupies, but I don't really count those.'

'Do you think Sophie would count them?' Mark could not resist.

'Fuck off, Mark. That stays between you and me, OK?'

'All right, mate, no need to be oversensitive.'

'Well, you know what I mean. Girls don't see things in quite the same way as us, do they?'

'No. Probably not Sophie anyway.'

'Yeah, exactly, and there's Amy to think about as well.'

Mark found Johnny's attitude extraordinary really. It was not just his drunken fumbles on tour that were dismissed; Johnny clearly did not count his dalliances with Mark as transgressions either. The discussion was between men, he supposed, and in Johnny's world not relevant to his wife. Still, it must have been obvious that Mark would never have told Sophie about him and Johnny, or Johnny and the groupies for that matter, so these secrets were safe with him. He looked covertly at his friend as he watched the television, his gaunt profile intent on the football. He wondered what really went on in that head of his. Sometimes he thought that it might not be as much as he had always supposed. Well, the others would be back soon, so he needed to enjoy these fleeting moments they had alone together.

***

The orange winter sun was just disappearing behind the trees as they waved goodbye to their guests, leaving a cold night ahead. Sophie had felt chilled to the bone since that morning. She had no idea what to do or say now that she was alone with Johnny. She had managed to get through the last few hours without anyone noticing her mood, but now the others had left she felt paralysed. She had kissed Mark goodbye, but she had wanted to spit in his face.

'I think I'll have a lie down, Johnny. I'm really tired,' she said. 'Can you look after Amy?'

'Yeah, sure, no worries.'

She went upstairs to their bedroom and got straight under the covers in her clothes. She could feel herself shivering. She tried to wrap her body into a tight ball, but the shivering wouldn't stop. Then the tears came, thick and fast, as she sobbed into her pillow. How could they? How could they both abuse her trust like that? How could they? Just as things had been going well with Johnny, this happens. Was Johnny gay? Was he bisexual? How long had this been going on with Mark? Since they were teenagers? And Mark? He was supposed to be her friend. How could he do this to her? And Amy? Had Johnny thought about her, about how she might be affected? She had no idea how to even start to answer these questions. Meanwhile, downstairs was an oblivious Johnny. She could not possibly confront him. She could not bear the idea of it. She would have to try to behave as if nothing had happened until he went back up to London in a few days. All she had to do was to get through the next few days, and then she would think about what she could do. She could feel the damp pillow against her cheek. She closed her eyes as the sobbing subsided, trying to sleep to relieve the pain, but all she could see was Mark's head as it bobbed up and down and the expression of pure pleasure on Johnny's face. It was the way he looked when he was with her. She tried to put it out of her mind, but it just would not shift. She heard footsteps coming up the stairs. It was Johnny.

'I've made you some tea, love. How are you feeling?'

Fortunately the room was dark as she had drawn the curtains.

'I've got a bit of a headache. I think I'm going to go to bed early. I just need some quiet.'

'OK, love, I'll let you sleep. Don't worry about Amy. I'll look after her.'

He closed the door after him. She felt relieved; she now had from this evening until tomorrow morning to try to make sense of the situation.

***

Sophie looked at her watch. The luminous hands glowed five o'clock at her. She had slept a little, but had spent most of the evening and then the night tossing and turning as she replayed the scene in her mind over and over again. At least the crying and the shivering had stopped. As the shock faded she was able to think slightly more rationally about the situation. Her conclusion was that while Johnny was a feckless waster, Mark was a fucking cunt. The C-word was not one that she used lightly, but if ever she felt justified it was now. She got up as quietly as she could, put on her dressing-gown and slipped out of the bedroom. She crept along the landing to Amy's room and peeped around her door to check on her. She was sleeping soundly. An expression of guiltless innocence covered her face. It lifted Sophie's spirits a little. She walked downstairs to the kitchen, filled the kettle, made some tea and sat down with it on their deliberately battered leather armchair. The Aga opposite warmed her bare feet. She felt an anger rising within her. She felt humiliated and disrespected, almost as if she had been violated in some way. She would have liked to have talked to someone about it, but who? Her mother? She would drum Johnny out of town in an instant, and it was not as simple as that. Her father? He was not good at confrontation, and she had inherited his weakness. He would listen with an understanding ear and would certainly keep a secret if she asked, but what help would he be? He was a procrastinator; he was built for inaction. She needed action, but what kind of action? What about Henri? Now there was a thought. He knew them both, for a start. She certainly respected him, but did she trust him? She trusted him enough to keep her horrible secret to himself. But he would be in Geneva and she in Rye. This was not something that she could discuss over the telephone. If she was going to talk to Henri about it she needed to see him face to face. Where? London maybe, or Geneva, or even Paris? She could do with some more of those wonderful clothes, but most of all she needed something to look forward to. She would start planning straight away. She would call Henri at Emily's later. There was no need to make any excuses to Johnny about another trip; it was a business trip after all. Anyway, why the fuck should she make excuses to Johnny? She had another flashback; she was standing in front of the mirror again. She would have to move that mirror or every time she looked in it she would see the same thing over her shoulder. She looked at her watch; it was coming up to six o'clock. Today was Saturday, and Johnny was due back in London on Monday. Only a couple more days to get through. Saturday! She realised that she had planned to open the shop today and start a sale of the old stock. She could call Henri in a couple of hours from there. She would need more stock if she sold off most of what she had in her sale. The perfect reason for a trip to Paris. A plan was starting to form. That's what she needed, a plan. She could even open tomorrow as well. Opening on the Sundays before Christmas had worked well. She would hardly see Johnny if she opened both days. Another cup of tea then she'd go to the shop. Maybe getting out of the house would get rid of the flashbacks. She had to keep busy. That was the answer. And telephone Henri. How early could she call him without it looking a bit odd?

***

Henri heard a telephone ringing somewhere; it sounded like it was in the distance at first, but as it got louder he realised that it was the telephone by their bed waking him up.

'Hi, Sophie, you're an early bird.' Emily had picked up. 'Thanks so much for New Year, by the way. We had the most fabulous time. I'll pass you over, he's right here.'

Henri took the telephone and sat up in bed. This was unexpected.

'*Salut*, Sophie. This is a nice surprise. A little early, but a nice surprise all the same.'

Emily got out of bed next to him, and his eyes followed her pert bottom across the room. Perhaps she objected to him talking to another woman while he lay naked in her bed.

'I'm sorry. I'm at the shop already, sorting out my winter sale. I'm reopening later this morning. It suddenly occurred to me that if I sell the things I'm putting into the sale I'll be short on stock. I'd like to go back to see Juste and Véronique, quite soon if possible.'

Henri sensed that Sophie was talking more quickly than usual. She did not seem quite as measured. He wondered what was bothering her. He had noticed that she had seemed a little odd when they left Rye yesterday. A little distracted.

'Sounds like a good idea,' he replied. 'Why don't you call them? Have you got the number?'

'I was hoping you might call for me. You remember there was that scene in the club last time. I'm not sure if Véronique has forgiven me. I was hoping that you might come to Paris again too. It was much easier with you there.'

Now this was unexpected, particularly after what had happened last time. Maybe she had changed her mind. If she had, he was very happy.

'I'm sure Véronique has forgotten all about your little problem at the club. I'm just as sure that Juste has made plenty of passes at other girls since then. Are you sure you really need me to come?'

It would be easy for him to go to Paris for a couple of days, but he wanted to be more certain that Sophie might succumb to his charms this time.

'Yes, I don't think I'll go unless you're there. Actually, there's something I want to talk to you about. I can't really discuss it on the phone.'

Curiouser and curiouser.

'Well, that sounds intriguing. How can I refuse? When were you thinking of going?'

'As soon as possible really. In a week or so. What do you think?'

'Maybe. I'll have to look at my diary.' He was pretty sure that he could convince his boss that he had enough potential new clients to see in Paris. It was only three and a half hours on the train.

'When are you back in the office?'

'On Monday. I'm flying back to Geneva tomorrow night.'

'OK. Will you call me from the office on Monday to let me know?'

'Sure. How's Johnny?'

'He's the same as he was when you saw him yesterday.' The tone of Sophie's voice had changed completely when she said this. Henri wondered what had happened.

'I'll call you on Monday. *À bientôt,*' he said and put the telephone down. Emily came back into the room.

'What did Sophie want?' she asked.

'She just wanted to talk about ordering more stock from my friends in Paris, Juste and Véronique.'

'Oh, right. Why did she call so early?'

'She was already at her shop. Some people have to work at the weekend, you know.'

He could tell that this explanation was good enough for Emily to lose interest.

Emily got back into bed. She really did look very sexy. She was wearing a white T-shirt that almost covered her bum and some skimpy pale-blue cotton knickers. The short conversation with Sophie had piqued his senses. He was sure that what she wanted to discuss was something to do with her and Johnny. Should he call Johnny to do some more fishing? Probably not a good idea. Anyway, he only had another twenty-four hours in Emily's nice warm bed. He'd better make use of them.

***

It felt good to be back with the band after a couple of weeks off. By the end of the tour they had hated each other, but he had been really pleased to see his old mates again when they all returned to the rehearsal rooms in Crouch End. Leaving Sophie and Amy had tugged at his heartstrings, particularly as he and Sophie had been getting on so well over the holiday, but he was equally happy to be back. He was doing what he loved to do, playing his Telecaster, losing himself in the music. The band had got together straight after New Year for a number of reasons: one was to work on material for a new album, but the most pressing was to rehearse for a slot that they had been asked to play at the *Feedback* magazine awards the following week. They were all trying to be quite cool about this, but it was a seriously big deal and would really raise their profile among their peers.

'OK, guys, let's just run through "Does She Believe?".' Alex was taking charge as ever.

Johnny took a sip of his Jim Beam and Coke and a last drag on his Marlboro Light. With his right foot he first pressed the button on the echo box and then the fuzz box and then launched into the opening riff. As he finished the last note of the riff and strummed the first chord, the drums, bass and vocal boomed in right on cue. He smiled at Alex as he sang the first verse, his voice as haunting as ever:

> 'There's a mystery in her walk,
> There's a distance in her talk.
> Is there an answer in her eyes?
> No, she has them well disguised.
> Is there an answer in her smile?
> No, I'll have to wait awhile.
>
> Does she believe?
> Does she believe in me?
> Does she believe?
> Does she believe in me?'

As Alex sang, Johnny mouthed the words, only singing harmonies into his microphone for the second two lines of each chorus. At the end of the last chorus they all finished together, right on the button.

'That was great, guys, nice and tight,' said Alex.

'Yeah, really crisp,' said Johnny. He had really enjoyed it.

'Let's try "Lost In Space". We all know we're going to have to play it at the awards next week.'

There was a knock on the door. It was Andy, who ran the rehearsal rooms.

'Urgent message for Johnny. Can you call Sophie at the shop?'

'Sorry, guys, I'd better call before we start the next song.'

'OK, Johnny, but be as quick as you can please.' Alex made clear his annoyance at the interruption.

'I've already apologised, Alex. You heard what the guy said. It's urgent.'

Johnny went to Andy's little office at the entrance to the rooms. He was normally pretty relaxed about occasional use of the telephone. Sure enough, he passed it over to Johnny as he came in. He hoped nothing had happened to Amy – or Sophie, for that matter. Sophie answered the telephone almost before it rang.

'Hi, babe, I just got your message. Andy said it was urgent.'

'Yes. It'll have to be quick, there's someone in the shop. I just wanted to let you know that I won't be able to make it to the awards next week. I'm going to Paris again to buy some more clothes.'

'Oh, OK, babe. Is that all? Andy said it was urgent, I was worried that something had happened to Amy.'

'Well, I thought you'd want to know that I'm going to Paris, that's all.'

'Sure. Maybe I'll invite Mark to the awards instead.'

'What do you mean?'

'Well, we can each invite one person each. If you can't come, I'll invite Mark.'

'That'll be cosy.'

'Oh, he'll love it, Sophie, he's really into the band.'

'Well, you two have a lovely time then. Sorry, I have to go. Bye.'

He was left with the dialling tone. Sophie had been a bit abrupt. He supposed it was just that she was busy in the shop. He couldn't wait to tell Mark. He'd piss himself when he heard that he was going to the *Feedback* Awards.

He went back to the rehearsal room.

'So, has the crisis been averted?' Alex asked.

'There's no crisis, fortunately. It's just that Sophie can't make the awards next week. She has to go to Paris. She wanted to let me know.'

'I'm not sure why that was so urgent. She never comes to our gigs anyway. I don't think we're posh enough.'

126

'Alex, can you lay off Sophie? She is my fucking wife, after all.'

'You wouldn't think it, the amount you see of her.'

'You little fucker.' Johnny walked over to Alex and squared up to him menacingly.

'Chill, you two. We're here to play some music.' Johnny felt Dave's arm around his shoulder. He was right. Johnny should be used to Alex's jibes by now. Alex was grinning at him. Johnny did sometimes wonder if he deliberately wound up the other members of the band; Alex loved to be in charge, and he loved to remind the others that he was in charge, even if it meant resorting to low blows. Sophie always seemed to be his target; he appeared to resent the fact that Johnny had ended up with a well-bred, independent wife.

He gave Alex a last scowl then went straight over to his guitar, threw it on and launched into the opening riff of 'Lost in Space'. He felt his anger flow into his playing as he began to lose himself in the music.

***

And in a few days the forty-second president of the United States will be inaugurated. Bill Clinton, former Governor of Arkansas, is the first Democratic president since Jimmy Carter, and at forty-six years old, the third youngest in history. After the news headlines we profile the man and the impact he is likely to have. You may or may not know that from the 1st of January we have had a single European market among members of the European Community. Again, following the news headlines we look at what this means to British businesses.

Well, that's pertinent, thought Sophie as she headed towards Folkestone in their Volvo estate. Anything to make doing business with France easier. She had decided that now she knew she was definitely going to buy from Juste and Véronique, she may as well take the clothes away with her rather than waiting for a delivery. This meant driving to Folkestone, taking the ferry and then driving to Paris. It was a big deal doing this trip on her own, but she wanted to test herself. She had no idea how things would be resolved with Johnny, or if they ever would, so she needed to make sure that she could manage everything on her own. Not that he had ever been much help from a business point of view, but what he had helped with recently was money, and if that source dried up she needed to make sure that the shop was making a decent profit. In a short time she had become very used to living in their comfortable new house.

She flicked the radio over from Radio 4 to Radio 1 while the shipping forecast was being broadcast. A familiar guitar riff jumped out at her, followed by Alex's querulous vocals. It was the last chorus of 'Does She Believe?'. She felt a slight shiver as she quite clearly heard her husband's voice on the harmonies as the song closed. It was the first time that she had heard Swerve on the radio.

That was Swerve with 'Does She Believe?', the third single from their smash-hit debut album, Lost in Space. *These boys are going to go a long way. In fact, tomorrow night they're going as far as the Grosvenor House Hotel, Park Lane, London Town, playing live at the* Feedback *Awards, and we'll be there to hear them as we broadcast live from the event.*

Sophie turned back to the shipping forecast. She was on her way to Paris to try to forget about Johnny for a couple of days; the last thing she wanted was to be reminded of the award ceremony where Mark would be acting as a surrogate wife. She felt a lump in her throat. At least she felt better than she had done a week ago; the flashbacks had fallen away, but they left behind a deep lasting pain, a kind of numbness. She was hoping that putting some distance between herself and the scene of the crime would help. She was also hoping that talking to Henri about it would have some benefit. She felt butterflies in her stomach; she was not quite sure what she was looking for from Henri. Was it just a shoulder to cry on? She knew that he was attracted to her, but was she ready to sleep with him? If she did, what would the consequences be? Would he then walk away, or would it be the start of something? He was so difficult to read. She would just have to trust her instincts.

***

It had been Henri's idea to invite Juste and Véronique to the hotel for dinner. He had told Sophie that he thought that it would help the '*entente cordiale*'. She thought it would be an opportunity for her to relax a little over dinner before talking to Henri about Johnny and Mark once the others had left. She was too worried about everything else to be worried about whether or not Véronique bore her a grudge; she had simply mentioned this to Henri to try to convince him to come to Paris. As it turned out, the atmosphere was anything but frosty. They were sitting in the grand dining-room at Le Meurice. It was a spectacular room, with gold, marble, wood panelling, huge mirrors, beautiful hand-painted walls and ceilings, all in that French style that reminded Sophie of Versailles. She supposed that must mean that the style was Louis XVI, but she was not sure; she was not going to ask either, as it would probably mean a little lecture from Henri or Juste.

The *maître d'* appeared silently to take their order.

'Would you like me to order for you, ladies?' Henri asked.

'Certainly not,' said Juste. 'I will order for myself and Véronique, and I should hope that Sophie will order for herself. Where did you pick up those old-fashioned manners? Old-fashioned Geneva, I suppose?'

'I think it was probably from my father, who happens to be Parisian.'

'Well, whoever it was, it belongs to the last century.'

Sophie smiled. Juste clearly did not see the irony in her own presumption that she would be ordering for Véronique.

'For mademoiselle the red mullet salad followed by the Bresse chicken, and for me the lobster followed by the *filet de bœuf*. I'd like the beef blue please.'

It was Sophie next. She had finally started to regain her appetite, having eaten like a bird for a week or so.

'I'll have the lobster too, and I'll also have the *filet de bœuf* but rare please.'

'I'll have the same,' said Henri.

'You don't have to be like sheep,' said Juste. 'Have some imagination.'

'You have impeccable taste, Juste, so it's easy to follow your lead.'

'You are an incorrigible charmer, Henri, but remember you have no chance with me.' Juste cackled at her borderline comment. Sophie smiled and noticed Véronique also allowing herself a little coquettish chuckle.

Juste was slightly reminiscent of David Vanian of the Damned tonight, thought Sophie. Her blonde hair had now been dyed dark and was slicked back away from her pale face, which was deliberately made up to accentuate her high cheekbones. She wore a black suit, possibly a man's suit, with a white blouse and a black bootlace tie. Sophie almost fancied her. Véronique was wearing an impossibly short black skirt, black stockings, impossibly high black stilettos and a tiny sleeveless silver blouse. Her long hair tumbled over her shoulders. She really was beautiful. Sophie herself had also dressed in black, having brought with her a little black fifties Chanel cocktail dress from her own stock. It was sleeveless with a high neck and a tight fit around the bust and hips. It fitted her like a glove, which gave her back some of the confidence she had lacked since New Year's Day.

'You know that this hotel was the favourite of the Rosbifs in the last century, Sophie?' asked Juste.

'Yes, I did. It's fabulous. I feel very spoiled staying here.'

'I used to come here with my father sometimes when I was growing up. He was descended from Russian aristocracy. His family came here after the 1917 revolution, and he liked to pretend that he was still important, so we would come here for lunch sometimes. He couldn't really afford it, but I used to love it. The grandeur.'

'You say that you used to come here with your father. Does that mean you don't any more?' Sophie asked.

'He drank himself to death,' Juste replied.

'I'm sorry to hear that.'

'Don't worry. It was the best thing that could have happened to him.'

'And your mother?'

'We don't speak. She does not approve of my sexual preferences.' Juste turned and smiled at Véronique, who smiled back, her eyes looking downwards.

The sommelier poured more wine. Sophie sipped at hers. It was delicious, rich and buttery.

'What's this wine?' she asked Henri.

'It's a 1988 Meursault.'

'That's a white burgundy,' explained Juste.

'It's wonderful. How about you, Véronique? Where are you from?'

'She's from the *banlieue*. I rescued her from a life of multiple pregnancies by multiple fathers.'

'Don't exaggerate, Juste. But it's true, I do come from the other side of the Périphérique.'

'That's the ring-road that runs around Paris,' said Henri.

'Yes, I know,' said Sophie. 'I am a little bit French, you know.'

'So, how French are you?' asked Juste.

'My mother's name is du Pont. Her father was a Frenchman who married an Englishwoman, my grandmother. So I suppose I'm a quarter French.'

'You know you speak very good French with no accent.' Juste paid her a rare compliment.

'Well, I used to come to France at least once a year when I was growing up, and my mother often spoke French to me at home in England.'

'So where did you two meet?' Sophie asked.

'I thought I told you. We met in the lesbian bar in Geneva,' said Henri.

'No, Juste and Véronique.'

'I saved Véronique from an ugly heterosexual. She immediately fell in love with me.'

Véronique giggled into her hand.

'She was with her boyfriend from the *banlieue* at a club in Les Halles,' Juste continued. 'He was drunk, they were arguing, and I was worried that he was going to hit her. I had been looking at her all evening; she was the most beautiful girl in the club. I didn't want to risk any damage to that beautiful face.'

Juste stopped for a moment as their first courses were served. Sophie looked at Véronique, whose face was now as pink with embarrassment as the lobster they had just been served.

'*Bon appétit*,' they all said. Sophie noticed how the food had suddenly taken precedence. They were in France after all.

'*Magnifique*,' said Juste as she tasted her lobster, before continuing. 'So, I tapped this arsehole on the back, told him what I thought of him, grabbed Véronique by the hand and walked straight out of the club with her. The arsehole just stood there with his chin on the floor.'

Véronique was giggling again at the memory.

'As soon as we got to the street we started running, and we didn't stop until we knew the arsehole would not catch us. We've been together ever since.'

'I've never heard that story,' said Henri. 'That's wonderful.'

'Was it the first time you'd had a relationship with another woman, Véronique?' Sophie regretted the question as soon as she asked it.

'That's a little forward,' said Henri.

'No, it's OK. We have nothing to hide, do we Véronique?' said Juste.

'Absolutely nothing,' said Véronique. 'Yes, Juste was my first girl. And my last, I hope. You should try it, you know. We all know in our hearts that men are not to be trusted.'

Henri started to make noises of protestation.

'I'm sorry, Henri,' Véronique continued, 'but you know it's true!' Véronique smiled at Henri. The fine wine and haute cuisine had clearly loosened her up.

'Why do you ask anyway?' said Juste.

Now Sophie was on the spot.

'I just wondered if being gay is something that you always know from a young age or if it depends on whom you meet. If you feel sexual attraction generally for the opposite sex, can you still be attracted to a particular person of the same sex?'

'And why are you wondering this?' Juste raised one eyebrow at Sophie as she asked this question.

'Oh, a friend of mine asked me about it.' Sophie tried to brush off the enquiry.

'Who was that?' asked Henri.

'Oh, it's an old school friend, no one you know.' She knew that she sounded unconvincing.

The sommelier arrived and began the ceremony of opening and decanting the bottle of Bordeaux that Henri had ordered. This took the pressure off Sophie. Shit, she thought, I hadn't meant to get into this conversation. It's too late now, though.

'The Cheval Blanc 1982, sir.'

'You spoil us, Henri,' said Juste. She clearly knew enough about wine to know what they were about to drink. Sophie's choice of red wine had until recently been Bulgarian Cabernet Sauvignon at one pound ninety-nine a bottle.

The waiter poured the wine and left.

'In answer to your question, Sophie, I have never felt sexually attracted to a man. Maybe it will happen one day, but not so far. My view is that in life people are attracted to other people; sometimes this attraction is platonic, sometimes it is sexual; the gender of the person is not necessarily relevant. In my case I would say I am exclusively sexually attracted to women, and, if I can speak for Henri, I believe that he is also exclusively attracted to women?'

Henri smiled and nodded. Juste continued.

'But for others the attraction is not so concentrated. I believe it is quite normal to be sexually attracted to both sexes. I think this is the case for Véronique, is it not, *ma puce*?'

'I'm only attracted to you, *mon amour*.'

Juste smiled at Véronique then looked straight at Sophie.

'If you wish to confess that you are hopelessly attracted to me then now is the time. It is quite understandable.'

They all laughed apart from Véronique, who looked daggers at Juste. Sophie was laughing nervously; she knew that Juste was only half joking.

'So, what do you think your *friend* would make of that?' asked Henri. The emphasis he put on the word friend let Sophie know that he thought she was lying.

'I think my friend is normally heterosexual but has had relationships with her own sex. I think she's not sure what to make of it.'

'Maybe she should make nothing of it. It's just the way she is,' said Juste. Sophie felt like Juste was addressing her directly. It sounded like an invitation to treat. Time to change the subject.

'Yes, I think you're probably right, Juste. I'll tell her not to worry.' Juste smiled, a little half-smile, a reassuring smile, a smile that said 'I understand'. Sophie looked away. She sipped at her wine.

'The wine is delicious by the way, Henri.' This opened a discussion on the 1982 vintage Cheval Blanc and on Bordeaux in general, much to Sophie's relief.

***

Sophie and Henri sat at the bar of the hotel. Sophie was sipping on a Cointreau with ice, Henri on an old Armagnac. Sophie was not sure what to do. She was physically attracted to Henri, and she felt inclined to cheat on Johnny as some kind of payback. She had come to Paris with that in mind, but there was something inside her that still made her hang back. On one level she trusted Henri – she found his company reassuring and his self-confidence relaxed her – but on another level she did not trust him at all. She needed the intimacy that sleeping with him might bring, but would she regret it? When she had imagined telling Henri about Johnny and Mark it was as she lay with him after sex, the intimate post-coital moment allowing her to open up.

'So, *chérie*, now that we are on our own, what was it that you wanted to talk to me about?' Henri had beaten her to it. She must have sounded serious when she told him that she had something to discuss with him. He clearly expected a discussion. The drinks had loosened her up, but was she really ready to talk about it?

'It's about something that happened at New Year.' Now it was too late.

'I thought you seemed a little distracted when we were leaving. What happened?'

'You remember that we went for a walk on New Year's Day.'

'Yes.'

'Do you remember that I went back to the house for hats because Amy and I were cold?'

'Yes, now you mention it.'

'I saw something when I went back to the house.'

'What do you mean?'

'Well, Johnny and Mark had stayed at the house.'

'Yes, to watch the football.'

'Well, they weren't watching the football.'

'What were they doing?'

Sophie felt the tears running down her cheeks as she spoke.

'They were having sex.'

'What do you mean?' Henri's jaw suddenly went slack.

'Mark was giving Johnny a blowjob.'

'Shit.' Henri was now ghostly pale. 'Are you sure?'

'Yes, shit. And yes, I am sure.'

'But how did you see them without them seeing you?'

'That doesn't matter, but unless I was hallucinating I saw them.'

'What did you say to them?'

'Nothing, they didn't see me. I ran out of the house.'

'But, what about since then? What have you said to Johnny?'

'Nothing. I couldn't bear to.' The tears continued to roll down her face, but despite this she felt remarkably calm.

'Oh, Sophie.' She felt Henri take her hand in his.

'You're the first person I've told. It's been pretty grim, but thankfully Johnny left for London a couple of days later, so I haven't had to spend much time with him.'

'What are you going to do?'

'I still don't have any real idea. It's not something I've ever had to deal with before.' She managed a smile despite herself.

'Now I understand your questions over dinner a little better. But I'd never have guessed. It's so typically English.'

'What do you mean?'

'Well, Johnny and Mark went to an all-boys school, no?'

'And?'

'Well, from what I have heard, this kind of thing happens all the time at these schools.'

'Does it?'

'Yes, you know all this stuff with fags and everything.'

'They went to Hastings Grammar School not Eton.'

'It's not the same?'

'No.'

'Well, I must say that we French do think of English men as being quite homosexual, so in a way it does not surprise me. But Johnny and Mark, now *that* surprises me. Particularly Johnny. Incredible.'

Henri was not helping. Sophie felt her anger rising.

'Yes, fucking incredible. Incredible!' She realised that she had raised her voice but not by how much. Suddenly everyone in the bar was looking at them.

'Why don't we go upstairs? I can see you're really upset, Sophie.'

She was still angry, but she let Henri take her up to her room. The last thing she wanted was to be the object of some upmarket rubbernecking. She gave Henri the key, and he put his arm around her and ushered her quickly up in the lift. Once she was in the privacy of her own space she sat on the bed and began to cry. The sobs came from deep within her – uncontrollable, heaving great sobs. She felt like they would never stop. It was as if she had never cried before, as if she had saved up all her accumulated grief and self-pity for this moment. She was aware of Henri sitting next to her on the bed and aware of his arm around her shoulder, but he seemed a long way away. She felt more alone than she ever had. More alone than when she discovered she was pregnant. Even more alone than she had as a small girl. After a while the sobs began to die down.

'I think you should get into bed,' she heard Henri say.

She let him unzip the back of her dress and help her wriggle out of it. He found her nightie and put it on over her underwear. Then he pulled back the covers of the bed and let her slip in between them.

'Don't leave me, Henri,' she said quietly.

'Don't worry, I'll stay for a while,' he replied, and she watched as he went and sat in the armchair in the corner of the room.

She felt her breathing start to become slower and more even, more under control, and gradually she drifted towards the solace of sleep.

***

Later Sophie woke up. The room was still dimly lit by a table lamp. Henri was asleep in the armchair, his suit jacket screwed up in his lap, his head flopped to one side. She knew what she wanted to do. She walked over to Henri, held his hand and woke him gently. She took the jacket from his lap and hung it on the back of a chair. She helped him to his feet then started to undress him. First she unbuttoned his shirt, took it off and tossed it to the ground. Then she unhooked the waist of his trousers, unzipped the flies and let them drop to the floor. He stepped out of them, and she walked him to the bed, sat him down and took off his socks. He seemed to be half asleep still, and that was exactly what she wanted. She wanted this to feel like a dream. She laid him down on the bed and began to kiss his chest and then his stomach softly. She moved down to his penis, which was already firm, waiting for her. She put her mouth over it and began to move her head slowly up and down. She heard Henri moan softly. She wished that Johnny could see her now.

***

Mark was trying desperately to concentrate on what his client was saying, but he was finding it unusually difficult. He was so excited. This was not a normal state of mind for him, and it was causing him considerable anxiety, but there was no getting away from it. Tonight was probably going to be the best night of his life. Fortunately the meeting was drawing to a close, and he would soon be able to change his clothes and head for Park Lane.

'So, I was hoping that what we might be able to do is revalue the stock downwards, generate a loss and claim a repayment of the corporation tax that we paid last year. What do you think?'

The Finance Director of the client company was no fool, and Mark needed to concentrate quite hard on a normal day to keep up with him. Unfortunately, he had only really heard the last four words, and he was not sure what to think. His colleague from the Tax Department stepped in, saving his blushes.

'Well, provided the stock write-down is acceptable from an

accounting-standards perspective, the tax treatment would follow the accounting treatment, so, in principle, the result would be a loss in the current year, which we would be able to carry back to last year. This would reduce last year's profits and result in a repayment of at least part of the tax paid by the company last year. What about the write-down, though, Mark? Do you think that complies from an accounting perspective?'

Mark had heard what his colleague had said and had managed to concentrate to the end of the sentence, so now he could reply in an informed way. He needed to be careful, though; he should not let Johnny and Swerve start affecting his career. He really needed to focus for the rest of the meeting.

Once it had finished Mark waited for the office to clear out before he changed his clothes. Fortunately there did not seem to be anyone burning the midnight oil tonight, so by six-thirty the coast was clear. Once he had passed his exams he had quickly been promoted to Assistant Audit Manager, and that meant that he was entitled to a desk in an office. He shared this with a colleague; it would require a couple more promotions before he had one all to himself. He closed the blinds on the goldfish bowl of a window that looked out on to the audit room and pulled out his sports bag from under his desk where he had discreetly hidden it early that morning. He did not like his colleagues knowing about his personal life, particularly anything that might seem too racy for his profession. Victoria was sworn to secrecy, not only about their relationship but also about anything to do with Johnny. The last thing he wanted was people in the office knowing that his best friend was a musician, a member of Swerve. He unzipped his bag and took out his outfit for the evening. It had been difficult to decide what he should wear in the company of the band and the other music industry glitterati. He had decided in the end to wear a double-breasted blazer, a white button-down shirt and a pair of jeans. The blazer–jeans combo was quite daring, he thought. While he could not compete with

Johnny in looking trendy, he did want to make an attempt not to look too stiff. He changed quickly and then walked down the back stairs of the building to ensure that he did not bump into anyone he knew. Once on the pavement he walked up to Fleet Street and hailed a taxi. As the taxi driver lowered the window, he took great pleasure in requesting the Grosvenor House Hotel, Park Lane, as his destination.

Mark had been bowled over when Johnny had phoned him to invite him to the *Feedback* Awards. He had been smiling ever since, as Victoria had pointed out to him. He could tell that she was disappointed there was no extra place for her, and he had commiserated with her, but secretly he revelled in being Johnny's partner for the evening. He was also still in the warm glow of their covert sexual tryst at Johnny's house at New Year. Things were happening that he had never allowed himself even to dream of. Despite what Mark had said at New Year, Victoria had moved in with him at his flat in Islington. Since then it had become harder for him and Johnny to spend time together, so the moments that they could spend alone had become more precious. Certainly for Mark they had; Johnny never discussed how he felt, at least, not since he had tried to put a stop to things last year. That had not lasted long. Still, he had to be more careful himself now that Victoria was around more. He liked being with her, but it just was not the same as being with Johnny. Even not being with Victoria was not like not being with Johnny. When he was not with Victoria, he hardly thought about it; when Johnny was not with him, he was still on Mark's mind the whole time if he allowed it.

The taxi pulled up at the back of the hotel – where the ticket had instructed him to enter – or it tried to. There were security, paparazzi and crowds of people everywhere. Not for the first time Mark felt in his pocket for his official invitation. It was still there. He read it again; he had been given a specific arrival time. Johnny had told him not to be late, as the organisers tried to get all the ordinary civilians into the venue before the celebrities arrived. He paid the cab and pushed his way through to the red carpet. Johnny had warned him that Swerve were playing to open the ceremony, so he and the rest of the band would be joining them at the table once they had finished. Before the ceremony they would be waiting backstage. This meant that Mark would have to find their table on his own then make small talk with the other guests until Swerve arrived. The paparazzi had set up their gear at one end, but unsurprisingly there was a distinct lack of flashes as he walked towards the entrance. He reached security, gave them his ticket and breathed a sigh of relief as they let him through. He was then approached by a charming mini-skirted helper who escorted him through to his table.

The table was one of maybe a hundred in a vast ballroom with a large stage at one end. Mark seemed to be the first to arrive at his table, and he walked around looking at the place names. There were ten places, and he smiled as he found his name next to Johnny's. There were also places for Alex, Rob and Dave from the band as well as Charlie, Alex's girlfriend. These were the only names he recognised. The table was awash with booze: vodka, gin and cognac; bottles of champagne, white wine and beer in a vast ice-filled silver dish; red wine; mixers. Enough to sink a battleship, Mark thought. He helped himself to a beer, then sat down and waited. The Auteurs song 'Showgirl' was playing loudly, and he sang along to it under his breath; he had noticed in the newspaper that the Auteurs were up for best group. He had bought their album himself, so he definitely approved of that choice. Swerve were nominated for best new group, and, according to the newspaper, were in with a chance of winning. He sat back and watched the room slowly fill up, the hair on his arms standing up with the excitement of it. Suddenly there was a tap on his back.

'Hi, Mark.' He recognised Charlotte's voice. 'Alex told me that Sophie couldn't come, so Johnny asked his boyfriend instead.'

The other girls with Charlotte started tittering. Mark tried to ignore the rather puerile remark, although he thought it a little strange. Surely Alex could not have known about him and Johnny? He was sure he did not. He must try to control his paranoia.

'Hi, Charlie,' he said, giving her the obligatory rock-star air kisses.

'This is Wendy and Amelia. They've come with Rob and Dave.'

Mark gave the new girls the same kissing treatment. They both had long straight hair, like Charlotte, and were, like Charlotte, wearing short floaty dresses with biker boots. They were pretty, but neither of them was as pretty as Charlotte, who looked stunning. Mark imagined that Alex would not take kindly to the bassist and drummer having better-looking girlfriends than him. Come to think of it, that was probably one of the reasons that Alex resented Sophie – her looks – as well as the fact that she refused to be pushed around.

'Can I get you a drink, ladies?' he asked, doing his best to be charming.

'We'll have some champers. Thanks, Mark.' Charlotte answered for all of them. She seemed to be in charge of their little pack.

He poured the champagne while the girls talked among themselves then handed them the glasses.

'We were just backstage, Mark. The boys are really nervous,' Charlotte said.

'I'm not surprised. This is a massive night in the history of Swerve. This has to be the biggest gig they've ever played.'

'Quite right, old chap. And you are?' a new voice interjected.

Mark immediately recognised the tall, elegant figure of Charles Cooper-Smythe, the head of Paisley Records, Swerve's record company. He was accompanied by a rather fierce-looking short, stocky woman with a jet-black bob and bright-red lipstick. Mark put out his hand to greet them.

'Mark Arnold, Coopers & Lybrand. I'm an old friend of Johnny's.'

'I'm surprised they let an accountant in,' said Charles. Mark could have kicked himself. Why had he told him he was an accountant?

'This is Gretchen, my assistant.' Mark shook hands with Gretchen. The handshake was firm and dry.

'Pleased to meet you, Mr Arnold.' Gretchen's accent was from Eastern Europe, Mark thought, probably not Germany but maybe one of the newly independent countries such as Poland.

'Good evening, ladies,' Charles greeted the pack of girlfriends. There was lots of hair tossing as they twittered back their coquettish hellos. They seemed to be slightly in awe of him.

'A glass of that fizz wouldn't go amiss, Mark.'

Mark poured Charles and Gretchen a glass of champagne each.

'I'll have a brandy chaser with mine, if I may, old boy,' said Charles.

Mark poured a large measure of brandy out too.

'Here's to a jolly evening. Start as you mean to go on, that's what I say.' Charles raised his glass and downed the cognac in one. This was swiftly followed by the champagne. 'First drink of the day; always tends to go down rather quickly,' he continued. 'So, Mark, do our boys have a shot at this award?'

'Absolutely. I think they have a great chance; they're heavily tipped in the papers.'

'Yes, absolutely,' said Charles. He seemed somewhat disdainful, as if he were above the whole thing. 'Let's go for a wander, Gretchen.'

Charles and his stiff-backed gait drifted off into the throng with Gretchen at his shoulder. Mark assumed that Charles did not consider him sufficiently interesting or potentially useful enough to spend any more time with. Paisley Records would make an interesting client, though; he should try to arrange a meeting with Charles at some point in a more business-like environment. He sat back and continued to watch the room fill up, sipping on his champagne. He felt no obligation to talk to the girls, who were gossiping and pointing people out quite happily. He started to star-watch himself and noticed how, as the evening went on, the celebrity status of the guests changed. First came the C-listers, who in the main he did not recognise apart from the odd minor television presenter or weather girl. Then the B-listers: he spotted the Auteurs – or at least Luke Haines and Alice Readman, who, if they won their award, might just be on the brink of becoming A-listers – and Brett Anderson of Suede. The B-listers looked pretty sure of themselves as they strutted in, like peacocks displaying their recent success. But when compared with the A-listers, who were last to arrive, they appeared as young pretenders. He saw Bob Geldof's thatch of brown hair in the distance accompanied by Paula Yates's peroxide blonde bob. The two of them and their entourage cut an effortless swathe through the crowd. David Bowie followed shortly afterwards, again surrounded by flunkies, sauntering to his table as if he were at his local restaurant. Mark was pretty blown away by the whole thing and almost had to pinch himself to remember that this was not some aspirational dream. He really was here at the *Feedback* Awards.

Before he knew it the lights were dimming, and their compère for the evening was introducing Swerve: 'The latest sensation from the south coast, Swerve, with their huge hit "LOST … IN … SPACE".'

Charles and Gretchen slipped back into their seats at the table as the four boys ran on to the stage. Mark's heart missed a beat; he always felt incredibly nervous for Johnny when he watched him play live, and this was as nervous as he had ever felt. He also fell in love with him again each time he saw him play. He did not always allow himself the self-indulgence of admitting that he was in love with Johnny, but when he was watching him on stage it was impossible to deny it to himself. He was hopelessly in love with his rock-star friend; he had been for years. Johnny represented everything that Mark admired but knew he could not have: a rebellious nature, a devil-may-care attitude, the ability to take risks, a sense of cool. These were all things that Mark envied but did not really want for himself. Instead, he could have them by proxy through Johnny. When Johnny was on stage his admiration seemed to be amplified, and this in turn multiplied the physical attraction that he felt. As Johnny played those opening chords, in one glorious instant the music brought into focus the way Mark felt about him. At this precise moment he could forgive Johnny anything.

The band played their hit song to rapt attention from the audience of musos and to a rapturous reception as they finished. Mark felt a shiver of pride; he took enormous pleasure from his personal connection with the band but also from his secret relationship with its guitarist.

As the applause died down Charles gave his verdict. 'Well, I must say, I thought they absolutely tore the arse out of that,' he said loudly, speaking over the compère.

'They were fucking brilliant,' said Mark a little more quietly.

Before they knew it the boys were among them. They had dashed off stage, straight to the table. They arrived to a ripple of applause from the tables around them and to much hugging and backslapping. Mark gave Johnny a huge hug and a kiss on the cheek before letting him sit down next to him.

'Steady, Mark. I'm not fucking queer,' Johnny whispered loudly to him.

Johnny certainly knew how to push away the people who loved him. Mark hated the way he did this, although he had admittedly probably got a little carried away with his greeting. He was pretty sure no one had noticed among the general euphoria of their arrival at the table in any case. He decided to ignore Johnny's comment.

'Anyway, mate, that was fantastic.'

'Cheers. Any chance of a drink?' Johnny replied, lighting a cigarette.

'What do you want?'

'A large vodka tonic would be good. Heavy on the vodka.'

Mark made the drink and looked at Johnny as he did so. His expression was pretty glazed. He wondered if he was back on the booze in a big way. Maybe it was just to control his nerves.

'Are you OK?' he asked him as he handed him the drink.

'Yeah, all good,' he said, taking a large slug.

Their table was being hushed by the tables around them, so they quietened down while the ceremony continued. Johnny leaned behind Mark and whispered something into Charles's ear. Charles felt in his pocket and handed something to Johnny. Johnny immediately got up and left the room. Mark wondered what that was all about. Anyway, within a couple of minutes Johnny was back. The award for best new band was one of the early awards, so it was quickly upon them in no more than a couple of vodka tonics.

'Good luck, boys,' said Alex to his fellow band members. They all leaned forward and clinked their glasses together.

'You don't need luck, boys. You're going to win,' said Charles.

The compère, the well-known alternative comedian Ronnie Kemp, handed over to Andy Parkins, lead singer of the Kestrels, who had won the award the year before. He introduced the contenders in Hollywood style.

'And finally, those south-coast rockers, Swerve. And the winners are ... Swerve.'

The table erupted in a huge cheer. Even Mark found himself on his feet, hugging Gretchen of all people. Johnny was in his face, wide-eyed, shaking his fist in triumph. Eventually the table celebration broke up, and the band made their way to the stage to be presented with the award. Mark thought it seemed to be very well received, as applause as well as whistles and cheers rang through the room. Alex accepted the award and stepped forward to the mike.

'This is only the beginning,' was all that he said.

It would have had a good deal of resonance had Johnny not stepped forward straight afterwards.

'Fucking right,' he yelled.

This fell rather flat, but the boys left the stage quickly, raising their arms in triumph.

'That friend of yours needs to know when to keep his mouth shut. He also needs to know when to lay off the sauce,' said Charles.

***

Mark looked at his watch. He would have to leave the party pretty soon to have any chance of getting to work tomorrow. He had, at least theoretically, managed to arrange a meeting with Charles at a later date, which was something of an achievement. He had been working a little on Gretchen, as he figured that she was the way to make sure he got the meeting. The after-party was at the cocktail bar at the top of the Hilton, Park Lane. Charles seemed somehow to have managed to book the whole bar, allowing a total exclusion of the general public. From what Mark had seen this had permitted proceedings to degenerate somewhat. He had finally worked out why there were so many frequent trips to the toilets; it had been naïve of him not to have picked up on it before. All had soon become clear, as once the happy throng realised that it was a private party the snorting of cocaine became totally open in the toilets. He had watched Johnny's condition deteriorate fairly rapidly at the hands of booze and cocaine, and while it bothered him a little he also thought that Johnny deserved to celebrate. It was when he saw the groupies hovering that he decided that he should definitely think about making tracks. He was pretty sure that Johnny was in no condition to turn them down, and from what he had witnessed so far these girls were definitely available. He was used to seeing Johnny with other women – latterly Sophie, of course – and while he felt a little jealous he was resigned to Johnny's heterosexual side and to the fact that he could do nothing about it. He took a last look around the room. Alex was holding court on one side, distancing himself from the obvious groupies, with a crowd that included Charlotte as well as what looked to Mark like journalists and/or record company-types or wannabe musicians who had not made it and so had found another way to make money from the music business. Johnny, Rob and Dave were at a nearby table that seemed less aspirational and more hedonistic. The preoccupations here seemed to be booze, drugs and girls. Mark noticed that, although the crowd of girls at this table included Wendy and Amelia, neither Rob nor Dave was devoting his exclusive attention to either of them. Now that they were *Feedback* prize winners the competition among the girls was hotting up. Mark tried to catch Johnny's eye rather than interrupt, but it proved impossible. He slipped away quietly, rather looking forward to his cosy flat in Islington and to Victoria's homely body heat.

LAUSANNE, SWITZERLAND

23 JULY 1993

After spending some time mulling it over Sophie had decided not to go to the Paleo Festival to watch Swerve play, but she had decided to come to Lausanne anyway. Amy was too young really to go to an event like that – or at least that had been Sophie's excuse – but a daughter needs to see her father, and this was one way of seeing Johnny while he was on tour. The honest truth was that Sophie hated being backstage at Swerve gigs. The tabloid-press view of young bands on tour, fuelled by a cocktail of drink, drugs and groupies, was not so far from the truth, but that was not the reason she hated being backstage. What really irritated her was the way that the band members were cosseted by their management, their every whim pandered to. It was not an environment that she wanted Amy to be exposed to and not an environment that she wanted to spend time in herself. Frankly, Johnny didn't deserve it. He didn't deserve to be spoiled, and she was not going to condone it by joining all the sycophantic hangers-on backstage. She was not even sure that it had been a good idea to come to Switzerland at all; it had been Henri who had talked her into it. Fortunately, he had also talked Johnny into making the band stay at a decent hotel for the night. This had enabled her to now be sitting on the evening-sun-drenched terrace, looking across Lac Léman to the high Alps on the other side of the lake. As the sun descended on her right the lake was gradually turning through a rainbow of colours, from aquamarine through pink to crimson. It was an unforgettable sight and one that had gradually lulled Amy to sleep in her pushchair as Sophie sipped on a couple of glasses of champagne. They were staying at the Beau Rivage Palace, a very grand belle époque hotel right on the edge of the lake in a chic suburb of Lausanne. Sophie had to admit that, despite her reservations about Johnny's rock-star lifestyle, the hotel alone had made it worth the trip.

Henri had come up with the original idea. Apparently he and Mark were doing some business with Charles Cooper-Smythe, and they had arranged to meet him in Geneva before Swerve played at the festival in nearby Nyon. Henri had then suggested that they all meet up in Lausanne after the gig for a poker game, just like the old days. Well, none of it felt much like the old days to Sophie. Since that slightly tragic night in Paris in January she had not seen Henri, but they had talked quite regularly on the telephone. Were they having an affair? She was not sure really. Yes, they had had sexual contact, and yes, she had kept that secret from anyone else, but it didn't feel like an affair. They hardly saw one another for a start, and their telephone calls were more as friends than lovers. It was a strange situation. She was not sure that she could really trust Henri, but he knew about Johnny and Mark, and that was important to her. She needed to know that there was somebody else out there who knew about it. She hadn't seen Mark since New Year, and she had hardly seen Johnny, particularly given that they were a married couple. He had been recording the new album in London up until March, and since then he had been on tour promoting it. This time it wasn't just in the UK; it was a tour of the whole of Europe. Swerve were now quite famous, and Johnny had become a minor celebrity. The funny thing was that the escalation of Johnny's fame seemed to have conveniently allowed her to avoid him. The few times so far that year when he had been able to come down to Rye she had deliberately kept her distance, busied herself with the shop and let Johnny spend time with Amy, his mother and the Jim Beam bottle.

He called her quite regularly, maybe once or twice a week, always relatively early. He said this was to speak to Amy before she went to bed, but Sophie knew that if he phoned any later he would probably be too wasted to make any sense. During his brief stays she had given way and had perfunctory sex with him a couple of times. The first time, a couple of months after the blowjob incident, had been pretty grim, but the memory had gradually receded. She still had no clue what to do about what she had seen other than to sweep it under the carpet for the moment. Inaction seemed to be the best action. Henri thought that she should confront them both; he had even suggested that she do it while they were here in Lausanne. But she was not one for confrontation, and Johnny was Amy's father after all. It was important that Amy had a father in her life, even if he was a feckless, unfaithful waster. The air was starting to cool down a little, and the sun had almost disappeared behind the mountains, so Sophie decided to go up to their suite, put Amy to bed, order some room service and then break out a pack of cards to warm up. Despite everything, the one thing she was really looking forward to was some poker.

***

Henri was not quite sure what to expect from the meeting with Mark and Charles Cooper-Smythe, so he had decided to hold the first meeting without his boss present. Given his relatively junior status at the bank he would have been expected to take his boss along, but he was concerned about making the wrong impression. He did not know Mark anything like as well as he knew Johnny, although he had always seemed a pretty serious guy and highly motivated professionally. But, and it was quite a big but, the blowjob thing had surprised him. He had no difficulty with the sexuality of it – if Mark was gay or bisexual then he had no problem – what he had a difficulty with was the deceit. If Mark was going to introduce a client to him, then he needed to understand Mark and understand what made him tick. This was where he was having a problem. It was not the lack of honesty per se, it was the lack of predictability. He was quite happy to deal with someone who was dishonest as long as he understood their dishonesty. Dealing with someone who was unpredictable was much more difficult. Mark's poker, however, was totally predictable and made him a bad player, so maybe he was predictable in business but unpredictable when it came to sex. As this was quite plausible, Henri had agreed to meet Mark's client. It was also a good thing for him at this relatively early stage in his career to be seen to be bringing business into the bank. All in all he was prepared to take a risk. The telephone on his desk rang.

'Mr Cooper-Smythe and Mr Arnold are waiting for you in the meeting-room.'

'Thank you.'

Henri walked out of his open-plan office, told his secretary that he was going to his meeting and took the lift down to the first floor. The first floor contained the meeting-rooms at Lagrange et Cie. Henri had specifically chosen one of the rather grandly decorated rooms, as he thought that this might impress the Brits. These older meeting-rooms in the bank's *fin-de-siècle* building had changed little over the last hundred years or so. They had tall double doors that opened on to large spaces with intricate parquet floors and high ceilings, which dangled antique chandeliers over their occupants. Henri liked the sense of history that these old-fashioned chambers engendered; it created a feeling of security and well-being, and that was good for business.

He opened the doors to find Mark and Mr Cooper-Smythe sipping on their espressos.

'Henri, great to see you.' Mark was all bonhomie and firm hand-shake. Cooper-Smythe seemed more reserved.

'M. le Cerf, pleased to meet you,' he said curtly.

Cooper-Smythe was wearing a three-piece tweed suit and

brown brogues. The suit was quite extravagantly tailored, and the tweed had highlights of purple and bright green. English gentleman on acid, thought Henri. A monocle would not have looked out of place. Mark was wearing the pinstripe uniform of the accountant and adopting a slightly fawning manner.

After some small talk about weather, airports and journey times, Henri got down to business.

'So, what can I do for you today?'

'Well, old chap, there may be any number of things that you can do, but the most pressing is to take care of these.'

He put an attaché case on the table, snapped it open and lifted the leather bottom of the inside to reveal a secret compartment. It was filled with jewellery. To Henri's amateur eye it looked like highly valuable jewellery. The stones were large, and there were a lot of them, set in a variety of different ways – rings, pendants, brooches. It was quite a collection.

'Jesus Christ, Charles, I didn't know anything about those.'

'There's a reason for that, dear boy. You would have had kittens if you'd known that I was bringing these through customs.'

'May I ask where they came from, sir?' asked Henri.

'Well, I didn't steal them, if that's what you are intimating.'

'Certainly not. I'm afraid we need to know the provenance of these kinds of items before we can consider safe-keeping.' This was not a particularly good start.

'They're an inheritance from a great-aunt. I have a valuation here somewhere. It comes to a couple of million sterling. I thought it might be helpful. An old school chum of mine works at Christie's. He sorted it out.'

Cooper-Smythe dug out a document and passed it over. Henri inspected it. It was correctly addressed to him, and it was on paper with a Christie's letterhead. Everything looked to be in order. He turned to the final page, and sure enough the valuation came to a little over two million sterling.

'Thank you, sir. This all looks to be in good order. What would you like us to do? Hold the collection in a safety-deposit box?'

'That would be ideal.'

'Well, we can organise that straight away.'

Henri called down to his colleagues to organise a safety-deposit box. He could hear Mark muttering to Cooper-Smythe in the background. He was clearly a little disgruntled.

'Perhaps we could now discuss the reason that I thought we had come here,' said Mark.

Cooper-Smythe produced another document from his attaché case. He passed it over to Henri. It was a share certificate for five million one hundred thousand shares in Paisley Records Plc.

'Charles's main business is Paisley Records, which, as you know, is Swerve's record label. They have a number of other successful bands signed to the label, and Charles took the decision to take the company to the stock market at the end of last year. Charles is still the majority shareholder, and he wants to keep things that way. He owns 51 per cent of the company, and the rest is owned by the public. It's mainly in the hands of pension funds; there are just a few private investors. Charles's problem is that he is asset-rich and cash-poor. The current price of shares in Paisley Records is about two pounds per share. This means that in theory his holding is worth over ten million pounds. The problem is that the ten million is all tied up in one company, and he can't sell any of it on the open market without losing his majority stake. What Charles would like to do is to borrow, say, a million or two against the value of the shares so that he can give himself some liquidity and invest in some other assets.'

'I wouldn't mind buying a big fuck-off house, for example,' Charles interjected.

'Why don't you sell the jewellery?'

'Well, my great-aunt is still alive and wouldn't take kindly to a sale. The idea is that the future Mrs Cooper-Smythe wears the jewels and then we pass them on to our progeny. She's given them to me now so that we can avoid paying death duties not so that I can sell them and buy myself a few toys.'

'Inheritance tax,' Mark corrected.

'Whatever it's called,' said Charles.

'OK, I understand. Well, I'll have to talk to our credit department, but I would hope that we can lend against the shares. We can normally lend up to 50 per cent of the value of quoted shares that we hold for customers, using the shares themselves as security. As this is a large holding in quite a small company the percentage would be lower, but I'm pretty sure we'll still be able to do something.'

'That would be nice. So I might be able to borrow a couple of million?'

'It certainly sounds feasible.'

'That sounds very promising, Henri. What do we need to do to get the ball rolling?' Mark asked.

Henri began to explain the various bureaucratic hoops that they would have to jump through. This could actually be quite promising business, he thought. Things had turned out better than he had expected.

***

Henri had arranged for a car to take him and Mark from Geneva to Lausanne so they could check into the hotel, change and then take them to the festival at Nyon. Swerve were playing at around eight o'clock, and finishing at around nine-thirty. Charles had left them in Geneva to go to another appointment and then make his own way to Nyon, leaving Henri and Mark to make the trip to Lausanne alone. Mark was quite pleased with the way that the meeting had gone – apart, of course, from the matter of the jewellery. That was the kind of thing that would have got him into a lot of trouble back in London. He had known that Cooper-Smythe was slightly risky as a client, but he would have to keep a closer eye on him than he had previously thought. He relaxed into the comfortable leather of the back seat of the car. The business was out of the way now, and he could look forward to the gig.

'So, have you seen much of Johnny since New Year?' Henri asked him as they drove along.

'Yes, we see each other in London. Not often, though. He's been really busy with the album, then touring. I did go to the *Feedback* Awards. That was pretty amazing. That's when I realised that Johnny really was a star.'

'Yes, I remember. Did you know that Sophie came to Paris at the same time to meet me?'

'I think Johnny mentioned it.'

'I've introduced her to some friends of mine, lesbians who sell clothes.'

'That's very good of you.' Why mention that they were lesbians, though? thought Mark.

'Yes, she really is a lovely girl, Sophie. Very friendly, if you know what I mean.'

Henri winked at Mark. What on earth was he on about?

'What do you mean, she's friendly?'

'Well, you used to live with her at college, no? You must have discovered her friendly side?'

Henri started to poke his tongue backwards and forwards into the inside of his cheek, mimicking someone giving oral sex.

'I don't know what the hell you're on about, Henri, but Sophie's married to Johnny, so I think you ought to shut up.' Mark was furious.

'Just a little joke between boys.' Henri grinned back at him and punched him on the shoulder.

Mark was not sure what to make of Henri. Was he just joking, or had he really been blown by Sophie? He was pretty smooth. Maybe he had managed to talk her into it. The stupid bitch. He could feel the emotion rising in him. 'Not as a lover. I love you dearly as a friend but not as a lover.' He still remembered the brush off she had given him as if it were yesterday. Well, she better not have been up to anything with Henri, he thought. If she had, he might feel obliged to tell Johnny.

'So, tell me more about Mr Cooper-Smythe. How did he start Paisley Records, do you know?'

Henri had changed the subject. Good, thought Mark. I'll ignore what he said before. For the sake of everyone.

***

Johnny drifted back into consciousness and looked out of the window. The countryside flashed by, reminding him where he was, or at least reminding him that he was on the tour bus. The reality was that had no idea where he was. Somewhere in Europe? Where had they been the day before? It was coming back to him – in the mountains, Austria. That was it. He could still see a few mountains from the window, but they were in the far distance. Switzerland, that's where they were headed. His head was throbbing a little, his mouth was dry and he had a cold sweat on. He leaned forward and pulled out the bottle of Jim Beam from the pocket attached to the back of the seat in front of him and took a hefty swig. Then he opened the cooler on the floor next to him, took out a can of Heineken, pulled the ring pull and put it to his lips, taking a long draught. Next he felt in the inside pocket of his jacket and found one of the wraps that were located there. He unwrapped the small package and poured out the white powder on the table next to him. Then he took out his wallet, pulled out a credit card and began to arrange the powder into two lines, each maybe a quarter of an inch wide and three inches long. Finally he took a fifty-Deutschemark note from his wallet, rolled it into a cylinder, put the note to his nose and inhaled the two lines of cocaine. He was at a low ebb physically and mentally; it was a level of tiredness that he had not experienced before. Touring with the band was an exhausting round of incredible highs followed by incredible lows, made endurable by his consumption of alcohol and cocaine. He knew he was fucking himself up, but he couldn't really see any other solution until the end of the tour. He felt the cocaine quickly start to ease the cold sweat and perk him up. He took another slug of Jim Beam. He remembered now. He would get to see Amy soon, and Sophie; they were staying at the hotel tonight. He would see them soon after the gig. He and Sophie were pretty distant at the moment. Another thing to try to sort out at the end of the tour. Absence should have been making the heart grow fonder, but this did not seem to be the case with Sophie, only with Amy. He put his headphones on and pressed play. They were filled with melancholic acoustic guitar; he had been listening to a lot of Nick Drake recently. He just seemed to connect with it. But he had too much cocaine in his system right now, so that was enough of *Five Leaves Left*. He sorted through his CDs and spotted the cover with a single banana. That was what he needed; the rhythmic distorted guitar of the Velvet Underground would see him through the next hour or so. Another Jim Beam and another can of beer and he would be back to where he needed to be.

***

'So, are we going to play cards or what?' Johnny was on the wrong end of a lot of Jim Beam and probably some class-As, thought Sophie. At least she had managed to keep him away from Amy so far. He was being unpleasantly loud, and even though the hotel suite was large she was worried that he was going to wake their daughter up.

'Yes, come on, it's time to play some cards. It's been too long.' Henri was also acting as though he was under the influence of something; he seemed louder than normal. They all seemed to have come back from the gig in a state of high excitement.

'Well, I'm ready. How about you, Sophie?' Mark was just a bit pissed, she thought, but Henri and Johnny had definitely been on the charlie. She wondered how it might affect Henri's game. She was not expecting much from Johnny in any case.

'That's what we came for after all. I'll just do a final check on Amy before we get started.'

'Why don't I do that?' said Johnny.

'I don't think that's a great idea, Johnny, do you?'

'What the fuck does that mean? She's my daughter.'

Sophie ignored Johnny and walked through the suite to the bedrooms. There was no point arguing with Johnny when he was in a belligerent mood. Ignoring him was a much better choice, as he soon moved on to the next thing. Cocaine did not help his attention span. There were two closed doors between Amy and the area where they were playing cards, so it shouldn't be too loud, Sophie thought, trying to convince herself that she wasn't being a bad mother. She really fancied the adrenalin buzz of some poker, and nothing was going to get in the way of it, especially Johnny. She opened the door to Amy's room just a crack; she was sound asleep, clutching her favourite teddy. Sophie felt a maternal pang. She kissed Amy on the cheek and then closed the door quietly on her way out of the room.

She walked back into the main room of the suite, ready for action. Smoke was already hanging in the air, and Henri was unpacking some gambling chips and a piece of green baize that had been provided by the hotel.

'So, has anyone been playing any poker?' she asked as she returned to the main room.

'I haven't since we last played. I've been boning up on my stats, though,' said Mark.

'You and your fucking stats, Mark. No wonder you never learned how to bluff!' Johnny was on Mark's case now.

'We've had a few hands on the tour bus, but the guys are pretty useless. Normally everyone's either too tired or too wasted to play cards.'

'Well, I must admit that I've got a little school going in Geneva. Just to keep my hand in for the main event, you understand.' Sophie looked at Henri and smiled as he said this.

Henri had that arrogant glint in his eye. She had wondered if it might be awkward with him today, but it seemed quite normal to be back in their little group despite the year's earlier events. Even seeing Mark had not been the ordeal she expected. She had convinced herself that Mark was not competition as far as she and Johnny were concerned. But more than that, she had reached a point where she was almost past caring what happened to her and Johnny. There was residual resentment, but the fear and anxiety had disappeared. She felt a little sorry for Mark, and she realised that she always had done. As for Johnny, unless he straightened himself out he was likely to disappear into a rock-star's abyss of ego and self-abuse. She still felt that there was something between them but felt no obligation to help him rediscover it, particularly after what she had seen at New Year. Sooner or later she supposed that she would have to call a halt to the sham that their marriage had become, but she would need to build up some energy before she confronted that. Business at the shop was good, Amy was doing well, her life was back on track, but she needed a break from her routine. Tonight, she just wanted to play some cards.

'So what are we playing?' Johnny asked.

'I vote for Texas hold 'em, no limit,' said Henri. This meant no limit to the maximum bet. He clearly meant business.

'Fine by me,' said Johnny.

'I'm happy with Texas hold 'em, but I'm not playing no limit with you guys. I can't afford it,' said Mark.

'So what do you suggest?'

'A big blind of four pounds and a pot limit. That's already twice as high on the blinds as we played for last year at my place.' Mark had a point, thought Sophie. With blinds at four pounds and a pot limit, the pots could still build up quite quickly.

'OK, *c'est bon*,' said Henri.

'No problem,' said Johnny.

Mark looked at Sophie, and she nodded. I'm going to take as much of your money as I can tonight, you pathetic coward, she thought to herself as she smiled back at him. She had to admit to herself that maybe New Year was still bothering her more than she had thought.

'We're going to have to agree the exchange rate,' said Henri. 'I have Swiss Francs, which are worth about one-eighty to the pound. Is that rate OK with everyone?'

They murmured their assent. Henri gave himself some chips and in exchange put in a bundle of Swiss francs.

'I'm not sure what I've got.' Johnny removed a huge wad of multicoloured bank notes from the front pocket of his ripped 501s. There were Deutschemarks, French francs, some Italian lira. Henri counted them out, did some quick calculations and gave Johnny some chips back, adding the notes to the pile of Swiss francs.

'That's about three hundred pounds. The chips are a pound a chip.'

'It's a good job we have our Swiss banker for these exchange rates,' said Mark.

Sophie and Mark changed up two hundred pounds and received their chips in return. They were ready to go. They decided to use an empty ashtray as the dealer button and then cut for deal. Sophie cut the ace of diamonds, which was the top card and meant it was her deal. She hoped it was a good omen. First she moved the ashtray in front of her to remind everyone that it was her deal. Then she shuffled the cards and looked at the others. The chic panelled walls of the suite decor were hushed behind them with anticipation.

She dealt two cards down to each player. She reminded herself that in Texas hold 'em the dealer was in the best betting position after the first round. This was because in all subsequent rounds of betting it was the player left of the dealer who had to bet first and the dealer who would be betting last. Given the testosterone already pumping around the room she was expecting the early hands to be quite aggressively played, so, provided she was dealt some decent cards, she was looking to make some early headway, particularly when it was her deal and she was the last to bet.

She picked up her first two cards: a pair of tens. The poker gods appeared to be smiling down on her. Mark was the small blind to her left, then Johnny the big blind opposite her and Henri was to her right. Henri had the first bet in the first round only. Thereafter it would be Mark to bet first, then Johnny, then Henri, then her.

'Call,' said Henri, tossing in four chips, the amount of the big blind, to call.

'Call and raise four,' said Sophie.

'Blimey, Sophie, raising already? We've hardly started.' Mark threw his cards in, forfeiting the small blind of two chips that he had already anted.

'I'll call your four and raise ten,' said Johnny.

'*Trop pour moi.*' Henri wanted no further part in the hand.

Good, thought Sophie. She was quite happy to play head to head against a drunken Johnny and build up her pot for the real match against Henri and Mark.

'Call,' she said, adding another eight chips.

She then dealt three cards face up in the middle of the table. She looked at Johnny, puffing on his cigarette. She noticed as he inhaled that he still had those high cheekbones that had set her off in the first place, but they were not quite as pronounced as they had been. His face was a little puffy and blotchy. He looked tired too, really tired, the tiredness displaying itself in the dark circles under his eyes. She almost felt sorry for him until she remembered what it had been like to see Mark's head in his groin.

She looked at the flop: a three of clubs, a four of diamonds and a rather splendid-looking ten of spades. The gods were definitely on her side. A few minutes later she was raking in a large mound of chips. Her three tens had beaten Johnny's pair of kings. He had only made his pair of kings on the river card, the last of the five communal cards. It had not been the best hand he had ever played.

'Why did you stay in that hand, Johnny?' asked Mark. It was like a red rag to a bull.

'Because I thought I was going to win. Why do you think, fuckwit?'

Mark stayed silent. Johnny poured himself a large Jim Beam, opened a bottle of Heineken and lit another Marlboro Light.

'I was dealt ace-king. You would have folded, would you?'

'Well, I don't know. It seemed pretty clear that Sophie had something good.'

'Look, Mark, you play your cards, and I'll play mine. Just fucking deal the next hand.'

'Easy, guys. Let's try to enjoy ourselves,' said Henri.

'Tell fuckface to keep his mouth shut then.'

'Johnny, we're not on the tour bus now,' said Sophie. This quietened him down a little.

'Sorry, babe, but you know how annoying Mark can be. Well played anyway. I didn't see your three tens coming.'

'Well, being dealt a pair of tens helped,' she said self-effacingly.

Mark was still not saying much. Sophie could tell that he was stewing. He started to deal two cards to each player for the next hand. Before she looked at her own cards Sophie furtively glanced at each of the others as they picked up what they had been dealt. Johnny grinned, Henri's face was stoic and Mark grinned too, although he tried hard to stop himself. She looked at her own cards: a seven and a two unsuited. She was first to bet and first to fold. She watched the remainder of the hand play out. Henri folded quite quickly, but, as had been betrayed by their smiles, both Johnny and Mark had good cards. Johnny's betting was aggressive as ever, but Mark simply kept calling. In the end Mark won the pot with ace-king to Johnny's ace-queen. They both managed a pair of aces, but Mark had the higher card in his own hand. Johnny's mood was not improving.

'You jammy fucker,' he said to Mark.

'Statistically ace-king is a very strong hand. I had to back it,' said Mark.

'Statistically I had a very strong hand,' said Johnny, mimicking Mark monotone delivery. 'You're so fucking queer, you know that.'

This was a strange thing to say, thought Sophie. It was almost as if Johnny was outing Mark. She looked at Mark, who was turning a dark shade of beetroot. There was a silence. Johnny got up and went to the loo, no doubt to top up the charlie. Mark started to busy himself with the cards. Sophie looked at Henri, who raised an eyebrow at her quizzically. Was this the moment to tell Mark and Johnny that she had seen them together? She had the impression that Henri thought it was. Instead, she stood up, left the table and went over to refill her wine glass.

'That was a strange thing that Johnny just said to you, Mark,' said Henri.

Mark bristled. Sophie could see that he was trying to keep a lid on his feelings.

'Well, you know what he's like when he's off his face. He does tend to come out with some pretty weird stuff.'

At that moment Johnny came back in, sniffing a little and wiping his nose. Sophie could not help herself.

'Been to see Charlie, Johnny?' she asked.

This seemed to take the tension out of the conversation; both Mark and Henri chuckled.

'Well, I need to stay awake somehow,' he said with a grin.

She had not intended her remark to be funny, but as the others had laughed, Johnny had assumed that she had. It had certainly calmed them all down a little.

Sophie remained short of cards for the next few hands, folding early and watching as Johnny won some chips back from Mark and Henri took some from both of them. Some of the acrimony seemed to have dispersed. Winning seemed to improve Johnny's mood, but there still appeared to be something bubbling under between Mark and Henri.

It was Sophie's deal again. She looked at what she had dealt herself: a seven and a five. She needed better cards to be more involved. Henri was first to bet; he called and threw in four chips to stay in the hand. Sophie folded and put her two cards to the bottom of the pack. Unusually, Mark raised from the small blind; he must have a caught a pair, thought Sophie.

'I'm not playing with Mark if he's got a pair,' said Johnny, throwing his cards back to Sophie.

'How do you know I've got a pair?' asked Mark.

'Because the only time you raise is when you've got a pair,' said Johnny.

Mark shifted in his seat but did not rise to the bait.

'I'll call,' said Henri.

Sophie was pretty sure Johnny was right. She figured Mark for a high pair, probably picture cards, but she had no idea what Henri had to keep him in the hand. She dealt out the flop: a three of clubs, a six of diamonds and a nine of spades. Mark had probably not improved his hand; she didn't know about Henri. She looked at his face. His fringe dangled over his eyes, and he was slightly hunched over his cards; he was in his inscrutable position. She looked at Mark, who had a slight smile on his face, his body language keen and eager, but there was something else. Sophie sensed that it had become a little personal between Mark and Henri; there was more intensity than Mark would normally display, more aggression. He was left of the dealer and first to bet.

'I'll raise the pot,' he said.

This was unusual. Mark would not normally make such a large bet, even if had good cards. What would Henri do? He sat inert for some time. He was clearly deciding whether or not to take a risk, weighing up the likelihood of beating Mark against the potential return. Was there also something else, she wondered? He was trying to hide it and doing quite well, but Henri seemed a little more pumped up than normal. She was pretty sure he had been on the charlie too. She watched as he tapped out a Disque Bleu and lit it almost as if he was trying to slow himself down. She looked again at the cards. What might he have that would keep him in the hand? A high pair? Probably not. He would surely have bet more aggressively rather than calling in the last round of betting. The most likely scenario was that he was thinking about drawing to a flush or a straight. The flush was remote, as it would need two more cards to make. The odds were too high. But a straight, now that was possible, particularly if he was drawing to an open-ended straight. Then he only needed one more card to make it, and that card could be either at the top or the bottom of his current sequence of four cards. If Henri had been dealt a four and a five or a seven and an eight, particularly of the same suit, he might well have stayed in the hand to see the flop. She figured him for seven-eight, which together with the six and nine in the flop meant he needed a five or a ten to make a straight with two more cards to come. The odds were about two to one, so Henri was behind if he figured Mark for a high pair, but Mark was piling the money in rather complacently, so it might actually be a risk worth taking.

'Call,' said Henri. He clearly agreed. Sophie looked at Mark. A greedy little smile had appeared. If Sophie had read the hand correctly, Mark thought it was in the bag.

She dealt the next card face up. It was a queen. Mark was almost bursting to bet. So he had just added another queen to his pair of queens, thought Sophie.

'I bet the pot,' said Mark.

'I call,' said Henri.

It was no surprise that Henri had called quickly this time. If she was right, the two to one odds of making the straight were dependent on staying in until the last card. She dealt the last card quickly. It was a ten. She looked at Henri as she dealt it. His body language hardly changed, but she just caught a glimpse through the fringe into those well-protected eyes. She was pretty sure that he had made his straight. It beat Mark's three queens, and Henri knew it. She was sure that Mark had not spotted the possibility. He tended just to look at the other high cards rather than watching for his opponent's flushes or straights, and this straight was well concealed, so he had no chance. All he could see on the table, apart from his queen, were four cards lower than his.

'I bet the pot again.' It was definitely personal, thought Sophie. Mark had not even stopped to think. Even he must have begun to wonder why Henri was still in the hand.

'Fucking hell, Mark,' said Johnny. 'Where did you get that pair of balls from?' Mark looked daggers at him.

Sophie counted the chips in the pot. There were two hundred and seventy. Mark needed more chips to make his bet. He pulled out some more fifty-pound notes.

'Can you give me another three hundred please, Sophie.' She took his cash, added it to the pile of notes in the bank and counted out three hundred chips. She put two hundred and seventy in the middle and gave Mark the remaining thirty.

'I call, and I raise the pot.' Henri did not just put the knife in, he turned it as well.

'What?' said Mark. 'But you've been calling all the way through.'

'And now I'm raising.'

Mark was panicked. He looked at his cards again and then looked at the five community cards. After a while the colour drained from his face. The penny has finally dropped, thought Sophie. He's just worked out that there's a hand that beats his.

Henri was in the process of counting out more notes to make

his bet. Sophie counted out the chips. It was two hundred and seventy to call, which meant that there would then be three times two hundred and seventy in the pot, so eight hundred and ten to raise. They were running out of chips.

'The raise is eight hundred and ten. Shall I just write the bets down?' Sophie asked.

'Fine by me,' said Henri. 'I raise eight hundred and ten.'

'Well, I'm not re-raising,' said Mark.

'Pussy,' said Johnny.

'Shut the fuck up,' said Mark. 'I'm going to call, though. Can you write it down please, Sophie?'

Mark looked sick as a dog. He could have folded, thought Sophie. That would save him eight hundred and ten pounds – not exactly small change.

'You owe the pot eight hundred and ten to call,' confirmed Sophie. 'That's it, the betting's over. Time to show your hand, Henri.'

Henri laid down his two cards, a seven and an eight of hearts.

'I have a straight,' he said dispassionately.

He had the straight, just as Sophie had thought. Mark threw his cards down. A pair of queens, making three queens with the extra queen on the table; a good hand but not enough. She had read him like a book, and so had Henri. Henri had been a little lucky to draw the ten on the last card, but it had been a calculated risk. The return on his investment had been huge.

'You sly French fucker,' said Johnny.

'Yes, he is a sly fucker,' said Mark. 'More than you can imagine.'

'What is that supposed to mean, Mark?'

'You know what I'm talking about.'

'OK, boys, let's calm down.' There was an edge to the way Mark was talking that was unnerving Sophie.

'Yes, I'm sure you want me to calm down, Sophie, don't you? You're probably afraid of what I might say.' Mark was on the edge.

'What's he talking about, Sophie?' asked Johnny, in a suddenly accusative tone.

'I've no idea,' she replied. She wished he would shut the fuck up.

'Ask Henri. He knows what I'm talking about. The stuff that goes on in Paris behind your back. The *business* they have in Paris.' Mark sneered the word business.

Sophie felt sick to the pit of her stomach.

'Whatever business we have been doing in Paris, Mark, it's nothing compared with the business that you and Johnny have been doing behind Sophie's back. But what you don't realise is that it's not always behind her back. She's seen you sucking Johnny's cock, Mark. She's seen you doing it. In her own house.'

'Henri, that's enough.' Sophie had heard too much. She realised only later that she had shouted, maybe even screamed, the words.

A deathly hush fell across the table. The secrets were out. Sophie stood up, walked over to the drinks table and filled her wine glass back up again. She felt surprisingly calm and controlled.

'Well, I don't think we're going to be playing any more poker tonight, are we? You two had better go. I think Johnny and I have plenty of talking to do.'

Henri and Mark murmured their assent, grabbed their jackets and hustled out of the room as fast as they could. They clearly did not want to witness the conversation between Johnny and Sophie. The cards, chips and bank notes were left strewn across the table like an unfinished meal. Two of Mark's three queens stared unblinkingly upwards. Johnny was slumped across the table with his head in his hands. Sophie felt strangely relieved that their dirty little secrets were out in the open. Perhaps now there would be some honesty in their relationship – if there was anything left of their relationship. She stood next to the table of drinks, looking at the mess that was on the card table. She turned away and looked out of the tall, elegant window, across the dimly lit gardens of the hotel, beyond into the blackness of the lake. Yes, she thought, if there was anything left other than the emptiness that now seemed to be consuming her. She looked back over at Johnny. He was in a complete mess. It really was not the best time to talk things through, but when was there a good time? Tomorrow morning he would be back on the tour bus. She sat back down at the table, sipping on her wine. Johnny still had his head in his hands.

'Johnny, maybe it's better if we sleep on this. Why don't you sleep in the main bed? I'll go in with Amy.' She really did not want to have the conversation about their future now; she just did not know what to say. The only thing she knew for certain was that she did not want to sleep in the same bed as Johnny. She was not sure that she wanted to sleep at all. She had the feeling that tonight was probably going to be a bit of a watershed.

'You're probably right,' Johnny said. 'I'm pretty fucked anyway.' He got up, grabbed the remains of the bottle of Jim Beam and headed towards the main bedroom.

Sophie watched him shuffle off; those few short years since they had met had taken their toll. She looked at the chips and cards strewn across the table, and it occurred to her that someone needed to sort out who owed what. If she wasn't going to go to sleep she might as well make herself useful. She looked around the room. There was some hotel stationery. A plan was starting to form. She would have to send the bulk of the cash to Henri, and she would have to tell Mark what he owed Henri after that last bet. She might as well tell each of them what she thought of them at the same time. And as for Johnny, well maybe it would be easier to articulate how she felt if she wrote it down.

A few hours later she rubbed her tired eyes and looked at the three envelopes in front of her. One, quite a bulky package, was addressed to Henri le Cerf, Lagrange et Cie, Geneva. She had marked 'BY HAND' in the right-hand corner of the envelope. She

170

would ask the hotel to deliver it that morning. The next envelope was simply marked 'Johnny'. Johnny would find it when he woke up, by which time she and Amy would likely be at the airport. The third was addressed to Mark Arnold, and she would post it to his flat in Islington when she got back to England. She was tired but satisfied. She was ready to move on.

***

Henri sat at his desk sipping on an espresso and gazing in the direction of the *Financial Times*. He had the morning-after shivers. He shivered both when he had an attack of nausea and when he had an attack of paranoia. The nausea was the alcohol, and the paranoia was the cocaine. It would pass. He hoped the flashbacks to the previous night would also pass. That jumped-up arsehole Mark had deserved it; but he had felt a bit sorry for Sophie and Johnny. He hoped he had not ruined his relationships with either of them. Johnny was a cool guy. And Sophie? Well, he wasn't sure what to think about Sophie. He had been desperate to sleep with her at one time, but when she had seduced him in Paris it had all felt a little sad and tawdry. He liked her, and she was a beautiful girl, but she was Johnny's wife, and, unusually, that seemed to bother him, so he had backed off.

'M. le Cerf, this has arrived for you.' It was one of the concierges.

'Thanks, François.'

It was a small package addressed to him at the bank, with 'Private and Confidential, to be opened by addressee only' emblazoned on it. It also had 'BY HAND' written in capitals in the top right-hand corner. He didn't recognise the handwriting. And it was in English. Strange. He tore off the sellotape and shook out the contents. Banknotes in various denominations fell on to his desk together with a letter in the same handwriting. He realised who it was from as soon as he started reading.

Beau Rivage Palace Hotel
Lausanne
24 July 1993

Dear Henri

I can't sleep, so I've decided to share out the money and send it on to you. You seemed to forget to pick it up during your rather hasty departure. You may or may not remember, but the last pot before we started writing the bets down came to £810 in cash. You then raised £810, which I wrote down, and Mark called your bet, which I also wrote down. So this means that you are owed the £810 in cash and £810 from Mark. When I cleared up it also looked as if you had another £40 in chips left in front of you, so I am enclosing a total of £850 in cash now. I've given you all the foreign currency plus £250 in sterling, which I think is about right in total. I've also written to Mark reminding him that he needs to settle his debt of £810 to you.

Well, that's all the housekeeping out of the way. I'm not sure where we all go from here. There's a lot that Johnny and I need to sort out. I don't think it will help this process if you and I continue our relationship. (Did we ever really have one?!) I appreciate you helping me through a difficult time in my life; the support you gave me really gave me a leg up. Maybe it was wrong for us to sleep together, but we can't undo what's already happened, and it helped me at the time. For my part I have very fond memories of my visits to Paris and the Hôtel Meurice, and I'd like to thank you for being so generous.

Anyway, I think that whatever there was between us is over now. I'm sure you understand.

Bonne chance,

Sophie

P.S. I hope you don't mind if I keep up my business with Véronique and Juste.

Henri quickly counted the cash and stashed it in his back pocket. He was relieved. He had no real idea why he had been so desperate to out Mark and Johnny, but once he had done it he had been worried that there would be repercussions. He had also been worried that Sophie might think that he was doing it because he wanted to be with her, which was definitely not the case. He had just wanted to show Mark who was boss. He was sorry that Johnny had been dragged into it, but he was pretty sure he could smooth that over. He felt the paranoia lifting, and even the nausea seemed to be retreating. He had been meaning to ask Samantha in the Investment Department out for lunch. Maybe that was a good way to spend some of his poker winnings. The only other issue to resolve was to make peace with Mark so that they could go ahead with their business deal. He would put a call in to him later. He was pretty sure now that he could turn that around. Mark was a pragmatic individual, and business was business after all.

***

Johnny could hear a noise in the distance, a ringing; it was getting louder and louder. It took a while, but in the end he realised what it was and answered the telephone.

'Shake a leg, buddy. We're waiting for you in the lobby.' It was Dave.

'What time is it?'

'Time to get your arse down here pronto.'

'OK, I'm coming.'

He felt like shit again. Headache, dry mouth – no shivers yet, but, as night follows day, he was sure that they would arrive shortly. He eased himself out of bed and started to remember the previous night. He walked out of the bedroom in his underpants into the main suite. It was empty. There was a pile of cash on the table next to the empty bottles and glasses. He went over to pick it up and saw an envelope addressed simply to 'Johnny'. It was in Sophie's handwriting. He went back to the bedroom and dressed hurriedly, then put the cash and the envelope in the pocket of his jeans, picked up his holdall, untouched from where he had put it down the previous evening, and left the suite. Ablutions would have to wait. He arrived in the lobby and saw the tour bus parked outside. Alex and Dave were smoking by the steps.

'Nice of you to make it,' said Alex.

'All right, Alex, I feel rough enough as it is. Did anyone see Sophie and Amy this morning?'

They shook their heads. Johnny screwed up his eyes against the hot summer sun. He could feel the beads of sweat breaking out on his forehead. He felt in his jacket for his Wayfarers and put them on. The distance the sunglasses put between him and the rest of the world made him feel a little better. He got on the bus and walked to the back to his usual spot. The cooler was on the floor next to him, and he located a can of Coke. He'd lay off the booze for a little while and try to make a little sense of what had happened last night. He cringed as he remembered that Sophie now knew about Mark. But had she known already? He tried hard to remember the conversation, but it was all much too vague. One thing he was certain of was that Henri had outed them. There was more than that, though, something to do with Henri and Sophie? What was it? Suddenly he remembered the envelope and groped in his jeans pocket for it. He opened it to find a letter in Sophie's handwriting. He sparked up a Marlboro Light, inhaled and then shivered slightly as he started to read.

Beau Rivage Palace Hotel
Lausanne
24 July 1993

Dear Johnny

I'm not quite sure where to start. I can't sleep, so I thought I would at least try to lay out how I feel. It may not be the way I feel in the future, but right now this is the way I feel.

I'm not sure whether or not you realise, but you seem to be on a bit of a mission to self-destruct. I know that the touring is tough and your new-found fame means you have a lot to cope with, but you don't even really seem to be enjoying it. I had thought that we might be getting things back on track at Christmas, but then I saw you with Mark.

Oh shit! Now he started to remember the previous night's conversation.

You will probably never understand quite how much that hurt me. Infidelity is a difficult thing to cope with at the best of times, but to discover that your husband is both unfaithful and bisexual in precisely the same moment has proved to be insurmountable. I'm sorry that you had to find out that I had slept with Henri.

The bitch. He'd forgotten about that.

It happened only once, in Paris, not long after I had seen you and Mark together. I think in a way it was me taking revenge on you for what I had seen. It helped a little at the time, but I now realise it was a mistake. I'm pretty sure it would not have happened if I had not known about you and Mark.

I'm not sure where you and I go from here, but one thing I do know is that for the moment it would be better if we separated. I am desperate for Amy to have a father in her life, as I know you are, but I'm sure that you can also understand why I would not want our relationship to continue on the same footing.

I don't think separating will be particularly difficult, as we hardly see one another as it is. What will be difficult is how we deal with Amy. We need to think hard about this. I don't have a plan yet other than to try to make sure that she is never directly confronted with the idea that we have split up. This shouldn't be too hard to achieve, given that you are rarely at home anyway.

I hope you understand and agree that this is the best thing to do for the moment. It will be hard to talk about this on the telephone, so I think we should save any discussion for when we can see each other face to face. I expect you to keep calling to speak to Amy, but don't be surprised if I don't have much to say to you.

I am truly sorry that things have come to this.

Love

Sophie

PS I left what looked like your cash on the table. I hope you found it.

PPS we'll be on the way back to England very early in the morning, so don't worry if you can't find us.

Johnny drained the last of his can of Coke and sparked up another Marlboro Light. He folded the letter and put it back in his jeans pocket. A morning-beer buzz seemed his only real option. He retrieved a can of Heineken from the cooler, cracked it open and took a long slug. He was too tired and too wasted to think. A numbness had settled over him, and he intended to make it even number.

**

Mark put the key into the door of his Islington flat and felt the relief flood through him. He had had the weekend to recover from the trip to Switzerland, but Victoria had been with him. He really would have preferred to spend the weekend on his own, taking stock of the situation. Instead he had spent it telling Victoria what a wonderful time they had all had in Lausanne. Fortunately, Victoria had left that Monday morning to go up to Leeds to work on an audit of one of the subsidiaries of a large industrial client, so he would be alone in his flat for most of the week. He opened the door and leaned down to pick up the post from the doormat. There was one handwritten envelope. Whose handwriting was that? It looked vaguely familiar. He walked into the kitchen, put his briefcase down and had a good look at the postmark. It was hot in the flat; he loosened his tie and undid the top button of his shirt. The postmark was a bit smudged, but he could just about make out that it was marked Rye. Sophie. That's whose handwriting it was. He put the envelope down, opened a kitchen cupboard and took out a bottle of Lagavulin; he was pretty sure he would need a decent slug of malt to get through whatever the envelope contained. He walked through to the living-room and sat down on the sofa, opened the envelope, pulled out the letter, breathed in deeply and started to read.

Beau Rivage Palace Hotel
Lausanne
24 July 1993

Dear Mark

I can't sleep, so I have decided to sort out who is owed what from the poker table. I enclose £30 which you seem to have had left in front of you at the table. You also need to send £810 to Henri to settle the last bet to call in the last hand that we played. This is one of the bets that I wrote down, as you had run out of cash. I'm sure you remember what happened.

So, now you know that I know about you and Johnny. I came back to the house to get my hat when we were out walking on New Year's Day and saw you sucking his cock. I've spent the last six months gradually coming to terms with this. It hasn't been easy, and it is one of the reasons that I ended up sleeping with Henri. There is nothing between Henri and I; it just happened once in January shortly after I had seen you and Johnny together. I was lonely, and Henri made himself available.

I can't stop Johnny from having a relationship with you if that is what he wants to do, but I can stop you having a continuing relationship with me. As tonight's revelations mean that everything is out in the open, it also means that I don't have to pretend that I want to see you any longer, so I would appreciate it if you would stay out of my way. As you can imagine, I have spent a lot of time wondering how long you and Johnny have had a physical relationship. Since puberty? Since you were young adults? Since he married me? If I know that I am never going to see you again, in time I might stop asking myself these kinds of questions.

I would wish you a nice life, but I don't really want you to have a nice life. I would rather that you suffer some of the misery that I have suffered these last few months.

I am very sad that it has come to this,

Sophie

Mark put down the letter and exhaled. His eyes were welling up with tears. He felt a mixture of anger, hurt and relief. He could hardly blame Sophie for the way that she felt, he knew that, but the attack on him was pretty savage. Did the relationship they had had as students mean nothing to her now? Obviously not. Should he respond to the letter? A response did not seem to be expected. It was pretty clear what was expected: no further contact. He wondered what she had said to Johnny. He would have to wait to find out. Johnny was away on tour, and it was virtually impossible to contact him when they were travelling the whole time. He could try through Cooper-Smythe's office, but it would be hard to leave a message that meant anything to Johnny. In a way he was relieved and almost pleased that Sophie now knew about him and Johnny. It was revenge for her rejection of him, but it did not feel quite as satisfying as he had thought it might have done. It was too messy.

It wasn't only Sophie who had been affected, it was all of them. He did not want Victoria to find out about it, that was certain; if she did it would mean the end of their relationship and maybe even his career. This was what had been bothering him all weekend. Victoria had actually asked him what was wrong. He had made up an excuse, but it was difficult. He had to put Johnny and Sophie out of his mind for a while, focus on his work and be nice to Victoria. The only alternative was to give up on Victoria and concentrate on men. But that was a big step. It would have big consequences and might even lead to him coming out. He was definitely not ready for that. The only other related issue was Henri and their deal with Cooper-Smythe. Like the snake he was, Henri had been on the telephone earlier to make sure that events in Lausanne had not put a stop to their business dealings. Mark did not need to point out to Henri that Mark was hardly in a position to tell Cooper-Smythe that they would have to change banks because Henri had outed him as a bisexual to his gay lover's wife. Henri would have known that Mark was in a tight spot, that was why he had phoned to make up. Mark would just have to keep him at arm's length. He sipped at his whisky then he screwed Sophie's letter into a ball. He was going to have to be a little more careful.

THE WEST END OF LONDON

3 MAY 1994

Johnny had had a bad feeling about the meeting at Paisley Records as soon as Alex had told him that he did not know what it was about. Now that they were at the meeting he felt even worse. Cooper-Smythe's charm had completely disappeared to be replaced by an unpleasant brand of hectoring.

'What I'm saying, guys, is it's not working. It's too heavy, too druggy. It's out of date. Kurt Cobain died last month. Grunge is on the way out. It's Britpop that's selling.'

'I thought you believed in what we were doing,' said Alex.

'I did when I first met you, but you haven't developed.'

'Have you listened to the new tapes?' Alex was not happy.

'Yes, but nothing is grabbing me. There's nothing new. Look, when *Lost in Space* came out it sounded fresh, and it sold well for a first album. To be honest, when you came up with *Return of Swerve* we thought it was a bit lame, but we decided to rush it out anyway on the back of *Lost in Space*, but it hasn't sold that well. We then spent a lot of money on the *Return of Swerve* tour last year, and it tailed right off. Spring and summer were OK because people were still coming to hear the songs from *Lost in Space*, but first albums don't last for ever, chaps. *Return of Swerve* has been a bit of a flop. We've spent a lot of money on you, and we're not sure that we can afford to spend any more.'

'You told us you loved *Return of Swerve*,' said Dave.

'That may be so, David, but the public didn't, and that's what counts.'

This was not good news. Johnny could tell by the way Cooper-Smythe was speaking that this was likely to be the end of their contract. He had also heard on the grapevine that Paisley Records had a few financial issues, so they were hardly likely to throw money at Swerve when they weren't selling records.

'Have a look in the mirror, guys. Look at your biker jackets and ripped jeans. You're starting to look like old farts. Times change, tastes change and only the fittest survive.'

'So what does this mean?' asked Alex.

'Do you want me to spell it out for you, Alex? I'm afraid this is the end. We're not taking up our option on your album.'

'What do you mean? I thought we had a five-album deal.'

'Well, you'd better go away and read your contract then. You have a deal for *Lost in Space*, and then we have options on your next four albums. We took our option on *Return of Swerve*, regrettably, but we are no longer interested in taking options on anything else.'

'So what happens next?' asked Rob.

'You really want me to spell it out for you, don't you? This is it, gentlemen. We are no longer business partners. We don't like your new material, we don't expect it to sell and we won't be involved with you on a continuing basis. Gretchen will explain the financial implications to you.'

Cooper-Smythe sat back in his chair and put his feet on his desk. Gretchen had been standing silently at his side throughout the conversation. She picked up a clipboard from the desk and was about to speak, but she was interrupted by Alex. He was on his feet, jabbing his finger at Cooper-Smythe.

'You can't do this, you can't do this.' Alex was beside himself. His world was falling in on him.

'I think you'll find that I am perfectly entitled to do this.'

'I'm telling you that you fucking can't.'

Johnny stood up and tried to calm Alex, who was on the verge of climbing over the desk to stick one on Cooper-Smythe. That was the last thing they needed. Johnny found it pretty easy to pull back Alex's small frame. Dave and Rob seemed too dejected to put up much of a fight. They both stood up and helped Johnny with Alex.

'We don't need to hear what Gretchen's got to say,' said Rob. 'You'll be hearing from our solicitor.' As far as Johnny knew they didn't have a solicitor.

'By all means. I look forward to it.' Cooper-Smythe was not exactly cowed by their threat.

They wrestled Alex out of the door and down the stairs of the small offices back on to the streets of Soho.

'All right, you can let go of me now.' Alex wriggled free of their grip and patted himself down. His pride had taken a severe blow. Johnny could see that he was furious.

'I think we could all do with a drink. Shall we go in the Blue Posts?'

'You could always do with a drink, Johnny, but for once I agree with you.'

Johnny decided to ignore Alex's jibe as they all trooped into the small confines of the Blue Posts in Rupert Street. Johnny went to the bar as the others squeezed around one of the small tables. It was still only late morning, so the pub was almost empty, the stale air betraying the previous night's revelry. Johnny sparked up a Marlboro Light and pulled on it deeply as he waited for the barman to drag himself away from his crossword. He could hear Alex behind him chuntering away.

'Fucking cheek. Who does he think he is?'

He ordered two pints of Guinness, two pints of Timothy Taylor's and four Jim Beams. The barman raised a quizzical eyebrow at the order.

'It's been a bad morning,' said Johnny.

He handed the bitters to Dave and Rob; the Guinesses were for him and Alex. He then handed round the Jim Beams.

'I don't want a short, Johnny. It's not even midday,' said Alex.

'I thought it might calm us down a bit. Don't worry, I'll drink it if you don't want it.'

'I'm sure you will, but maybe we should have a sober conversation for a change. You were listening in there, weren't you? We no longer have a record deal. They dumped us.'

'Well, I didn't trust Cooper-Smythe from the outset. I said we needed a proper manager, and you said that we could manage ourselves. Look where that's got us.' Johnny was fed up with Alex's digs at him. It was time to remind Alex of his own shortcomings.

'That's typical, Johnny. You always think you know better, don't you?'

'All right, guys. Let's calm down. We need to think rationally about this.' Dave was the voice of reason.

'We need to go up there and kick that fucker's head in.' Rob was Dave's antithesis.

'Well, I was trying to do that, but for some reason you guys dragged me away.'

'I thought you would have thanked me for doing that,' said Johnny.

'You know what, Johnny, I wouldn't thank you for anything much. Your negativity is bringing this band down. I'm sure the amount of coke you stick up your nose doesn't help either. That's without even mentioning the booze.'

'I suppose you're some kind of saint?'

'No, but I know when to work and when to play.'

'And I don't?'

'No, I don't think you do any more.'

'You arrogant little shit,' said Johnny. 'I'm not sure why I stay in this band to spend my time with a bossy little fucker like you.'

'Well, why don't you leave then?'

'I might just do that. Is that what you two want?' Johnny stared at Rob and Dave.

'You haven't really been putting in a full shift for a long time, mate,' said Rob.

Dave just shrugged his shoulders.

'It seems I'm not the only one,' said Alex.

'You know what,' said Johnny. 'Fuck you guys. You can find another guitarist. I'm not having this. I'm out of here.'

He picked up his Jim Beam and downed it in one. Then he picked up Alex's Jim Beam and swallowed that too. Then, much to the astonishment of his now-ex-bandmates, he headed for the door. They had had arguments before, but Johnny had always backed down. He stood out on the street fuming. He was tired of Alex's constant sniping, tired of being the odd one out in all the arguments; just tired. This felt like it could be the end of the road. Where the fuck did he go now, though? He stood in the little alleyway by the side of the pub. He felt claustrophobic, as if the city's buildings were pushing down on him, squeezing the life out of him.

Suddenly he knew instinctively where he wanted to be, and he set off down the alley into Wardour Street towards Charing Cross Station. He needed some space, a calm environment, some sea air. He needed time to make sense of things. He could see lots more of Amy – maybe even sort a few things out with Sophie. Since they had separated last year he had either been touring or recording. He needed a break. Most of all he needed to be with someone who wouldn't judge him. He could feel the pace of his walk quickening. He needed to go and stay with his mother.

***

Mark picked up the telephone and recognised the voice straight away. It was the sly old fox from Geneva. He sounded more agitated than usual.

'Have you spoken to Cooper-Smythe lately?'

'No, not for a couple of weeks.'

'Have you looked at the markets today?'

'We don't really have access to the markets like you do. We don't have Reuters or Bloomberg. I've only had a computer for a couple of years.'

'Well, Paisley Records is tanking; the share price is down nearly 30 per cent today. Someone has dumped a load of shares, and it can't be Cooper-Smythe because we have all his shares in our safe-keeping account. I've tried to get hold of him, but he's unavailable, according to Gretchen. I've asked around, and the only thing I can pick up is that some of the brokers are saying there's a rumour that the company is in financial difficulty. What's going on?'

'Well, I don't know. The last audit we did was for the year to 31 December 1992. That's over a year ago now. We're due to start the 1993 audit in a couple of weeks, but I haven't had the advance information yet, so I don't really have anything more up-to-date. The company makes announcements about its results each quarter, and we check the management accounts then, but you would know about those already. They certainly haven't told the market that there are any problems.'

'Well, there obviously are some serious problems. If the share price goes down much more we're going to have to start selling Cooper-Smythe's shares to cover the two million pounds we lent him. If we start selling into a market that's already selling the shares off then the price really is going to go into freefall. I've already got my credit people on my back. Can you go round to the offices and find out what the hell is happening?'

'I can't just barge into the office and demand to see Cooper-Smythe.'

'Look, Mark, this is serious, and if we have a big problem I will hold you responsible. We better not have another Polly Peck on our hands.'

185

'It's hardly the same situation.'

'I don't see a great deal of difference.'

'All right, Henri. I'll see what I can do. Leave it with me.'

'I'm counting on you, Mark. We're both in deep shit if this goes down.'

'I said I'll see what I can do, Henri. Goodbye.'

Mark was sweating. He didn't like the sound of this. If Paisley Records really were having difficulties it would not be good for his career. Whenever a client company went bust there was an investigation into the auditors' work, and while he was pretty sure he had not done anything illegal he had always been pretty lenient with Cooper-Smythe, and he, in turn, had always pushed Mark to do things that were right on the limit. He was never very confident with the quarterly information that was provided to him, and certainly in 1992 there had been some big adjustments to the company's figures following the audit. But the market perception at the time was that the company was on a roll, so the share price had actually gone up. If he was honest, he was not that surprised that there seemed to be problems. He had just heard from Johnny that the label had dumped Swerve, who had been their most successful act in 1993. He needed to get over there quickly to find out what was happening.

***

Mark hopped out of the taxi in Wardour Street, right outside the Paisley Records office. He had not phoned ahead, as he wanted to surprise them. He buzzed the intercom on the street, and the receptionist let him straight in. The office was above the Paisley Records shop where the label had first started. Mark skipped up the stairs to the small reception area. Daisy, the receptionist, looked the same as ever. She had a short boyish haircut and a perky, slightly spiky demeanour. She projected an image that Charles would have liked.

'Hi, Mark, have you got a meeting with Charles? Gretchen didn't tell me, and Charles isn't here.'

'I was hoping to see Charles, yes.'

'He hasn't been in today.'

'Can I see Gretchen then?'

'I'll buzz her and see if she's free.'

Mark waited.

'I'm sorry, Mark. She's not available at the moment.'

'But you just spoke to her?'

'Yes, but she's not available.'

Mark knew where Gretchen's office was, next to Charles's suite. He got up and strode towards it.

'Mark,' Daisy called after him.

He ignored her and moved with purpose down the corridor. Charles was one thing – he could be a little intimidating – but Mark was not going to let Gretchen ruin his career. The door to her office was open, so he walked straight in. She seemed to be drowning under the sea of papers that covered her desk. She looked up when she heard him come in. She looked as fierce as usual, but Mark had learned that it was a bit of a façade; she was actually quite amenable once she started to trust you.

'I told Daisy I was busy, Mark.' At that point Daisy arrived at the door.

'I'm sorry, Gretchen, he just barged his way down here.'

'Don't worry, Daisy. I'll deal with him.'

'Come in, Mark, and close the door behind you.'

He sat down opposite her. She was just about visible through the piles of printouts and documents on her desk.

'So, what's going on, Gretchen?'

'What do you mean?' She pronounced her Ws as Vs.

'I've just had Henri le Cerf on the phone from Geneva. Apparently your company's share price is going through the floor, and he's been trying to get hold of Charles to find out why, but he's unavailable.'

'I see.'

'Well, what is going on?'

'Charles isn't here. You'll have to discuss it with him.'

'When is he going to be back?'

'I'm not sure.' This was proving to be more difficult than Mark had expected. He would need some leverage to get Gretchen to open up.

'You do realise that I'm the company's auditor, Gretchen, and you are required to let me know if the company is in any kind of financial difficulty. The company and its officers would have an obligation to make an announcement to the market if that were the case.'

'Mark, listen carefully. I'm not going to tell you very much because I don't know all the details, and I haven't been able to work out exactly what has happened yet, but what I can tell you is that Charles has gone missing. This is not a good sign.'

'Oh shit,' said Mark.

'I don't think I should tell you any more unless you are here as the official representative of Coopers & Lybrand.'

Mark understood what Gretchen was saying. If Gretchen gave him information that was price sensitive he would be become an insider and would not be able to discuss it externally without fear of prosecution for insider trading. So even if Gretchen did give him information he would not be able to tell Henri.

'Thanks, Gretchen. I understand. I'm not here officially, I simply wanted to meet up with Charles. If he's not here, I'll go. No doubt I'll be back again soon in a more official capacity.'

'No doubt.'

Gretchen was no fool. Mark had underestimated her. He got up and left.

Back at the office, there was a note on his desk. It was from his boss.

Mark

Please see me as soon as you are back in the office. There are problems at Paisley Records, and it seems likely that the shares will be suspended. Please do not talk to anyone there until we have discussed the issue.

Brian 2.30pm

Shit, thought Mark. It really did seem like there was no way back now. Should he call Henri? No, for his own sake he had better get straight round to Brian's office.

***

Sophie felt her eyes stinging as she finished chopping the onion. It was good that she and Amy could eat the same food now; there was no fun in cooking for one. She wondered what time Mary would be bringing Amy back. It should be quite soon. At the mention of Paisley Records on the radio Sophie's ears pricked up.

And, finally, the music news. The shares of independent record company Paisley Records were suspended from trading today, following rumours in the City that the company is in financial difficulties. You may remember that Paisley were in the news a few days ago when they dropped Alex Middlehead's band Swerve from their label. This was followed by guitarist Johnny Jones leaving the band for personal reasons. Paisley's dropping of Swerve caused some surprise in the music business at the time, but these latest revelations shed more light on what may have been behind it all. We have tried to contact the company's managing director, Charles Cooper-Smythe, for a statement, but he was unavailable. This is Melinda Freedom reporting for Radio 1 news. Now back to…

None of that sounded good, thought Sophie. She had read a couple of days earlier in the *Mirror*'s gossip column that Johnny had left Swerve and had wondered if she should contact him. She had decided to wait for him to contact her – in any case, she was seeing

Mary today, so she could find out from her what was happening. There hadn't been time for a chat that morning. It was strange how things had just fizzled out between her and Johnny since the trip to Lausanne. Her letter had made it clear how she felt, and he had done what she asked. He phoned from time to time to speak to Amy, and every now and then he came and picked her up for the day. When they met they were polite, but they never really spoke unless it was about Amy. Amy herself had picked up on the fact that her father no longer stayed with them or even really spent any time in the house, but after a while she too had stopped asking any questions. They were all in a kind of purgatory. Maybe now was the time to stop the silent suffering; she certainly thought that she was ready to move on. She stood at the sink, looking out into the garden, and saw Amy arrive with Mary. Amy ran up the garden path at full pelt, and Mary followed, smiling affectionately at her grandchild. It struck her that Mary was a very warm person, and some of this had rubbed off on Johnny. He had been rough around the edges when they had met, but he had been gentle and affectionate. The booze, cocaine and fame had put paid to that. She went to the door.

'Mummy, I saw Daddy today. He's staying with Granny.'

'Really? That was a nice surprise.' She would definitely find out what was happening by the sound of it.

'Hi, Mary, thanks for today. I don't know what I'd do without you.'

'I hope you don't mind. Johnny turned up on Monday at home. He's been sacked by the band. He was in a bit of a mess.'

'Why don't you go and watch telly, Amy, while I make your tea.' Amy skipped off, unused actually to being encouraged to watch the television.

'Have you got time for a cup of tea?' Sophie asked Mary.

They went through to the kitchen. Mary sat at the table, and Sophie busied herself first with the tea and then with the spaghetti bolognese as they talked.

'Yes, so Johnny turned up on Monday. I'm afraid that day was a write-off. He was tipsy when he arrived and paralytic by the time I put him to bed. I hadn't realised quite how bad his drinking was until then. I understand better now what you've had to deal with.'

'It hasn't been a bed of roses.'

'No, I can see that. He wanted to come and see Amy the next day, but I managed to put him off. To be honest, I read him the riot act.'

'Really?'

'Yes. Why are you surprised?'

'Well, he doesn't take kindly to criticism.'

'No, but I don't do it very often, and he knows he's overstepped the mark if I have to tell him off.'

Sophie passed a mug of tea to Mary. She was still a very attractive woman; looking at her made it obvious where Johnny had inherited his bone structure.

'I told him that he couldn't see Amy until he sobered up – and by that I meant really sobered up, not just taking a day off drinking because he had a hangover.'

'And he did it?'

'I told him that I'd be looking after Amy on Friday, and that if he was in a fit state by then he could see her. As far as I know he hasn't had a drink since Monday. To be honest, he hasn't done much other than sleep. He seems to be exhausted.'

'So how was he today?'

'Much better. He seemed more like his old self. I think it's going to take weeks or even months for him to really recover. And that's only if he really wants to straighten himself out.'

'Well, let's hope he does.'

'I think he'd like to see you, Sophie.'

'Really.' Sophie's tone was flat.

'I think he knows he's messed up. I don't know what happened between you two, and I don't want to know ...' (No, you don't want to know, thought Sophie.) '... but I get the impression that he wants to try to make it up to you.'

'That might be difficult.'

'But not impossible.'

Sophie smiled thinly at Mary. She had no idea whether or not she wanted the old Johnny back. She had assumed that the new pissed, drugged-up, rock-star Johnny was here to stay.

'What's happened with Swerve?' she asked.

'Again, I don't know all the ins and outs, but it seems that he had a big row with Alex, and they kicked him out because of it.'

'That figures.'

'Yeah, I never liked Alex either. But there we are. I suppose it was good while it lasted – in some ways anyway.'

'You don't think he'll try to get back together with them?'

'It doesn't look like it. I don't think he's been in touch. He's not phoning anyone as far as I know, and no one seems to be phoning him.'

'It's strange that it all ended so quickly. It seems like yesterday that they were playing the local pubs.'

'It's beyond me altogether. I just hope that he can get his health sorted out. So, will you meet him?'

'I'll think about it. Ask me again next Friday.'

'OK. I hope you didn't mind me giving Amy a surprise today?'

'Well, to be honest, Mary, I would rather have known, but, now I know he's around, it's not a problem, no. I don't really want her routine to be too disrupted, though.'

'I understand. You're a good girl, Sophie. I always thought you'd be good for Johnny, that you might cure that wild streak of his. Maybe you will in the end.'

As she showed Mary out it occurred to Sophie that she had never tried to tell Johnny what to do; she had been afraid to try to rein him in. Maybe she should have tried to be tougher with him. Was she up to having another attempt? She was not sure, but she knew who she was going to ask.

After they had eaten, Sophie put Amy to bed, installed herself on the sofa with a glass of Australian Shiraz and picked up the telephone.

'*Allo.*'

'*Salut, c'est Sophie à l'appareil.*'

'*Salut, ma puce.*' Sophie could hear the smile in Juste's voice. They continued the conversation in French.

'Do you have time to talk?' she asked.

'Yes, of course. I always have time for you, my dear.'

Sophie felt herself colouring slightly at the compliment, even though she was on the telephone. Juste had always known how to embarrass her.

'I need your advice.'

'I'll do my best.'

'Do you remember the conversation we had in Paris over dinner at Le Meurice last January?'

'I remember a lovely evening, but you may have to help me a little more.'

'I told you about a friend of mine, who was considering their sexuality.'

'Ah, yes. I assumed that you were talking about yourself.'

'Well, no, it wasn't me, it was Johnny.'

'*Les Anglais. Ils sont tous les pédérastes.*'

'What do you mean?'

'Well, we French, we believe that English men are all homosexual when they are young. They seem to grow out of it as they get older. It must be something to do with your single-sex schools.'

'Well, what would you say if I told you I had seen Johnny being given oral sex by his friend Mark last year?'

'Old habits die hard. I don't think it's anything to worry about. These things happen. As long as he stops if you ask him to stop. In some ways it's better than another woman.'

'You really think so?'

'I may not be the best person to ask, but I don't think you should worry too much about it. It's probably some adolescent crush they're still getting over.'

'You make it sound so ordinary.'

'I'm sure you're not the first woman to be betrayed in this way. Men are pigs, I'm afraid.'

'But we've separated because of this.'

'Well, then he knows that you are seriously pissed off. But you haven't divorced, have you?'

'No. He wants to see me again to discuss the future.'

'Then you should see him if you want to. If you don't want to, forget him and move on. Life is short, so it should be sweet, *ma puce*. Only you can decide if it can still be sweet with him.'

'You are a very wise woman, Juste.'

'Maybe I've just seen more things than you have. Be brave. Make a decision one way or the other.'

'Thank you. I will.'

Sophie put the telephone down and sipped at her wine. She went over to the CD player and put on Suzanne Vega, her current favourite for accompanying a reflective mood. Could she forgive Johnny? Juste was so blasé about sex. Maybe she was right – it was something and nothing. Even so, did she really love Johnny enough not only to forgive him for what had happened with Mark but also to want to stay with him? Was he the person that she wanted to spend the rest of her life with? What did she see when she thought about him? She saw the Johnny she had first met, a young man with a glint in his eye. She surprised herself when she felt a slight tingle as she thought about it. There was something there, but was it enough? Maybe she should give it one last chance.

***

The last few days had been the worst of his career so far, Mark reflected as he sat in the lobby at Lagrange et Cie. He had learned plenty of lessons, but the main one was not to be seduced by the romance of the music business. Cooper-Smythe could still not be located, the shares in Paisley Records had been suspended. His boss Brian was furious and Henri, and probably all his bosses, were also furious. So Mark had been summoned to Switzerland to face the music on behalf of the missing Cooper-Smythe. He had not wanted to hang around in Geneva, so he had caught the early flight out from Heathrow to make the meeting at 11 a.m. and still get back to London the same day. All he wanted to do was go to the bank, have the meeting and then get back to the airport. His last trip to Switzerland had included the introduction of Cooper-Smythe and the infamous poker session in Lausanne – and look how that had ended. He cringed as he thought about it. He had made a very early start from Islington, added to which he had hardly slept, so he was not on his best form. The lack of sleep had given him a tension headache, which his nerves were not helping.

Cooper-Smythe had given Mark a power of attorney over the account at Lagrange, and, at the time, he had been quite flattered that he would place that kind of trust in Mark. It now looked like more of a set-up. The power of attorney meant that Mark was the bank's only contact for the account. Henri had insisted that, in this capacity, he come to the bank to witness a valuation of the jewels that were now the only security for the two-million-pound loan that remained owing. The Paisley Records shares were now effectively worthless; by the time the bank had reacted to the fact that the shares were in freefall they had been suspended. The bank had been too late to sell any of the shares before the suspension, which would have enabled it to pay down the loan. As a result the ten-million-pound asset that had been securing the two-million-pound loan was now worthless, and the bank wanted its money back. Fortunately for them they also had safe custody of the jewels. The bank had been prudent enough to ensure that Cooper-Smythe had offered them as further security when the loan had been granted. So, it looked as if the loan at least would be repaid through a forced sale of the Cooper-Smythe family collection. But Mark was still nervous; he had had to explain to Brian why he had power of attorney on Cooper-Smythe's account. The truth was that he had done it to ingratiate himself with Cooper-Smythe; Brian's view was that he had gone too far for a client. They were the company's auditors after all, and they needed to be careful not to get too close. The reality was that many of the partners were too close to the senior executives of the companies that they audited; it was only when something went wrong that this was called into question. There was a reason why it had been Mark rather than Brian who had got too close to this particular client: Brian had deemed Paisley Records too small a client for him to bother with, and, as Mark had made the initial contact, he had delegated the management of the relationship with Cooper-Smythe to him. However, as Mark was still a manager rather than a partner at Coopers & Lybrand he needed a partner to oversee his work, so Brian ultimately remained responsible for any problems. This was not a situation he was particularly enamoured with, as he had made clear to Mark. It was not doing any good at all to Mark's aspirations to become a partner himself.

'Hi, Mark. Thanks for coming.' This was a warmer reception than he had been expecting.

Henri led him off towards the meeting-room.

'The valuer is here already. We just need you now so that we can open up the box in front of you as the account holder. We've got the box in the meeting-room together with the key. Let's hope the valuer comes up with a decent figure and then some of the pressure will be off. All we will need to do then is put the collection into an auction for sale. I hope we can finally sort this out. I've had all sorts of heat over this, you know.'

'I know how you feel.'

'That arsehole Cooper-Smythe has a lot to answer for.'

At least he doesn't seem to hold me responsible, thought Mark.

They went into the meeting-room. A large safety-deposit box was on the table with a key next to it. Two serious-looking men were sitting at the table, and both stood up as they came in. Henri made the introductions.

'Mark Arnold. This is François Blanc from Christie's and Urs Berner, our Credit Manager.'

They shook hands.

'If you don't mind, Mark, I think we'll get straight on with it. Can you open the box?' asked Henri.

'Mark picked up the key and put it into the small lock on the heavy metal box. It opened easily. Inside was the array of dazzling jewels together with the letter on Christie's paper. Henri took the letter out and handed it to François Blanc.

'This is the previous valuation, M. Blanc.'

Blanc looked at the letter.

'Ah yes. My colleague in London, Hugo Beddington. This all looks to be in order. It's from last year, so I wouldn't expect a dramatic change in value. Let me just look at the jewels.'

Blanc took out a jeweller's loupe and started to look at the jewellery. Mark knew nothing about the world of jewels and watched silently as Blanc picked up each of the sparkling pieces in turn, peering through the eyeglass into every stone. The other two also sat hushed; there seemed to be a tacit agreement between them that it would be rude to interrupt such serious work by talking. After what seemed like an age Blanc put the last of the pieces back down on the table and took the loupe out of his eye. He sat down, and it was a moment before he said anything. He took a deep breath.

'I'm not quite sure how to tell you this, gentlemen, but I'm afraid the news is not good.'

'What do you mean?' asked Henri.

'I mean that these are not the jewels that my colleague valued. They are made of glass. Hugo may have seen the real jewels, but these are not them.'

'I don't understand,' said Henri.

'They are copies, M. le Cerf, fakes, if you like. They are good ones, and they would still fetch a few thousand, but they are worth only a tiny fraction of the original valuation.'

'But how can that be?' asked Henri.

'It is not unusual for copies to be made of a valuable collection of jewels. It is unusual to keep the copies in a safety-deposit box, however. Normally the real ones would be in the box and the copies kept at home. The owner would then be able to wear the copies without worrying about security. It means that there is no need to have insurance for the real jewels.'

'So what are the copies doing in our safety-deposit box?' Mark looked at Urs Berner as he spoke. He could see the beads of sweat on his bald pate. Mark sensed a lot of fear in the room. He himself was contributing. He could tell that livelihoods were at stake here.

'I'm afraid I can't answer that question,' said Blanc.

'What would they be worth if they were real?' asked Henri.

'I think Hugo's valuation would still be about right. There are some very large stones here, and I would imagine the originals would be of a high quality.'

'What are these copies worth?' asked Berner. His face was a rather deathly pale colour.

'Maybe ten thousand pounds. There's a lot here, and they are very well-made copies.'

The room fell silent. Ten thousand did not go very far towards repaying two million.

'I think my work is done here, gentlemen. Obviously, if you wish to sell the originals then Christie's would be more than happy to assist.'

'Yes, thanks,' said Henri. There didn't seem much more to say.

'I'll see you out,' said Berner, and after cursory goodbyes he got up and left with Blanc.

'Why the fuck did you ever bring that arsehole Cooper-Smythe to this bank?' said Henri to Mark once they had been left alone.

'I can assure you, Henri, that I am just as unhappy as you are.'

'I could lose my job over this.'

'I'm sorry.'

Berner came back into the room.

'So, can you explain what is going on here?' he said to Mark.

'I'm afraid it looks as though Mr Cooper-Smythe has made us all look rather stupid,' said Mark.

'And that's it? You think the bank can afford to lose two million pounds just like that?'

'Well, I'm very sorry, Mr Berner, but I had no idea that the jewels were fakes.'

'I hope that is the case. You are lucky that you only have a power of attorney on this account, otherwise we would be asking you for two million pounds. That is still possible. I will have to talk to our lawyers.'

'But how can I be held responsible?'

'You introduced this customer to the bank. The customer seems to have defrauded the bank, so perhaps you are liable, Mr Arnold. If you knew that this was possible when you made your introduction you probably are liable. I suggest that it is in your interests to find Mr Cooper-Smythe and his jewellery as soon as possible.'

Mark was pretty sure that he could not be sued for the two million, but it did not seem like the time or the place to put forward his case. The best thing he could do would be to take the first plane back to Heathrow. At least there was no suggestion that he would be prevented from doing so.

'Do you have any idea where Cooper-Smythe is?' asked Henri.

'I'm afraid not,' said Mark.

'Then I suggest you start looking,' said Berner. 'Henri, we need to talk.'

Mark gratefully took his leave.

***

Sophie had decided on lunch rather than dinner for her date with Johnny. He had suggested dinner, but that had seemed too intimate somehow; lunch was more business-like. She parked the car in the Rock-a-Nore car park and strolled along past the Stade towards Hastings old town. The tar-covered fishermen's net huts towered above her like a miniature shed Manhattan, and the smell of fish guts hung in the air. The gulls circled around overhead, shrieking in anticipation. Sophie always connected this area to her childhood. Her father had brought her here to the Fish Market once when she was very young. He had woken her in her bed early one winter's morning while it was still dark, and they had driven the short distance over from Rye to buy some fish. She was not sure now why they had come so early in the morning to the market rather than simply going to one of the fishmongers later in the day, or, indeed, why they had come to Hastings rather than Rye, but the memory had stayed with her vividly. She remembered the wet concrete floor of the market, the noisy racket of the fisherman hawking their wares and throwing the crates of fish around, the smell, the cold and the warm feeling created by the knowledge that she was on a secret adventure with her father. It was a feeling that she no longer felt when she was with him. She had admired him so much when she was younger, but adulthood had delivered the realisation that he was not quite what he had seemed when she was younger. She now knew that he had weaknesses. He was not that confident around other adults, and that was probably the reason that he had never pursued a serious career. His academic studies were something that he could hide behind. She still loved him and enjoyed his company, but he was not quite the hero that her younger self had imagined.

She turned inland towards the High Street and Porters Wine Bar, where they had agreed to meet. She was still in two minds about meeting Johnny on her own like this. If she was honest, she had been talked into it; Mary had not been pushy, that was not her way, but she had gradually worn Sophie down. She had helped her feel sympathy for Johnny where previously there had been only anger. Sophie had spent the previous couple of days thinking about what to wear and how she wanted to look. Strong and confident was the theme she had decided on. This was reflected in the black suit that she was wearing; it was something that she was selling in the shop, fifties Chanel, not *haute couture* but elegantly tailored. She had teamed it with a modern white blouse from Next. The blouse had a large collar and long cuffs that peeped out of the suit jacket; the suit itself was cut tight, but not too tight. On her feet she had a pair of plain black Russell and Bromley court shoes. She felt good, confident, attractive and in charge.

She opened the door to Porters and saw Johnny at a table in the corner of the room. He stood up smiling, and they kissed once on the cheek. He looked so much better than she remembered him looking for a long time; the shadows beneath his eyes had gone, his skin looked clean and tight to his face and he seemed comfortable. The haunted gaze had gone.

'You're looking well,' she said to him.

'Thanks. You look amazing. What a fabulous suit.'

Johnny was not big on compliments, so she realised that he must mean it and glowed slightly.

'I hope you don't mind coming here. I wasn't sure where to go. I wanted somewhere relaxed but not a pub, somewhere a bit more chilled than a proper restaurant.'

'Well, there aren't many of those in Hastings anyway, are there?'

'No, I suppose not. Anyway, the food's supposed to be OK here, and you can have a decent glass of wine if you want one.'

'Yes, thanks. Good idea. What are you having?'

'I've got a Virgin Mary. I'm off the booze at the moment. I thought it was about time.'

'Yes. I'm not, though. I'll have a glass of dry white wine, preferably French.'

'OK, I'll get you one.'

She watched as he walked up to the bar. He was still wearing his ripped jeans and biker jacket; the image was starting to look a little dated, but it suited him. He still had a nice bum. It was a strange situation they were in. She could not help but think that they still did not really know one another, despite the amount of time that they had been married. Four years. Was it already four years since that small ceremony at Rye Town Hall, her outfit barely covering her swelling tummy, and her mother's embarrassment plain for all to see? She shivered a little at the memory as Johnny returned to the table with her glass of wine. Maybe they had been doomed from the start.

'So, how's Amy?' Johnny asked.

'Oh, she's fine. She's not quite sure why you're living with Granny, but other than that she's fine.'

'What have you told her?'

'I've just said that you're looking after Granny at the moment. She seems to have accepted it.'

'I'm afraid the reality is that Granny's looking after me.' Johnny grinned at her sheepishly. Was it that self-deprecating side to him that had attracted her? There was an underlying neediness to it, which made her want to mother him a little.

'How are you doing anyway?'

'I'm still not drinking, as I said. I'm not sure how long I'll keep it up, but I think I need to stay off it for the foreseeable future. I haven't touched any charlie either, although in a way that's easier to give up once you're out of that rock-star environment.'

It was the first time that he had openly discussed his cocaine use with her.

'All I have left are these,' he said, lighting a Marlboro Light. 'And I've even cut down on them.'

'And how do you feel as a result of all this abstinence?'

'Better. Sober. Less tired. I'm starting to realise that I've been behaving pretty badly for quite a long time. I've let a lot of people down, but the ones that matter the most are you and Amy.'

While Sophie appreciated his sentiment, the frankness was making her a little uncomfortable. She swigged on her wine glass. The waitress came over to take their orders, saving her from Johnny's confession. Sophie chose the fish pie from the blackboard; she needed some comfort food to settle her nerves. She began to chat about Amy and what she'd been up to. She felt like she needed her food and at least one more glass of wine before she could tackle anything more serious, which she drank while she ate the fish pie and Johnny had another saintly Virgin Mary. They managed to avoid discussing their relationship until they had finished eating.

'Oh, I don't suppose you've heard. Mark and Henri have got themselves into deep shit.'

'No, I hadn't heard, but I do hope it's something quite nasty.'

'It doesn't sound great. I was pretty surprised Mark had got involved.'

'Yes, Mark's full of surprises.' The wine was now having an influence. Johnny looked embarrassed, but he continued.

'I don't know whether or not you knew, but they were doing business with Charles Cooper-Smythe at Paisley Records.'

'No, I didn't know that, but I do know that Cooper-Smythe's gone missing. I heard it on the radio.'

'Yeah, I still don't think he's turned up. No loss as far as I'm concerned. Fucking arsehole. Anyway, I talked to Mark the other night.'

Sophie really did not want to hear about Mark, but it seemed that she had little choice.

'It's top secret, but Cooper-Smythe has scammed Mark and Henri. He borrowed a load of money from Henri's bank and put up Paisley Records as security plus his family's jewellery. Well, Paisley Records has gone bust, so it's worth nothing, and it turns out that the jewels were fakes.'

'Oh dear, such a shame. It couldn't have happened to two nicer people.'

The penny seemed to drop with Johnny.

'Sorry, I wasn't really thinking. I don't suppose you really want to talk about Mark and Henri, do you?'

'It wouldn't be my first choice as a conversation topic, but it does at least sound as if something bad is happening to them, which *is* a consolation.'

'Mark's worried that he's going to lose his job. Henri's already lost his.'

'My heart bleeds.'

'We've never talked about that night in Lausanne, have we?'

'No.' Sophie felt frozen to the spot. She hated this kind of confrontational frankness. She wanted to put her fingers in her ears and scream to block out what Johnny was saying, but that would have been a little childish.

'Do you think we should?'

'Yes, I suppose so.'

There was a silence. Sophie was certainly not going to start, but Johnny seemed more courageous.

'Well, I just want to say sorry.'

'Well, that's a start.'

'I'm sorry for lots of things really, over the last couple of years particularly, but before that too. I don't think I've been a very good husband or father.'

'Oh. I thought you were talking about Mark.' Sophie could forgive the booze, drugs, the not being there; she had accepted that it was part of being a successful musician. At a push she might even be able to come to terms with the idea that he might have messed around with the odd groupie. What she struggled with was the idea of her husband having sex with his best friend.

'Well, of course I'm sorry about that. That's part of it.'

'But, Johnny, that's the most important part of it.' Finally she was saying what she actually felt. She felt her eyes filling with tears, and her voice faltered. 'I'm a pretty tolerant person, and I know that I need to apologise too, but Mark? Really, why did it have to be Mark? It's not just that he's a man it's also that he's your best friend. He was one of my friends. Imagine how I felt, how it seemed so wrong on so many different levels, and in our house ...'

Her voice tailed off. She took a tissue out of her bag and dabbed at her eyes. Johnny was silent opposite her, looking down at his feet. She looked around the small bar; it was busy enough for no one to have noticed them.

'I know, I'm sorry. It's not easy for me to talk about. I don't think I'm gay; I don't really know how it happened. It was only a few times and they were in the last couple of years, normally when I was pretty out of it. I can imagine how you feel, and all I can really say is sorry. It's not really something that I can explain because there doesn't seem to be an explanation.'

'So, is Mark gay?'

'I don't know. It's not something that we ever discussed. As I said, it just kind of happened a few times. There was never any discussion afterwards. We just carried on as normal without talking about it.'

'Really?' Sophie found this hard to believe.

'Really. It was like being friends but with a bit of occasional messing around.'

'So how do you feel about it now?'

'Pretty weird.'

'But you still see Mark.'

'Yeah, but there's no messing around.'

'And what does he say about it?'

'Well, like I said, we haven't really discussed it. He told me you had sent him a letter saying you didn't want to see him again, but other than that we haven't talked about it; we just stopped the messing around and carried on as friends. I haven't seen much of him, to be honest. We talk on the phone. Things have changed since Lausanne. It was a bit of a watershed for all of us, I think.'

Sophie was a little lost for words. Johnny seemed contrite, but there genuinely didn't seem to be any emotional connection with Mark other than their friendship.

'I gather you sent a similar letter to Henri.'

'Yes. I suppose if we're apologising I should say sorry too. How is M. le Cerf? Are you still in touch?'

'Yeah. Henri always was a bit of a slimeball, so I wasn't surprised that he tried to seduce you. You're a beautiful woman, Sophie. Most men would.'

Somehow Johnny had managed to compliment her while commenting on her infidelity; this was not a trait to be undervalued.

'I regret what I did, but I'm afraid I was in a bit of a mess at the time. It happened just after I'd seen you with Mark. I was feeling pretty vulnerable.'

'Yes, I know.'

'How do you know?'

'Henri told me. I saw him in London not long after Lausanne, and he apologised. He gave me his version of what had happened. I took it with a pinch of salt; he always tried to get off with my girlfriends when we were younger. It's not the first time.'

'And you think that's OK?'

'No, I don't think it's OK, I just accept him for what he is. He's an old friend. I decided to forgive and forget.'

Was it Johnny, or was it a male thing? He just didn't seem to care about any of this stuff as much as she did.

'So, you've just forgiven him? He screws your wife, and you just forgive him?'

Now a couple at the next table turned around to take a surreptitious look at them. Sophie decided she really did not care. Johnny did not seem to have noticed.

'I just think that if I want other people to forgive me for the mistakes I've made it would be a bit hypocritical of me not to forgive them for theirs.'

Begrudgingly she had to admit that he had a point.

'I'm just surprised that you would want to carry on seeing him.'

'Well, I'm not sure I've even seen him since that time in London anyway, so in a way I haven't carried on seeing him.'

'So it looks as though we've established that you're more forgiving than me. Where does that take us?'

'Well, I'm just pleased that we've finally talked about a few things. I'd like to see you again, for lunch or dinner, whatever, just spend some time together. I don't want to let you go, Sophie, not if I can help it. Getting sober has made me realise how good you and Amy are for me.'

'I'll think about it.' She had to admit that despite everything there was still something there. He was naturally indolent, but in a charming way. She watched as he lit a cigarette and leaned back languorously in his chair. Something stirred a little within her. Yes, there was definitely still something there.

'What time did you say they were coming?'

'I told them to get here around five. So I would imagine that Mark will be here at five and Henri will be fashionably late.'

'And why am I inviting them again?'

'Because you want to forgive and forget. It's good for the soul. We've spent too many important moments with these guys to write them out of our lives.'

Sophie finished putting on the rest of the hair dye and then checked the packet. She had to let it take for half an hour or so; she still had plenty of time before they arrived. She sat down at her dressing-table to do her nails while the dye took hold. She just wanted to lighten the dark brown a little; she wanted to look her absolute best tonight. She was still wondering why she had agreed to invite Mark and Henri for New Year. Johnny had ground her down, just as he had gradually worn her into accepting him back. It had started with the lunch at Porters then a couple of dinners. After that he had stayed overnight in the guest room a few times. Then, finally, one night after a few glasses of wine she had succumbed and invited him back into the marital bed. It had then only been a couple more weeks until he moved in again. Amy was delighted, of course; Sophie could not say that she was. After everything that had happened she still had difficult moments. If she was honest with herself she knew that she would never quite trust Johnny in the same way, but she was enjoying being a couple again. He was trying to be more understanding; he still had his impulsive and slightly reckless side, but it was kept in check for the most part. They were on a very even keel. The shop was working well, and Johnny was around to help with the childcare. Life was good. He had even started drinking a little again with no ill effects, and he had started playing guitar with some local musicians. Nothing too serious, he said, but the odd guest appearance at a live gig as well as a few jam sessions. This time she tried to be more interested in what he was doing. She realised now that she had left him too alone before; he seemed independent on the surface, but in reality he was quite emotionally needy. She had been doing her best to fulfil this need, and she noticed that he, in turn, was far more considerate in his treatment of her.

She stopped filing her nails and inspected them. Johnny had talked about closing the circle: they had got back together again, so it would be a shame to continue to exclude their old friends. If they were able to forgive each other then they should be able to forgive their friends as well. Johnny had become almost evangelical with the whole forgiveness thing since he had sobered up. In the end, in a weak moment, she had agreed to invite them for New Year's Eve. To her surprise they had both accepted. Now, a couple of hours from their arrival, she was dreading it.

***

A couple of glasses of wine over brunch always did the trick, thought Henri, as he lay there on the brink of dropping off to sleep. He listened to Emily's breathing as it evened out gradually until she sounded as if she were asleep. He was glad that he had called her this morning when his plane landed. He had time to kill before he was due down in Sussex, and what better way than to spend it in the company of the lovely Emily. He had neglected her rather in recent times. Moving to the new bank in Paris had meant that his trips to London were less frequent. But she had jumped at the chance of a reunion over lunch, and it had not been too difficult to convince her to go back to her flat for a siesta afterwards. He loved the smell of her, that unmistakeable, slightly exotic smell, like an orange grove in Provence. He still felt that she really was a lovely girl, and in a way he wished that he could fall for her, but he knew, as he always had, that it was never going to happen. She was just too nice.

But Sophie, he remembered now why he had felt she was a woman to admire, sexy and tough at the same time; she had a real inner strength. It was such a shame that when they had finally slept together her neediness had put him off. It really was ironic that the only time it had happened was the only time that he felt like she had needed him, and it had sapped his desire. Now that she was back with Johnny he already knew that he would find her desirable again. His chances of a fling were pretty remote now, though; in fact, he could hardly believe that he had been invited for New Year. After the Lausanne débâcle he had assumed that she would be true to her word and would cut him out of her life altogether. Then, when Johnny had told him that they were getting back together, he had assumed that was the last he would see of his old friend. A few months later, out of the blue, he had got a call from Johnny asking him to come over to stay with them for New Year's Eve. Even more astounding was the fact that Mark had been invited as well. He had not seen Mark since the Cooper-Smythe problem had blown up earlier in the year. At the time he had been furious with him, had blamed him for the loss of his job at Lagrange et Cie, but now he felt a little more sanguine. The move to Paris had been good for him. A new bank, a new city – a familiar city, but one that was far enough away from his family for him to feel like he was making his own way in life.

He rolled on to his side, facing Emily's back as she lay on her side away from him. He smelled her hair as she slept and put a hand on her one of her slim hips; he felt himself hardening immediately. He probably just about had time for another coupling before he had to get the train southwards. She rolled over drowsily, and he kissed her softly on the mouth; she kissed him back, also softly at first and then a little harder. She really was such a sweet girl.

***

Mark had decided to drive down the A21 today rather going on the M20 to Ashford and then on to Rye on the A259. After a study of the map it had seemed to him that the A21 route was quite a bit shorter, although the roads were slower. It was on drives like today that he regretted parting with the MG, but once he had made the grade of audit manager he had become entitled to a company car. The chance to own a 3-Series BMW was too good to turn down, and he had to admit it was a very comfortable ride and much more suited to a long drive in the winter months.

It was, of course, only a couple of years since the last New Year's Eve get-together. There had been a lot of water under the bridge since then. Victoria was not with him this time for a start. They had agreed that it would be better if she moved out back in the summer. It had been a decision made by mutual consent. Mark had the impression that she had felt uncomfortable about their relationship since his Paisley Records problem had become common knowledge in the office. Rather than being looked at as a rising star his reputation was now somewhat tainted. Victoria had never specifically mentioned this as a reason for leaving, but he could tell that she no longer viewed him as a potential partner. Frankly, he had tired of her anyway, and the period of cohabitation had more or less confirmed to him that in the long run he was probably more likely to end up living with a man than a woman. The question then became, should he come out? He had concluded that if he were to he would probably need to leave Coopers & Lybrand to join a new firm as a gay man. He wondered idly how

Johnny might feel about him if he knew that he was publicly gay. Would it put him off or make him seem more appealing? He was very pleased that he had managed to talk Johnny into inviting him down for New Year's Eve. He knew that now Johnny was back with Sophie he would somehow have to make it up with her if he wanted to carry on seeing him. He had had to work on Johnny, but after a few telephone calls he had convinced him that it would be better all round if everyone made up. He had to tread carefully with Sophie; a large bouquet of flowers lay waiting for her on the back seat. He realised now that while they were never destined to be a couple their lives were fated to be entwined through Johnny. Sophie might not agree with him now, but as time passed perhaps she might be prepared to accommodate the idea that he too had an intimate relationship with Johnny. He understood that Sophie's discovery of the sexual side of the relationship had been unfortunate, but, in a way, he was secretly pleased that she had seen them together. Since that fateful New Year's morning Mark had no longer felt the need to take revenge for Sophie's rejection of his romantic advances. That festering old wound had healed; her knowledge of his intimacy with her husband had been enough to heal it. He knew that he and Sophie would never be friends again, not like they had been, but what he hoped was that they could coexist for Johnny's sake. He was convinced that Johnny wanted their relationship to continue, even if he was back with Sophie. Johnny was attracted to danger, and while Mark himself was not dangerous, the idea of a sexual relationship with him was, and Mark believed that Johnny would never be able to give that up. He hoped he was right.

***

Johnny uncorked two bottles of Château la Nerthe 1981 to give them several hours' breathing time. He had decided that now he drank a lot less he would up the quality of what he did drink, and he had started to buy wine from Berry Brothers of St James's.

It would have been difficult to get hold of a wine like this in the Hastings area, that was for sure. He knew that both Sophie and Henri would appreciate it; he was less sure that Mark would. Mark could never have been described as an epicure. It was strange then that Johnny had ever been attracted to him. Never mind the fact that Mark was a bloke, they were opposites too, although they had a shared interest in music. Whatever. He had given up trying to rationalise his relationship with Mark. What had happened had happened, and now he was back with Sophie. She and Amy were at the centre of his life again, and that's how he wanted it to stay. But he did want Mark to be around too, and he had agreed with Mark's suggestion that they all get together again. It had taken a while to talk Sophie into it, but she had come around in the end. He could even argue in a way that he was also being generous of spirit in inviting Henri – Sophie had, after all, kind of had an affair with him. But if he was honest with himself, and he had got used to being so recently, the fact that Sophie had slept with Henri and used him as a bit of an emotional crutch really did not bother him. He knew that he probably should have been incredibly jealous, but it was just not in his make-up; it was not the first time that Henri had shagged one of his girlfriends, and it might not be the last. That was just the way Henri was built. Henri was an old friend, and you didn't just give up on your old friends when they messed up. He felt a little tense about tonight, but it would be worth it. It just felt right to have Mark and Henri back around the table, whether for dinner or for poker. Sure, they had their foibles, but they were like family to him, and families should learn to forgive and forget.

He opened the second bottle of wine and sniffed to check whether or not it was corked. It was definitely not corked; he could smell the tarry, blackcurrant nose bursting out of the bottle. Maybe he should allow himself just a small taste of each bottle to make absolutely certain. He looked at his watch: four-thirty. They were due to arrive in a little while and then he would have a drink anyway.

One little glass of wine before they got here certainly wouldn't make any difference. He poured half a glass and quaffed it one mouthful. It was delicious, full of the fruit and herbs of Provence; he could almost hear the cicadas and feel the late-afternoon sun on his face. It brought back memories of Swerve's 1993 summer tour, the gig they had played at the Roman amphitheatre in Orange. What a cool venue. He missed the band but not that twat Alex. Rob and Dave had not turned out to be much better. Dave had at least called him a couple of times but not a dicky-bird from Alex or Rob. Wankers. He had heard that they were back in the studio with a new guitarist and would probably tour again in 1995. Fuck them. He had enough cash left to last another year or two; he could take that time to put a new band together. He could write songs; it had usually been him who came up with the melodies for Swerve anyway. He picked up each of the bottles of wine again and poured a little more from each into the glass. There was not enough gone for them to notice really. He quaffed it back. Now he should check on the champagne; it should be cold enough. Maybe he'd ask Sophie if she fancied a glass before the others arrived.

***

'That sounds like someone pulling into the drive,' said Johnny.

Sophie felt her heart miss a beat. They stood up to look out of the window, holding their champagne. Amy was playing with the Cabbage Patch doll that she had become besotted with since receiving it on Christmas Day. A black BMW pulled into the drive with Mark behind the wheel.

'Uncle Mark's here,' said Johnny to Amy. She carried on playing silently.

'She doesn't seem that interested,' said Sophie. 'She must take after her mother.'

'Come on, girls, let's be nice to Uncle Mark.'

Johnny opened the front door and walked out into the dark

early evening to welcome Mark. Sophie stood at the window watching, sipping on her champagne. Johnny gave Mark a big hug as he got out of the car, and Sophie winced. Mark had thickened out a little since she had last seen him; it made him look middle-aged too soon. His neck was starting to join up with his chin. The black polo neck he was wearing was not helping the overall effect. She watched as he took a large bouquet out of the back seat. Well, at least he had come with a peace offering. She put down her glass and walked to the front door. She was wearing a new little black dress by Jaeger, which she had bought on a trip to Tunbridge Wells. It was quite short and figure-hugging, and she felt the chill of the winter night as she stood at the door. Mark approached with the flowers in front of him and handed them to her. They formed a convenient barrier between them, as it was impossible for them to reach past the bouquet to kiss one another hello. Sophie wondered if it was deliberate.

'Mark, it's good to see you. What lovely flowers.'

'It's good to see you too, Sophie. Thanks for inviting me.'

Between the white lilies and pink roses Sophie could just about make out Mark's expression. He seemed quite sincere. She decided to assume that he was until proven otherwise.

She busied herself with the flowers in the kitchen while Johnny poured Mark a drink. She could hear them chatting away like the old friends that they were. She brought the flowers back into the sitting-room in a vase and sat down. She felt the atmosphere stiffen as she did so; there was an elephant in the room that was hard to ignore. Sophie realised that she was even sitting on the sofa where the act had taken place. Mark interrupted the silence that had fallen.

'Guys, I really want to thank you for the invite. Particularly you, Sophie. It takes a lot of courage to forgive what happened, and I really admire you for doing so. Cheers.'

Mark raised his glass, and Sophie and Johnny followed suit, Johnny grinning almost wildly and Sophie smiling a little thinly.

It's not quite as easy as that to receive forgiveness for sucking my husband's cock, she thought, but you do at least sound like you meant it.

'Cheers,' she said. 'Let's hope that 1995 is a little easier to deal with than the last couple of years.'

They raised their glasses again. She wasn't sure if it was just the champagne taking effect, but Sophie was starting to feel more relaxed. By the time they heard a taxi pulling up outside half an hour or so later it was actually her who got up to greet Henri. This time Amy was a little more excited about the visitor, and she came out with her to wait at the front door. At least she had committed adultery with a good-looking man, she thought, as Henri strolled insouciantly up the drive, flicking his fringe back over his eye as he approached, a designer leather holdall slung over his shoulder.

'*Bon soir, les filles*,' he said, kissing them both on each cheek. Sophie was almost pleased to see him, she realised. The animosity she felt towards him after Lausanne seemed to have dissipated. She was reminded that there was something about his indolent confidence to which she was drawn.

As she showed him into the living-room it suddenly struck her that he and Mark may not be the best of friends any longer either. How had the Paisley Records débâcle ended? she wondered, as Henri got a big hug from Johnny but just a handshake from Mark. She was perhaps not the only one who might begrudge Mark's presence.

Johnny opened another bottle of Veuve Cliquot, and the boys settled into some fairly inane banter, as seemed to be the wont of all males when slightly uncomfortable.

'So, I assume that you have brought your cheque book with you this time.' Henri looked at Mark.

'Are we playing poker then?'

'Well, that depends on our hosts, but it's quite rare that we four get together without a game of cards, *n'est-ce pas, mes amis*?'

'Well, I'd be up for it. What about you, Sophie?'

'I had more or less assumed that poker was an inevitability,' said Sophie. 'We'll be having dinner in a little while, once Amy has gone to bed. Then I would imagine that we'll be seeing in the New Year around the card table.'

'Too right. That was one of the reasons I wanted us back together again,' said Johnny. 'I've missed giving Mark a good pasting.'

Unfortunate turn of phrase, Sophie thought to herself, smiling at the double entendre. But she had to stop thinking about those two together. Sooner or later she was going to say something out loud, and it was her husband that she was making jokes about. Surely something was not quite right if she was making jokes to herself about her husband sleeping with another man. What a messed-up situation. But at least Mark seemed to want to be friends; he really was trying quite hard to be nice to her. She decided to excuse herself before she made another *faux pas* and went off to the kitchen to sort out the dinner.

***

After dinner, they sat around nursing their drinks.

'So what do you think of this new Labour guy, Blair? We're used to socialists who eat caviar in France, but this is something new for you guys, no?'

'We call them champagne socialists over here,' said Johnny. 'I think he's a breath of fresh air. I know he's a bit posh for Labour, but he's young and energetic. Someone like him is the only way to get rid of the Tories.'

'I read the other day that Labour is up to 60 per cent in the opinion polls. I must say, Major seems to have run out of steam. Blair does look as though he might be able to work with business, much more so than someone like Kinnock,' said Mark.

'Talking of business, Mark, has anyone found that arsehole Cooper-Smythe?' asked Henri.

'He's still missing. Paisley Records is now in liquidation. The whole thing has been most regrettable.' Mark was growing more pompous as early middle age approached, thought Sophie.

'Regrettable? It's a fucking disgrace. That fucker was the reason I was thrown out of Swerve, and it turns out that he was a thief all along. You know who introduced us to him? That wanker Alex, that's who.'

'OK, Johnny, let's not go over that ground again. We're here to celebrate a new year not to dwell on the past.' The last thing Sophie wanted was a fighting-drunk Johnny on her hands.

'You're right, babe. I shouldn't talk about Paisley and Swerve. It just winds me up.'

'Well, in a way, I'm quite happy that I met Cooper-Smythe. If it hadn't been for him I'd still be working at Lagrange in boring Calvinist Geneva. Instead I'm in Paris, the centre of the universe.'

Sophie thought that Henri seemed on particularly good form. There was something very attractive about a man who was confident and happy.

'Well, why don't we see if the centre of the universe has improved your poker,' she said, looking straight into those well-hidden brown eyes. He held her gaze and smiled.

'It would be my pleasure.'

'Let's do it,' said Johnny.

***

So here they were again. It was Texas hold 'em as usual. Sophie looked at the other three as they turned up their cards for the first time that evening: Henri was inscrutable, Johnny grinned and Mark grimaced. She turned up her two cards: a nine and a six. It looked like she would be watching the first hand. She had dealt the cards, so the small blind was Mark to her left, the big blind was Henri opposite her and the first to bet was Johnny to her right. They were playing pot limit with a big blind of two pounds and a small blind of a pound, so there were three pounds in the pot. It was two pounds to stay in.

'Two pounds,' said Johnny, throwing in the chips from the nice new poker set that Sophie had bought him for Christmas.

'I fold,' she said.

'Me too,' said Mark to her left.

'Call,' said Henri.

Sophie dealt the flop. A jack of diamonds, a six of spades and a ten of spades. Nothing too exciting. It was Henri to bet first now, as he was left of the dealer.

'Check.'

'Four,' said Johnny. He hadn't raised the whole pot, so he obviously had something, but perhaps his hand was not complete. Maybe he was drawing to the spade flush or a straight with the jack and ten.

'Call your four and raise six,' said Henri. It was the old check-raise routine. Check at first because you do not want to scare off your opponent by raising then re-raise once he has raised you. Henri had a strong hand, but he had not bet the pot, so perhaps he knew he could still be beaten.

'Call,' said Johnny.

Sophie dealt the next card. It was the seven of hearts. She saw Johnny's shoulders wilt a little. She was pretty sure that he was drawing to a flush or a straight, and he had just missed it. He would have one last chance to make it when the river card came next. It was Henri to bet.

'Check.'

'Check,' said Johnny. 'You're not getting me with the old check-raise again.'

Johnny had rather given the game away now by not raising in the last round of betting. He clearly had not made his hand yet. Sophie dealt the last card. It was the two of spades. She looked at Johnny. She knew immediately that he had made his spade flush; he was trying to hide it, but his shoulders were up again, and his wiry chest was pushed forward.

'Check,' said Henri.

'Raise five,' said Johnny.

'I fold,' said Henri, throwing his cards face down to Sophie.

'Where's the fucking check-raise when you need it?' said Johnny, slumped back in his chair, disappointed not to have made more money.

'Even I could tell that you made the flush on the river card,' said Mark, 'so it must have been pretty obvious.'

'At least you won the hand, Johnny.' Sophie felt a pang of sympathy for her husband. He had taken some of Henri's chips at least.

'Yeah, that's true. How's it feel to lose, Henri?'

'Poker is all about knowing when to fold, my friend. One day you will learn.'

'Well, you folded, and I won,' said Johnny, rather missing the point. Henri was right, of course. He had lost the hand but might well win the war. Lots of players would have carried on betting just to make sure that Johnny had the flush or would not even have known that he had a flush. It was a small percentage who had the ability to fold when they held a good hand themselves but knew that they were beaten. Henri was one of those players, and Sophie liked to think that she was another.

They played a few more hands, and their usual characteristics unfolded around the table. Sophie had to admit that the familiarity was comforting. Mark steadily lost; he won the odd hand, but he never won very much because if he was betting everyone else knew not to bet unless they had something very special. Johnny had the odd big win and the odd big loss but also lost steadily overall. He wanted to be too involved, to play too many hands; the reality was that he just wanted to have fun and didn't really care whether he won or lost. Her only competition was Henri. He cared, and not because of the money; with Henri it was a question of pride. He wanted to be the best around the table; he wanted to win to prove that he was the best. Sophie felt the same. Poker brought out her competitive instincts more than anything else, and a good poker player such as Henri brought them out the most. She had not felt like the best player in the group for years, perhaps ever, but tonight she felt like she was at the top of her game; she felt like she could look inside the other players again, like she could predict their moves. All she needed was the right situation. Sure enough, after they had been playing for a couple of hours that situation presented itself.

Johnny was dealing to her right, which made her the small blind. More importantly it meant that she would be the first to bet after the first round, which was normally a disadvantage. She checked her cards: a king of clubs and a ten of diamonds. She looked at the others. Mark and Johnny looked pretty uninterested. Henri, as ever, was hard to read. It was Henri to bet first; he had to match the big blind of two pounds to stay in. He threw in a couple of chips.

'I fold,' said Johnny. 'I've played too many hands with rubbish tonight.'

'Call,' said Sophie.

'Check,' said Mark. He was the big blind so there was no need for him to put in any more chips.

Johnny dealt the flop. A king of spades, a seven of spades and a ten of clubs. This gave Sophie a very nice concealed two pairs of kings and tens. She was the first to bet, but she did not want to reveal her strength at this stage.

'Check,' she said.

'Fold,' said Mark.

'Raise three,' said Henri. This was a tempter. It was not an aggressive attempt to snatch the pot – he would have bet more to do that – but Henri had a hand. She wondered what it was. Perhaps he was drawing to a spade flush, but he probably had a bit more than that. An ace maybe, or a pair as well as the two spades.

'Call,' she said.

Johnny dealt the fourth shared card. Sophie looked straight at

Henri as it was dealt. Nothing. He did not flinch. No information there then. She looked at the card. It was the queen of diamonds, irrelevant to her and probably irrelevant to Henri. She would have to buy some information.

'Raise the pot,' she said, putting in twelve chips.

Henri thought for a while, perhaps as long as a couple of minutes.

'Call and raise another twelve,' he said.

Maybe he was trying to buy information too. If Sophie was right, and he was still trying to make his flush, it was quite brave to raise. Maybe he was trying to put her off the scent. Maybe he was trying to work out what she had. She decided not to give him any more information.

'Call,' she said.

Now it was all on the river card. If it was a spade Henri had probably won; anything else and she would be in charge. She concentrated on Henri as the card was dealt face up with the other four shared cards. He was very still as the card was dealt, but she thought she saw it, that glimmer that she had seen for the first time in Wapping. It was almost a blink but not quite; almost a twitch but not quite; the faintest of movements but enough. She knew without looking that he had made his flush. She could feel her shoulders tighten a little. Shit, she said, to herself, I must try to control that. Then she looked at the card. It was the ten of spades. It had not occurred to her before, but this was the one spade that put her ahead. She now had a full house, tens over kings, very well concealed. Now she felt her shoulders slump as she relaxed into the knowledge that she was about to win.

'Check,' she said. She saw the tiniest of smiles at the corner of Henri's mouth. Perhaps he had seen her shoulders tighten before she had looked at the last card and was convinced he was winning.

'I bet the pot.' He had walked straight into the check-raise.

'Call and raise the pot. That's sixty to call and one hundred and twenty to raise,' she said, counting out the chips.

Henri sat back in his chair suddenly.

There were loud exhalations of breath from Mark and Johnny.

'Go for it, Sophie,' said Johnny. 'Know when to fold, Henri, eh?'

Henri sat very still for what seemed like an age to Sophie.

'Call,' he said finally, flipping over the ace and nine of spades.

'He's got the flush,' said Johnny.

'Well, evidently,' said Mark.

Sophie flipped over her cards.

'Full house,' she said. 'Tens over kings.'

'Sophie wins. That's fucking brilliant, babe,' Johnny gave her a big kiss. She was extraordinarily pleased with herself but trying not to show it.

'Well played, Sophie. I thought you were dead and buried there.' Mark seemed genuinely impressed.

'You made it on the river card,' said Henri.

'Well, so did you,' she replied.

'That was the only card that could beat me. Well played.'

Sophie raked in the chips. Three hundred and sixty pounds. That was a big win. She felt on top of the world; her heart was pounding as if it wanted to burst out of her chest.

'Shit, it's ten to twelve already. I'd better get some more champagne.'

Sophie smiled as Johnny leaped up and almost ran to the kitchen. Mark followed him out of the room. Henri lit a Disque Bleu and looked straight into her eyes.

'Not only are you beautiful, but you can play poker. It's quite a combination.' He took hold of her hand across the table. She tingled as he did so. Here we go again, she thought.

'*La plus ça change; la plus c'est la même chose,*' she said, smiling at him. '1995 is going to be an interesting year.'

***

Johnny stood at the work surface wrestling with another bottle of Veuve Cliquot as Mark approached. From behind Mark put his arms around Johnny's waist and pushed his groin into Johnny's buttocks. He could feel himself hardening instantly. Johnny gasped as he did so and turned around to face him.

'Not now,' he whispered.

'When?'

'Later. Don't worry, we'll find a way.'

'I knew it wasn't over.'

'No, it's not over, Mark, but we need to be careful. I can't afford for Sophie to find out again.'

'I know. Don't worry.'

Mark moved away and let Johnny open the champagne. He popped the cork and kissed Mark on the mouth as he did so. Mark's heart missed a beat. Johnny had never done that before. They heard Henri calling from the living-room.

'That sounds like music to my ears.'

They smiled at one another and left the kitchen. It definitely was not over, thought Mark.

Lightning Source UK Ltd.
Milton Keynes UK
UKOW03f2159040214

225897UK00012B/471/P